THE SECOND VICTORY

MORRIS WEST was born in Australia, where he served a six-year novitiate with the Christian Brothers but left before taking his final vows. He became a teacher and joined the army in 1940. After the war he moved to Europe, where he now lives with his family, and began writing: his fourteen books have been translated into twenty-seven languages. *The Devil's Advocate*, one of the most famous, is now a major film, and cinema versions of other novels including *Harlequin* are planned. His most recent novel is *The Navigator*, published by William Collins in 1976.

Morris West has always been renowned for the authenticity of his facts and settings, whether connected with diplomacy, religion, international business or science, and each of his books was written after extensive travel and research in countries throughout the world.

MORRIS WEST

The Second Victory

Any man's death diminishes me, because
I am involved in mankinde.
                    JOHN DONNE: *Devotions*

FONTANA BOOKS
by agreement with
HEINEMANN

First published in 1968 by William Heinemann Ltd
First issued in Fontana Books 1977

© by Morris West 1958

Made and printed in Great Britain by
William Collins Sons & Co Ltd Glasgow

For PAUL BRICKHILL

CHAPTER 1

THEY HAD left the lowlands and were climbing steadily on the narrow road that wound dangerously round the high flank of the mountain. Below them was the steep fall to the river rushing loud and boisterous under the overhang of ice and the bare branches of the alders. Above was the heave of the mountainside with its swathes of black pines, beyond which the snow ran clear to the summit and the blue of the midday sky.

The jeep skidded perilously on the icy surface and Sergeant Willis wrestled it away from the drop. They stopped, got out and jacked up the wheels to put on the chains. While Willis was fitting them, grunting and cursing at the cold, Major Mark Hanlon stepped out in the middle of the road and looked up at the mountain.

Straight ahead of him was a broad gap in the pines. On either side the dark trunks rose like pillars in an ancient nave and their diminishing perspective drew his eyes onward and upward to the sharp line where the sky and the saddle met. Under the trees, the snow was stained brown with fallen needles, but beyond, it was a white dazzle broken only by the grey of rocky outcrops and the organ pipes of the distant Grauglockner.

Then he saw the skier.

He was right on top of the ridge, a tiny black puppet, with his head in the blue sky and his feet in the white snow. Hanlon took the fieldglasses from the case round his neck and trained them on the motionless figure.

A moment later the puppet began to move, slowly at first, thrusting himself forward with his stocks, then gathering speed as he hit the steeper fall. At the first outcrop he checked and made a tight turn that brought a whistle of admiration to Hanlon's lips. The glasses showed the wild flurry of snow and the precarious angle of the skier's body. Then he righted himself again and headed downhill in a long, diagonal *schuss*, straight for the opening in the pines. When he reached them, he would be doing seventy miles an hour.

Hanlon's shout of surprise brought Willis racing to his side and together they stood and watched the wild, suicidal plunge down the dazzling hillside. He did not check or turn at the humps, but took them, flying like a skeleton bird, his stocks trailing like wing-tips to balance his landing.

The two men watched him, breathless, waiting for the fall that would send him tumbling and broken down the slope. But he did not fall. He came onward, faster and faster, until they could see the grey of his uniform and the green flashes of the Alpenjäger regiment and the rifle slung between his shoulder-blades and the gleam of his polished pistol-belt.

Hanlon lowered the glasses for a moment and looked at Willis in surprise. The war was over, months now. All Austrian units were reported to be disarmed and disbanded. The Occupying Powers were spreading their authority into all the corners of the land. What was this one doing, armed and in battledress, in wild career down the mountain?

Hanlon raised the glasses again. The skier was nearing the end of his run. He was going like the wind and they saw that he would overshoot the clearing and end up behind the barrier of pines. A moment later they lost him and they stood, staring up through the colonnade of trees, waiting for the crash and the cries. But there was no sound, except the thunder of the river and the faint whisper of the wind in the branches.

It was perhaps thirty seconds before the skier came into view again, sliding easily down the transverse slope behind the grove. He was carrying his two stocks in one hand while the other held his rifle at the trail. At the focal point of the long perspective of trees he stopped, dug his stocks into the ground and stood watching them. A shaft of sunlight fell on his face and they saw the lean sunken jaws darkened by stubble and the red weal of a freshly-healed scar running from eye to chin down his right cheek.

Hanlon raised his hand and shouted in German:

"*Grüss Gott!* Come down here a minute! We'd like to talk to you."

Before the words were out of his mouth he saw the rifle thrown up—as a trapshooter throws it—fast, sighting and swinging in the same movement. He yelled and threw himself against Willis to drive him off balance, but before they hit the ground the shot rang out, and as Hanlon rolled spinning towards the shelter of the jeep he saw more bullets chipping

6

up the ice by his face and heard the wild echoes thundering round the valley.

He wrenched his pistol out of its holster and eased himself cautiously back in the shelter of the bodywork. The echoes were still shouting from hill to hill, but the clearing was deserted and Sergeant Willis lay on the road with a bullet in his head. When Hanlon bent over him he saw that he was dead and that the blood was frozen already on his cheek and on the ice beneath him.

After a while he stood up, finished putting on the chains, let down the jack and hoisted Willis's body into the jeep. Then he climbed into the driver's seat, started the engine and drove, very slowly, up the mountain road towards Bad Quellenberg.

Bad Quellenberg—so the legend says—was founded by a holy hermit named St Julian, who lived in the mountains with the deer and the bears and the eagles and the golden pheasants for company. He was a gentle man, it seems, a kind of Gothic St Francis, whose life was a protest against the violence of his times. When a stag was torn by a wolf, Julian struck the rock and a stream of warm, healing water gushed out, a perennial medicine for man and beast.

The legend suffers a little from the historians. There were men here in the Bronze Age. The Romans traded salt over the mountain roads from Salzburg and mined gold in the high passes of Naasfeld. The Goths were here and the Vandals and the Avars, and all of them, for health or comfort or cleanliness, bathed in the warm waters from which the town takes its name —Mountain of Springs.

Martin Luther came here too, but there is no record that he bathed. He seems to have spent most of his time hiding in log farmhouses high up on the slopes where the chamois came to graze in the bitter winter weather.

An enterprising peasant built an inn and a post-house at the neck of the pass, where travellers from Carinthia might change their horses and eat venison steaks and pinch the bottoms of the peasant girls before crossing into the troubled land of Salzburg, where Wolf Dietrich sat in his stone fortress with a crozier in one hand and a naked sword in the other.

Later, much later, a church was built and a monastery school, and a straggling town began to line itself down the banks of the torrent that gushed out of the mountain and went tumbling through the widening gorge into the lowlands. The inn became a hotel and canny Viennese and Salzburgers moved in to build guest houses and shops and terraced gardens and bath huts fed from hot mineral springs in the heart of the mountain.

The buildings spread themselves in a huge terraced amphitheatre round the throat of the valley, dwarfed by the peaks of the Grauglockner and the Gamsberg.

Later still they drove a tunnel through the mountain to make a railway link with Klagenfurt and Villach and Trieste and Belgrade and Athens. With the railway came Baedeker and Thomas Cook, so that soon Bad Quellenberg blossomed like a gentian patch under the golden rain of tourism.

They came in the summer to take the waters, to sit on the terrace for *Kaffeeklatsch*, to walk under the pines on the promenades, to flirt in the evening while the orchestras played Strauss waltzes and the peasant troupes came in to dance the *Schuhplattler* and play the zither for local colour. They came in the winter for the ski-ing and, in between, for the shooting, so that the hoteliers grew fat and the peasants rich and the woodcutters were hard put to it to feed enough pine logs into the mills to keep pace with the building.

High up in the mountains they built a power station to light the town and electrify the railway. When Austria was annexed to become a part of Greater Germany, the Party pundits came here for holidays and the youth groups marched singing through the valleys and Reichsmarschall Göring arrived, resplendent as a peacock, to sun himself and take the baths.

Then came the war, with England first and later with Russia, and the youth of Quellenberg were enlisted into Alpenjäger regiments and sent off to the Eastern front. As the years went on, the little forest of headboards grew and grew in the churchyard of St Julian. The hotels were turned into *Lazaretts* for the wounded and the shops closed one by one because there was nothing to sell and nobody with money to buy.

The trains ran erratically because Villach was bombed and Klagenfurt and the junctions at Salzburg and Schwarzach. When they did run the compartments were full of haggard, bitter men pulled back from the Udine and from Greece. The trucks were loaded with battered vehicles and guns that were useless because there was no fuel to run them and no ammunition left for the breeches.

Finally, there came a day when they heard on the radio that Germany had surrendered. The Quellenbergers gathered in the streets and the wounded sat up in their beds in the big hotels and on the lips of each one was the same frightened question: What now?

No one was in a hurry to answer them because Bad Quellenberg was a small place, a bath town, a cure resort, of no military or economic importance. So they waited, stunned and fearful, for a month, two months, until a company of troops arrived from Occupation Headquarters at Klagenfurt. The captain was a tow-headed youth with a wispy moustache and cold eyes. He presented himself and his orders to the Bürgermeister.

The Sonnblick Hotel, largest in Quellenberg, would be evacuated immediately and prepared as a headquarters for the Commander, Occupation Forces, Quellenberg Area. The commander himself would arrive in forty-eight hours. The Bürgermeister would see to it that all preparations were complete by that time.

The last maids were being hustled out of the corridors, the first guard was being mounted outside the entrance, as Major Mark Hanlon drove up the mountain pass with a dead man at his side.

Bürgermeister Max Holzinger stood at the big picture-window of his lounge and looked down over the pine tops to the snowbound valley.

It was a prospect that had rarely failed to please him: the broad meadow-reaches with the river winding like a black snake between the stripped alders, the log barns crouching under their snowy roofs, the thin lines of the fences, the peasant village huddled round the spire of the old church, the pines marching like spearmen along the mountainsides, the high saddles rising for ramparts against the world outside, the defiles with their treacherous mists and down draughts. No gunfire had startled the eagles nesting on the crags. Men had died, to be sure, in Russia, in Rumania, in Hungary, in Crete. His own son had died with them. But their dying had been a distant thing. Its tragedy had been dwarfed by the towering majesty of the mountains.

The Party leaders had come here to relax and play. The wounded had been sent here to recover—and forget if they could. Right to the end, Reichsminister Göbbels had controlled the Press and the radio, so that the pogroms and torture chambers and concentration camps became musty legends, and the tally of death, defeats and ruined cities reached them only as travellers' tales, fearful but far away.

Life in the valley had followed the old, old pattern. Winter passed and the meadows were green again and the sleek cattle grazed halfway to the peaks. The peasants came still to the market with milk and meat and eggs. The convalescents walked in the dappled sunlight of the promenades, and made love to the hungry girls in the grass. The sound of the axes rang cheerily enough from the timber slides, beating out the time for the melody of the running waters. At summer's end there was the mowing, when the women in bright dirndls tossed the grass into sheaves and hung it on the drying poles, fragrant as apples. And when the first chill returned to the hills the cattle were brought down, garlanded with the last flowers, the best milker crowned with a headdress of blooms and tinkling her bells in triumph.

Bells! They too were part of the life of the valley—part of its peace: cowbells clapping dull yet musical from the high meadows, sleighbells in winter, the angelus floating out from the church tower, morning, noon and evening, small silver bells when Father Albertus carried out the body of Christ for the blessing of the crops, the ominous slow tolling of the passing knell, more and more frequent as the end of the war drew near.

The mountains caught at their chimes and shuttled them back and forth, weaving a pattern of sound which was like the pattern of the old faith, familiar, repetitive, threatening and cajoling by turns, often ignored but never quite forgotten.

There had been a time when orders had come from the Party to silence the bells and send them as a gift to the gunsmiths, but he had set his face against it as he had set his face against so many other demands, and in the end he had won. It was a small victory when you laid it against the great compromise to which he and others had committed themselves. But he was glad that he had won it, because the bells had helped to maintain, almost to the end, the small illusion of peace in the valley.

Now there were no illusions left. The ramparts had been breached, the conquerors were coming in. A blond boy with a handful of troops sat in the hotel where Reichsmarschall

Göring had lodged and a nameless man with an ominous title was driving up the road to become the new ruler in the mountains.

Bürgermeister Max Holzinger wondered how he should greet him and how he would be answered. One thing he knew with certainty: he must preserve his dignity, because dignity is the last possession of the conquered.

He had been conquered before and he understood how important it was.

In the first war he had fought in a Carinthian cavalry regiment and he still walked stiffly from the bullet that had smashed his knee. He knew what it meant when a man could talk only of the battles he had lost and of the inglorious survivals of defeat. *Vae victis!* It is only the victors who are absolved by history.

Better than any, he knew that this time would be worse than the last. The ghosts were rising now in accusation. The living were crawling out of the cellars and the concentration camps. The judges were assembling already, lean and pitiless. Men like himself who had closed their eyes hopefully and too long were to be joined as accessories in the indictment. They had eaten the fruits of conquest, now they must be crammed with the dust of defeat.

He stared out across the white valley and wished the day were over.

He was a man of middle height, black haired in spite of his fifty years, with a lean, intelligent, Magyar face inherited from his mother, who was a Harsanyi from Buda before she married Gerhardt Holzinger from St Veit on the Glan. He himself had married a girl from Hamburg, tall, blonde, deep-bosomed, and the son she had given him had died in the first descent on Crete. She had given him a daughter too, dark, slim and vital. They had named her Irmtraud, because Valkyries were in fashion then, but the name matched oddly with her restless gipsy beauty. She was twenty-six years old, ripe to be married, but all the men she might have wed were dead or prisoners, or wandering lost and leaderless about the country.

He turned back from the window and saw them both sitting in their chairs, watching him.

His wife was working placidly over a piece of embroidery, but her hands were unsteady and her troubled eyes flickered back and forth from the work to himself. Her hair was greying now, and her waist thickening, but she was still strong boned and firm bodied, for all the years and the griefs. A vague regretful desire stirred in him as he remembered their youth together and wondered about their future.

Irmtraud sat sprawled in a deep armchair smoking a cigarette. She was dressed in a ski-costume that emphasised her long, slim legs and her flat belly, and the thrust of her youthful breasts. Her full mouth quirked into a malicious smile and the expression in her dark eyes was half hostile, half amused.

Holzinger wondered how one explained these things to the young—defeat, despair, betrayal and disillusion!

He faced them squarely, straddling a little to ease the weight of his stiff leg. He spoke quietly, piecing out the phrases with care, as if afraid they might mistake his meaning.

"I think you should both understand our situation."

"I'm sure we do, Max," His wife's deep, placid voice reassured him.

He shook his head.

"I'm afraid it's worse than you think, Liesl."

"How much worse?" His daughter sat up suddenly and her voice was sharp with curiosity.

"As a Party member I shall most certainly lose my job. Our money and property are liable to confiscation."

"*Du lieber Gott!*" Liesl's lips trembled and she bent quickly over the embroidery to hide her tears.

"But they can't do that!" Traudl's voice was firm but angry.

"They can do anything they wish, child," he told her soberly. "We should thank God we have the British and not the Russians. They have a respect for law and for the rights of the subject. More than we, I think. However . . ." he shifted uneasily, "I've tried to take precautions. I had Kunzli draw a deed of gift making you, Liesl, the owner of this house. It is pre-dated to 1938. I have hopes that it may survive an investigation—unless Kunzli decides to blackmail me, as he well may do. The rest I'm afraid we'll have to let go if they claim it."

"What's going to happen to us then?" She put the question coolly, as if it were a simple household matter.

"We'll survive, my dear." He smiled at her with thin irony. "Whatever happens, we shan't starve. I can still get a job sweeping the snow outside the hotels or spreading gravel on the promenades. We'll pocket our pride and . . ."

Sharp and sudden the telephone rang and Holzinger hurried

to the table and lifted the receiver. The women watched him, wide-eyed and tense.

"This is Holzinger. . . . Yes?"

They saw his face blench as the voice crackled through the receiver and they strained forward to catch the words, but could not hear them.

"When? . . . Where? . . . God in Heaven! Yes, yes, I'll come immediately. . . . *Auf Wiedersehn.*"

He put down the receiver and turned to face them. His face was grey and little beads of perspiration broke out on his temples. His wife started out of her chair towards him but he thrust her back with a gesture.

"What is it, Max? What's happened?"

"The worst, Liesl, the very worst." He passed a weary hand over his forehead. "The Occupation Commander has arrived. On the way up his driver was shot dead by a skier in Austrian uniform. I am ordered to wait on him immediately."

Without another word he turned on his heel and walked from the room. The two women followed him with wide, frightened eyes. When the door closed they looked at each other and Liesl Holzinger buried her face in her hands and wept. Her daughter came and knelt in front of her, stroking her hair and soothing her with little gentle words out of a forgotten childhood.

After a while she stopped weeping and raised her head. The girl wiped the tears from her face with a lace handkerchief; then her mother reached out and gripped her shoulders with urgent hands. Her voice was low and bitter and her eyes were strange:

"Twice in my life I have seen this happen, Traudl. Twice the men of this country and mine have made wars and lost them. They took our husbands and our brothers and our sons and let them die on the beaches and on the steppes. Those who were left came limping home, like your father, to lie with us again and breed again—new sons for a new sacrifice. They build us homes, only to destroy them again. We planted gardens, to find them trampled by new armies. Now we're too old to breed and too tired, I think, to build any more."

"No, *Mutti*!"

She disengaged herself from the urgent hands and stepped back.

"Yes!" Liesl was passionate and insistent. "Yes! They

make the messes and they expect us to clean them up. They make the ruins and expect us to patch them up. But they give us no voice in the decision. It is a man's world, so long as there are victories. But in defeat it is a woman's, because the best of the men are dead.

"The lips you might have kissed are cold. The arms that might have held you are buried under the snow. The bodies that might have warmed you are eaten by the wolves. Only the maimed are left, and the old, to give you children you will never love—because there will be no passion in their begetting. The strong ones are gone, who might have treated with the conquerors. The good ones are lost, who might have established a new faith with them. There is only you and the millions of women like you. . . . Do I frighten you, Traudl?"

"No." The girl's full lips curved into an ironic smile. "You don't frighten me. All men want the same thing. It's up to the woman to get the best price she can. I'll do as well as most."

Liesl Holzinger stared at her in momentary surprise. Then she too smiled and nodded slowly.

"I'm glad. That makes it easier for you—for all of us." With an odd, shy, sensual gesture, she reached out and let her hands rest for a moment on the thrusting breasts of the girl, then slide down slowly over the flat belly and the slim, boyish flanks. "In the end, it is the women who win, because they have the strongest weapon of all. The conquerors come like kings and end like children, naked in your arms, with their lips against your breast. They are young and they are lonely and they are afraid because they are strangers far from home. The life they bring you is robbed from their own women, and that is your revenge on them for all you have lost, on the folly of your own men who followed the trumpets while you were crying in a cold bed, all alone. Can you understand that?"

Wide eyed, wondering at the unfamiliar eloquence of her mother, vaguely stirred by the touch of her hands, the girl nodded slowly.

"Yes, I understand. But . . . but . . ."

"But what, child?"

"How do you know all this? How do you feel it?"

The ghost of a smile lightened the drawn face of Liesl Holzinger. Her eyes seemed to look beyond her daughter, beyond the valley and ridges, backward to a distant time, a distant country. She drew her girl close to her, pillowing the dark head on her breast.

Then, simply and flatly, she gave her the answer.

When Holzinger walked up the steps to the entrance of the Sonnblick Hotel, two guards stepped forward and barred his way with crossed bayonets. They were muffled to the ears in greatcoats and gloves and balaclavas, but their faces were pinched with cold and their eyes were blank. Even when he had identified himself in terse but halting English, they kept him standing in the wind while one of them went to fetch the sergeant of the guard.

The sergeant put him through a leisurely interrogation and finally admitted him. As they walked across the foyer to the lift, he saw Franz Mayer, the manager, and old Wilhelm, the porter, peering at him from behind the potted palms. He nodded a greeting, and saw them pop back into shelter like rabbits. He smiled bleakly at their retreating backs.

Helmut, the little lift boy, gave him a shy *"Grüss Gott"*, and Holzinger rumpled his hair affectionately as they rode upwards to the fifth floor, where the suites, he remembered wryly, had always been reserved for visiting dignitaries.

In spite of the fuel shortage, the central heating was turned up full and the big stone urns were full of hothouse flowers. Mayer was a good hotelier. He understood the refinements of service.

The sergeant led him briskly along the carpeted corridor and stopped outside the suite which Reichsmarschall Göring had occupied not twelve months before. He pressed the buzzer and a muffled voice said "Come in!" The sergeant opened the door and stood aside to let him enter. Then he closed the door, snapped to attention and announced the visitor.

"This is the Mayor, sir. He says he has an appointment with you."

"Thanks, Jennings. You may go."

"Very good, sir."

Another salute, the door opening and closing again, and Bürgermeister Max Holzinger stood in the presence of the Occupying Power.

He was seated at a big buhl desk, his back to the window, so that the shadows deepened the network of lines about his brown eyes, and the creases at the corner of his wide, quirky mouth. He had a high forehead and strong nose and there were small flecks of grey in his unruly hair. In spite of the grey hair and the lines, Holzinger put him at no more than thirty.

He wore fresh battledress and a starched shirt and his face had been newly shaven. The major's crowns on his shoulders were brightly polished and his long expressive hands were relaxed on the manila folder in front of him.

At his side stood the tow-headed captain who had come in with the advance party. Holzinger clicked his heels and bowed stiffly and waited for the opening gambit.

"My name is Hanlon, Occupation Commander for this area. You, I understand, are Bürgermeister Max Holzinger. Please sit down."

The voice was crisp and authoritative. The German flowed out, easy and pure, with a Viennese lilt to it. Holzinger was surprised, but he kept his face studiously blank and sat down. He put his gloves and his hat on the corner of the desk and waited. Hanlon opened the manila folder and spread the pages in front of him. He asked formally:

"You understand the terms of the Armistice and the status of the Occupying Forces?"

"I have not yet been informed of them."

"Very well. First, Austria is occupied by units of four Allied Armies: British, French, American and Russian. Bad Quellenberg is in the British Occupation Zone."

"Fortunately for us," murmured Holzinger dryly.

Hanlon ignored the comment and went on in the same detached tone.

"Occupation forces, their billeting, messing, transport and general maintenance, are a charge on the Austrian Government, through local authorities. The representative of the Occupying Power has the right to requisition such property or supplies as he may deem fit or necessary from time to time. He may recruit local labour and fix equitable wages. Local administrations and local police units are required to co-operate with him in the maintenance of order and in investigation or pursuit of suspected war criminals. Am I making all this clear?"

"Perfectly. You speak excellent German."

"Thank you." Hanlon did not smile. His eyes were cool and his tone impersonal. "The representative of the Occupying

Power will, on his part, do everything possible to restore and maintain order, to assist in reconstruction of local industries and in the repatriation and re-employment of discharged troops, other than suspected war criminals—subject to such directives as may be received from time to time from the General Officer Commanding Occupation Area. . . ." He closed the folder and leaned forward across the desk, his brown eyes searching the impassive face of the Bürgermeister. "I'll send you a copy of the documents. There's a couple of hours' solid reading in 'em. But they all boil down to this: it's a two-way deal. The Allies are sympathetic to Austria. Play ball with us and you'll benefit. Obstruct us and you'll land in bother."

"There's something you've forgotten, Major." Holzinger spoke quietly but distinctly, mindful of his own dignity and of the respect due to the new masters in the land.

"What's that?"

"I am told that former members of the Party are ineligible for public office and are to be dismissed forthwith and replaced by non-Nazi personnel. I've been a member of the Party for a long time. I think I should hand you my resignation."

A wintry smile twitched up the corners of Hanlon's mouth and a twinkle showed in his brown eyes. He said blandly:

"The local commander has a temporary discretion in these matters. I propose to exercise it and ask you to continue in office for the time being."

"And if I should decline?"

"You would be doing yourself and your people a disservice."

"In that case, you leave me no alternative but to accept."

"I was sure you'd understand that," said Mark Hanlon softly. "Now . . ." He closed the manila folder and sat back in his chair. His eyes were grim again and his mouth was tight as a trap. There was anger in his voice and cold bitterness. "We begin our association with a murder. . . ."

Holzinger nodded gravely.

"I've been told about it. I—I ask you to believe me when I say that I am ashamed and deeply sorry."

"I believe you," said Hanlon curtly. "I take it I can count on your full co-operation in hunting down this man and bringing him to justice."

"You may count on it, yes. If you will give me a full description of the man, the exact location of the crime, I'll speak immediately with the police and arrange searches of the town, the hamlets and the mountain farms."

"Good!" Hanlon nodded briskly and hurried on. "Captain Johnson here will supply you with a full description, which I have just dictated to him. The road point is clearly marked on the map which he will also give you. I've already telephoned the police from here and asked for an immediate search of the area. There has been no snow. The ski tracks will be clearly marked. The man is a Quellenberger, so it shouldn't be too difficult to smoke him out. His face is badly scarred. He'll be quite conspicuous."

"How do you know he's a Quellenberger?" Holzinger looked up in sharp surprise.

"I saw his flashes. They tally with those of the Quellenberg regiment, which according to the order of battle was almost totally destroyed in the Ukraine. He's an excellent skier and he took that run as if he'd known it since childhood. He belongs here—no doubt of it."

"You're a very efficient officer," said Max Holzinger with sour admiration.

"I'm glad you understand it. I hope you'll make your police understand it too. I'll want reports twice daily, with full map references. If necessary local huntsmen and woodcutters are to be recruited to assist in the search. I want this man found and I'll give you forty-eight hours."

"I'll do my best."

"You yourself will report to me each morning at 0930 hours for discussion of town business and the planning of reconstruction operations."

"Anything else?"

"Yes. I want the parish priest to call on me at his convenience this afternoon."

"The—the priest?" Try as he might to subdue his curiosity, he could not avoid the question. Hanlon nodded.

"Yes. Sergeant Willis was a Catholic. We have no chaplain. I should like to arrange for his burial according to the rites of the Church . . . And another thing . . ." He broke off and seemed to hesitate over the next order. Holzinger prompted him gently:

"I'm at your service, Major."

"We need a coffin," said Hanlon with cold deliberation. "We

need it delivered to the hotel by 2000 hours this evening. We need coffin-bearers, six of them, who will be the principal citizens of Quellenberg. All shops and businesses will be closed tomorrow and all citizens will be required to line the streets from this hotel to the church. The procession will leave the hotel at 0900 hours and the coffin will be carried to the church for the requiem Mass. After which the burial will take place in the churchyard of St Julian. You will see that a grave-digger is in readiness for the final ceremonies. That is all for the present."

Every word was a slap in the face and the dismissal was a final contempt. Holzinger stood up and faced the Occupying Power. Try as he might, he could not control the tremor of his voice:

"We shall be there, Major, as you ask. We should have been there anyway without asking. You're new here. You can't be expected to understand that a soldier's funeral is an occasion for us. Most of our boys died a long way away and we don't know where they are buried—or whether they were buried at all. We—we have a sympathy for soldiers—all of them, poor devils—and we like to think they will lie in friendly earth and under the sound of the bells. We'll be there, Major. All of us!"

He bowed and turned away, and Mark Hanlon watched him limping, stiff and straight-backed, to the door. Then he slammed his fist on the table and swore bitterly:

"God damn him! God damn and blast them all!"

The blond captain watched him with faint amusement. He was twenty-three years old—too young for hate, and not yet ripe for pity or for tears.

CHAPTER 2

KARL ADALBERT Fischer was Chief of Police in Bad Quellenberg. He was a stubby man, with a small head that sat incongruously on his round barrel body. He had short legs and a long neck and bright, unwinking eyes like a bird's. When he walked the streets in his long cloak and his square peaked cap he looked like an amiable duck.

He was a good-humoured fellow with a taste for schnapps and bouncing peasant girls. He ran his command with a genial inefficiency that had endeared him to the Quellenbergers and kept him comfortably in office for fifteen years. He had survived a dozen purges under the Greater German administration and he had counted on his shrewdness and experience to keep him safe until his retirement. Now he wasn't so sure.

When Max Holzinger came into his office he was warming his bottom against the stove, drinking schnapps and munching a butter cake. He waved a vague hand and murmured:

"*Grüss Gott*, Herr Bürgermeister. Pour yourself a drink. Come and warm yourself."

Holzinger tossed his hat on the littered table and peeled off his gloves. He poured a glass of the white fiery liquor and tossed it off at a gulp. The little policeman watched him with canny, appraising eyes. He grinned and said:

"You're upset, my friend. I take it you've met the Englishman?"

"I've met him," said Holzinger curtly. "He told me he'd been in touch with you."

"Oh yes! He's been in touch." He chuckled and choked on his liquor. "I thought it was a joke at first. He talks like a Viennese."

"It's no joke. He means business."

"I know. I assured him of our full co-operation and our earnest desire to assist him."

Holzinger looked up sharply.

"Don't underrate him, Karl. He's shrewd and efficient. He knows what he wants and he'll stop at nothing to get it. This—this killing is a bad start for us."

"Very bad." Fischer put down his glass and wiped his mouth with the back of his hand. "I've sent my boys up to look at the tracks. I hope they get there before dark."

"Before dark?" Holzinger stared at him, puzzled. "It's barely midday. The place is not ten miles out."

"The car is old," said Fischer thoughtfully. "The tyres are worn. The steering-rod is defective. The roads are icy. If there were an accident the boys would have to walk—and the Occupying Power would have to supply us with a new car. We could use one! Besides," he tilted his comical head and sniffed the air, "it should snow this afternoon. If it comes early enough, there'll be no tracks left."

"No!" Holzinger gaped at him, half angry, half amused. "This is serious, Karl. We can't play games."

"I'm not playing," said Karl Adalbert Fischer.

"What then? This is murder. We're responsible—both of us—to the Occupation Commander."

Fischer took a cigarette out of a leather case and tapped it reflectively on his thumbnail. His eyes were blank and hooded. He said sombrely: "There have been a lot of murders in the past ten years, Max. In a way we've been responsible for those too. I don't see why one poor, crazy devil should be hanged for all of them."

"He killed a Britisher."

"Until two months ago he was paid to do just that—and would have been shot himself if he hadn't. Maybe he didn't know the war was over. . . ."

"The court would accept that as . . ."

"What court!" The little head jerked up, wagging angrily on its long neck. "The drumhead! Where the judges sit with the stink of the concentration camps and the smell of the crematorium in their nostrils and lump us all together as torturers and sadists. I don't blame them for that either. But I'm not going to hand them this boy's head on a dish. Look. . . ." He turned away to the farther wall, on which still hung a map of the battle areas of Europe, stuck with little coloured flags. The flags were drooping and the map was stained with flung wine and coffee slops from the last despairing party before the Armistice.

It was typical of Fischer that he hadn't thought of tearing it down. Now he stood beside it, tracing the lines with his blunt finger, while the Bürgermeister watched him with growing wonderment.

"I'll show you where he came from and what happened to him on the way. He started here in the Ukraine at Mukachevo, which was the regimental hospital for our Quellenberg boys. He was a doctor, you see, young, not very experienced. But then none of our boys were old, were they? He soon got all the experience he wanted, what with amputations, belly wounds, frostbite and typhus, and all the other damn things that came when the Russkis started to roll us back all along the line. When the regiment was cut off he kept working night and day, with no drugs, no anæsthetics, until he dropped on his face in a dead man's blood. That probably saved his life, because when the Cossacks broke through, they went through the *Lazarett* with the bayonets, shouting and singing. That's how he got the scar on his face. Had he been awake, he'd have got it in the guts. When he woke, he was lying with the dead and even when he screamed there was no one to hear him because the Cossacks were a long way forward now and the snow was falling and the wind driving it across the steppes. His face was hanging open, but the cold had stopped the bleeding and he rummaged through the wreckage to find a hand mirror and sutures so that he could sew it up. Then he went through the pockets of the dead to find food scraps and cigarettes. He stripped the woollen clothes off those who had them and padded himself with bloody underclothing. Then he picked up a rifle and a bayonet and a dead man's pistol and set out to fight his way home. You know how long it took him?" Fischer's hand stabbed accusingly at his friend. "Twelve months! Twice he was taken, and twice he escaped. He walked from Mukachevo to Budapest, which is halfway across Hungary. The Russkis were round the city in a week, so he turned back east and came to Salonta in Rumania. Then he went south into Yugoslavia and headed north again towards Carinthia. He killed three men. He hunted like an animal for his food. He slept with prostitutes and seduced peasant girls so that they would feed him and hide him. In Yugoslavia the Chetniks took him and tortured him, so that he would never be good to a woman again. Then they laughed in his face and turned him out to die. By some miracle he survived. His wounds healed but his face was scarred into a Krampus mask. And, like all hunted, hungry men, he became a little mad. He saw enemies behind every tree. All his dreams were full of monsters . . . they still are, though he has been home a month. He wakes in the night screaming. The house seems like a prison to him and sometimes he goes out, with his gun and his pistol, ranging the mountains. They've tried to disarm him but he snarls like a cornered wolf. Lately they thought he was getting better. The nightmares didn't come so often. The wanderings were not so frequent. . . . Then, this happens. . . ."

"You talk . . ." said Holzinger, slowly, "as if you know him well."

"I do," said Karl Adalbert Fischer, "he's my sister's son."

"God in Heaven!"

"You—you see now why I can't let them have him?"

"I see it, yes. But I don't see how you can hold him safely. The Occupation may last for years."

The comical head nodded grimly.

"I'll hold him. I'll shift him from valley to valley, from farm to farm, and I'll have the English scouring every mountain but the right one. I'll keep him for ten years if I have to—and Hanlon will never come within a shot of him."

"You'll never keep a secret like that, Karl. People talk—our people more than most. Hanlon will come to hear of it, then you'll be the one he'll take."

The face of the little policeman relaxed again into a good-humoured smile. He poured himself another schnapps and savoured it slowly. Then he crossed to a steel cabinet in the corner of the room, unlocked it and took out a large folio bound in leather. When he spread it on the table, Holzinger saw that every page was covered with small Gothic script.

"What's that?"

"This?" said Fischer with a grin. "This is why a no-good fellow like me has held a job like this for fifteen years—and never a black mark against him. My office records are six months behind, but this has been written up every evening for all that time."

"What is it?" Holzinger looked puzzled.

"Dossiers, Herr Bürgermeister! My personal record on every man, woman and child in Quellenberg and the valley. Fact, gossip, suspicion, guesswork. Things I've heard in bed. Whispers I've picked up at funerals. All there. All mine. Most of it I've never used. But it's there when I want it."

"Have you got me there too?" Holzinger laughed uneasily.

Fischer nodded. "You and your wife and your daughter—and your son, God rest him. You're in good company. You have the page next to Father Albertus."

"Have you got Kunzli too?"

"Kunzli!" He spat contemptuously into the wastepaper basket. "I've got a long chapter on that one. Why do you ask?"

"I might want you to use it one day," said Holzinger softly.

Fischer made an emphatic gesture of refusal.

"Not even for you, Herr Bürgermeister. There's a lifetime of work in that book. I've never used it for blackmail, and I hope I never shall. But I intend to make a profit out of it—one way or another."

"You're making a profit out of it now, Karl."

"I am?" He cocked his head like a restless bird, ready to fly off at the slightest stir of danger.

"Yes. You see, I've forgotten all about your sister's son. So far as I know he died in Russland."

"Good!" The word came out on a long breath of satisfaction as Fischer bent over the table to pour two glasses of schnapps. "I was sure you'd understand, Max . . . And if you have any trouble with Kunzli, let me know."

"I'll do that," said Max Holzinger calmly. "*Prost!*"

"*Prost!*"

They raised their glasses and drank, standing in front of the fly-blown map where the wine was like spilt blood and the little flags drooped in drunken defeat.

'We deserve it,' thought Holzinger bitterly. 'We deserve everything that happens to us—the rulers we get, the sons we lose, the woman who betrays us. We've lost the war. The yoke is on our necks again—and we're still conspiring one against the other. God damn our miserable souls.'

He drained his glass, picked up his hat and gloves and walked out to discuss funeral arrangements with Father Albertus.

The door of the Pfarrhaus was opened by an apple-cheeked widow with an acid tongue. The Father wasn't there, she told him. He was down in the churchyard, shovelling snow like any labourer. Before he could check her she was launched into a clatter of dialect mourning the follies of the clergy and the burdens they laid on her own broad shoulders:

"He'll kill himself, that's what! And him old enough to know better. If he goes down with pneumonia, who has to nurse him? Me! He's hard enough to handle when he's well— God knows. Eats enough for a sparrow, waters his wine till it tastes like dish slops, sleeps maybe two hours a night. I wouldn't mind that if he'd let me sleep too. I'm two floors down but I hear him pacing up and down, muttering and praying. Sometimes he beats himself so that his shirts are bloody. Then it's me that has to wash them. You've only got to look at him to . . ."

"All right! All right! It's none of my business." Holzinger's patience was fraying thin. He had troubles enough of his own without peasant gossip on the ascetic oddities of an old priest. He turned away brusquely and the housekeeper shut the door with a bang and went back to her kitchen, mumbling unhappily about officials who got too big for their boots and whose womenfolk were no better than they should be anyway.

The Quellenbergers had never approved of the deep-voiced blonde from Hamburg and the escapades of the daughter had made meaty gossip round the farmhouse stoves.

Holzinger thrust his hands into his pockets, twitched his fur collar up round his ears, and walked with head thrust forward and eyes downcast to the solid ice of the roadway. Idling townsfolk raised their hats and '*Grüsse*'d him, but he neither saw nor heard them, and they turned away troubled, because normally he was a polite man who never failed to acknowledge a salute.

When he came to the high wall that hid the churchyard of St Julian from the roadway, a tiny blonde girl stepped out and held up a bunch of snow roses, begging in her piping voice:

"*Schneerosen*, Herr Bürgermeister! For the poor?"

Her sudden presence startled him, but there was so much innocence in her small, glowing face that he forced a smile and fumbled in his pocket for change to give her.

She curtsied and thanked him prettily, then thrust the roses into his hand and went skipping off towards the valley. Holzinger looked at the tiny white blooms with their waxy leaves, and wondered what the devil to do with them.

As he walked into the churchyard he saw the old wooden crucifix rearing itself among the forest of headboards. Acting on a sudden impulse he laid the flowers at the feet of the Christus, crossed himself awkwardly and turned away, feeling faintly guilty, like a boy caught at the jam jar.

Then he saw Father Albertus.

He was chipping the ice away from the grey stone steps of the entrance and shovelling it into a heap behind one of the buttresses. With his mane of white hair and his stooped shoulders, his threadbare cloak and his heavy boots, he looked like any aged peasant from the hills. But when he straightened at the sound of the footfall and turned to greet Holzinger, he was another man entirely.

The first thing one noticed was the extraordinary transparency of his face. It was as though a lamp burned behind it— a fire slowly consuming the flesh, so that there were only the fine aquiline bones and the old, translucent skin stretched over them.

Then one saw his eyes, cornflower blue, limpid as a child's, lit with an eager tenderness as a child's are lit when it has a secret to share with someone beloved. The mouth was firm but quirked upwards into a smile that belied the lines of suffering cut deep into the cheeks. The voice that issued from it was deep as a bell.

It was only afterwards that you remembered his hands.

They were gnarled and crooked like the talons of a hawk, the joints enlarged and anchylotic, so that the only movement left was in the thumbs and the forefingers.

Early, after the Anschluss, when he had been Rector of the Jesuit Novitiate at Graz, he had been taken to Mauthausen, for a course of 'corrective treatment'. One of his gaolers was a former pupil who had conceived the gentle revenge of breaking one of his fingers each week, and tormenting him with the thought that in the end the consecrated fingers would go too, so that he would never again be able to say Mass.

Father Albertus was a man who believed in prayer—and in Mauthausen there was nothing left to do but pray. Before six weeks were out, the Cardinal in Vienna had had him released and prudently offered him, through his superiors, the choice of expulsion from Austria or a parish appointment in the mountains.

So now he was in the churchyard of St Julian, leaning on his shovel like a peasant and listening to Holzinger's querulous report of his interview with Mark Hanlon. He heard him out in silence, then his eyes clouded with gentle regret and he said slowly:

"You must understand, Max, it's hard for any of us to behave well in a situation like this."

That was another characteristic of the old man. He never said the expected thing. He never wasted words on courteous preludes. He had no time now for anything but the truth.

"Harder for us than for him," said Holzinger sourly.

"No. Power is like the king's new clothes: an illusion that leaves a man naked to the laughter and the swords."

"You'll go to see him?"

"Yes."

"Try to explain to him that while I can direct the people to come to the funeral, I can't guarantee a full attendance. I can't force my colleagues to act as pall bearers."

"Forget your vanity, Herr Bürgermeister." There was a

gentle irony in the old man's smile. "Forget that this is an order from the Occupying Power. Make it a personal request from yourself, a suggestion that courtesy and charity are involved. Our people understand these things—most of the time."

"It gives Hanlon an easy victory."

"Hanlon . . . ?" He seized on the name suddenly. "That's not an English name, is it?"

"I don't know. I'm not so familiar with the language. Why?" Father Albertus shrugged.

"A passing thought. A tag of memory. It doesn't matter."

"By the way," Holzinger glanced around the churchyard, at the old headstones in the family plots, at the small forest of pine slabs that were the memorials of the unburied regiment, "where do we bury this man?"

"Over there." Father Albertus pointed to the big crucifix standing among the headboards. "At the feet of the Christus."

"In the middle of our boys?" Holzinger was alarmed. "The people won't like that."

"We are all one family in the womb and in the tomb," the old man admonished him gravely. "We are all brothers in Christ. The sooner the people understand that, the sooner they will come to peace."

Holzinger looked down at the gnarled and broken hands of the priest and knew that he could not gainsay him.

Major Mark Hanlon sat in his big lounge at the top of the Sonnblick Hotel and discussed the future with Captain Johnson. A white-coated waiter had just taken away the remains of their lunch and they sat sprawled in the big armchairs, drinking coffee and sipping a strong, sweet Austrian liqueur. The meal and the wine had relaxed them, the first strangeness of the place had worn off and they were beginning to be at ease with each other.

Johnson took out his cigarette case, offered it to Hanlon, then lit up for both of them. They smoked a few moments in silence, watching the blue spirals drift drowsily upward to the coffered ceiling. Johnson grinned boyishly and murmured:

"This is the life, Mark; I can take lots of it."

"You'll get it, Johnny," said Hanlon with cool good humour. "We're going to be here a long time. Are the boys settled in?"

"Yes. I've bedded them on the first and second floors, NCOs on the ground level. They'll eat in the main dining-room and use the *Stüberl* as a canteen. The NCOs can use the cocktail bar. The ballroom we'll turn into a theatre, the lounge and writing-room will do as they are. I thought you'd be happy with what we've got up here—there's room enough for a regiment."

Hanlon nodded reflectively and drew on his cigarette.

"They'll start getting bored in a week. We'll need some entertainment. See if Mayer can rake up some musicians for us. I'll write to Klagenfurt and ask 'em for a projector and a regular supply of films. You can probably find a ski-instructor for those who want to learn. We'd better close the bars at eleven. Lights out at midnight. All troops to be back in quarters by then."

"What about the non-fraternisation order?"

"It can't work, Johnny. They'll have to cancel it sooner or later. Probably sooner. Meantime . . ."

He broke off and stared up at the gold traceries of the ceiling. Johnson prompted him curiously.

"Meantime?"

"We don't want a bunch of pregnant servants in the hotel. So we'll make our own rules. All bars and *Stüberls* in the town are out of bounds to troops. If they want to take the girls walking or ski-ing, that's fine. If they're entertained in private houses, that's fine too. But no public fraternisation and no women on the premises here, unless we organise an official entertainment—which won't be for a while yet."

"Aren't you sticking your neck out, Mark? Don't misunderstand me," he amended hastily. "I think you're right. But what will Headquarters have to say about it?"

"I don't propose to tell 'em," said Hanlon bluntly. "I'm leaving it to you and the NCOs to talk sense into the troops and see they don't abuse the privilege—or the girls. If there's trouble I'll use the chopper, without mercy."

"Fair enough." Johnson nodded agreement. "I'll ride 'em on a tight bit for a week or two, then gradually relax. I think it's better that way."

"It's up to you, Johnny. I've got my hands full already."

His eyes clouded and his mouth set into a grim line. Johnson looked at him with vague uneasiness.

"Something on your mind, Mark?"

Abruptly Hanlon heaved himself out of the chair and walked to the window, where he stood watching the grey clouds roll in from the defile and over the white shoulders of the Grauglockner. He said absently:

"It'll be snowing soon."

"That doesn't answer the question."

"It does, you know." Hanlon swung round to face him. "All tracks will be blotted out in twenty minutes. The police will come back and say they couldn't find any trace of the man who killed Willis."

"You expected that, didn't you?"

"I expected it. I don't have to be happy about it."

"He's dead," said Johnson with the unconscious cruelty of youth. "You can't bring him back. He was killed after the whistle blew—which turns an act of war into a crime. You've set the machinery in motion to catch the criminal. I don't see why you have to tear your tripes out. It's part of the job. We bury Willis decently and forget him—because we can't remember him any more than the millions of others who've died in the past few years. Here, have another drink."

He slid the bottle and the glass along the polished table towards Hanlon. It surprised him a little when Hanlon stepped back from the window, picked them up and poured himself a double measure. He cocked a sardonic eye at his junior, raised the glass and gave the toast.

"To the New Order! *Prost!*"

"There's no new order," said Johnson cheerily, "because men are always the same and girls are always different. But that's no reason to waste the liquor. *Prost!*"

Then the telephone rang, and when Hanlon picked it up the sergeant of the guard told him that Father Albertus was waiting to see him.

"Keep him three minutes, then bring him up."

"Yessir."

He put down the receiver and turned briskly to Johnson.

"Visitor, Johnny! The vicar's calling. Let's clean up the mess and make ourselves look respectable."

"Don't the customers ever see through it?" Johnson was full of food and wine, and he was feeling a little larger than life. Hanlon shot him a quick glance and answered sourly.

"If they do, it's our own damn fault! Jump to it, Johnny! Empty the ashtrays and get the liquor out of sight."

They bustled about the room like a pair of housemaids, and when Father Albertus was ushered in a few minutes later Hanlon was sitting behind the buhl desk and Johnson was standing beside him, the proper symbols of the Occupying Power.

The sergeant stood aside and the old priest walked slowly across the wide carpet till he stood in front of the desk. He held out his hand and said: "*Grüss Gott*, Major!"

Johnson jumped at the sound of his deep bell-toned voice. Hanlon stared at him, wide-eyed and gaping, as if he were a ghost. He made no move to touch the outstretched hand, but raised himself slowly from the chair, his eyes fixed on the spare, luminous face and the white silken hair that framed it. His voice was a whisper of wonderment.

"God Almighty! No!"

Johnson and the sergeant stared at him, and he turned to them with an imperative gesture.

"Leave us please. Both of you!"

They hesitated a moment, then saluted smartly and walked from the room. Only when the door had closed on them, did he take the old man's hand. When he felt the stiff, broken fingers he looked down at them in shocked surprise, then back again at the smiling eyes.

"The name meant nothing when I heard it, Father. I still can't believe it's you!"

"Brother Mark! The restless lion. I remembered the name when Holzinger told me. You've changed, my son."

"You too, Father. Won't you sit down?"

He came out from behind his desk and brought up a chair for the old man. He offered a cigarette and a drink, but Father Albertus refused them both. Hanlon pulled up another chair and sat facing him, as if ashamed to occupy the seats of the mighty in the presence of the worn old scholar.

"God leads us on strange roads, my son." The mild eyes were studying every line of his face. "I come to bend the knee to Cæsar and I find my old novice sitting under the eagles."

"I was more comfortable in your lecture-room," said Hanlon dryly.

The old priest smiled and shook his head.

"You were restless then, too. The habit of religion sat uneasily on your shoulders." He glanced up at the shining crowns on the epaulettes. "Does this one chafe you less?"

"It suits me better, Father. I was never made for a monk."

"I often wondered. You were unhappy when you left us. Are you happy now?"

"I'm older." Hanlon skirted the answer carefully. "I'm not unhappy now." He looked down at the twisted hands clamped like talons on the arms of the chair. "Tell me about yourself, Father. What happened to your hands?"

"Mauthausen," said Father Albertus briefly. "An unhappy man who thought that by tormenting me he could ease the torment of his own conscience. He had been a student of mine, before I was made Novice Master. I must have failed him very badly. This, I feel, is a kind of penance for it."

"It's a madhouse!" Hanlon's voice was soft and surprisingly bitter. "What's happened to these people that they can do things like this—slow torture, sudden murder? In the old days, when I was at Graz with you, they weren't like that. They were gentle, *gemütlich*, full of *Schmalz* as a suet pudding. What's happened?"

"Nothing," said Father Albertus gravely. "Nothing but the flowering of the evil that was already in our hearts. Nothing that could not happen to you also, my son."

"I don't understand you." Hanlon's head jerked up resentfully.

"I think you do. You lived among us a long time. You loved us enough to learn the language like our own children. Unless I'm mistaken, that's why you came back—because you wanted to see us again, help us perhaps. Is that true?"

"Truer than you know. It took me six months to prepare the ground for this appointment, Father. After all the bloody mess of the war, it seemed a chance to build instead of destroy." He smiled and spread his hands in ironic deprecation. "You taught me better than you know, Father Novice Master. You took the taste out of a lot of kisses and the savour out of the best wine. You left me with this itch to mend the world—but never taught me the art of living in it comfortably. That, I had to learn myself. But . . . you're right enough. I wanted to come back. I did want to help. I did love these people."

"Until one of them murdered your friend."

"That's right."

"One is not all."

"But all of them will hide the one, won't they?"

31

"Don't blame them too much for that. They've lost nearly all their young men. There will be many girls in the valley who will never have a husband. Can you chide them for wanting to save even this maimed one?"

"They won't save him this way. Don't they understand? There's the law . . ."

"The law has been a mockery in Europe for a long time, Mark. You should understand that."

"There's a new law now."

The old man smiled with gentle irony and shook his head.

"The law of the conqueror. That is suspect from the beginning."

"I know that as well as you do. But don't you see they've got to give it a trial? Otherwise there's no hope of a new start. You, of all people, should have respect for the law, Father."

"I do, my son, but I've never believed the hangman was its best interpreter."

"For God's sake! I'm no hangman." Hanlon's voice was harsh with anger. "I'm here to see justice is done. And I remember enough of my life in Austria to temper it with mercy."

"You can't guarantee either justice or mercy," said Father Albertus bluntly. "You're a man subject to authority—like the centurion. You may arrest this fellow. You may arraign him. But you can neither plead his cause nor change the code by which he will be judged."

"Spare me the dialectics, Father!" Hanlon exploded impatiently. "It's a practical problem. A murder has been committed. If the people don't co-operate in bringing the murderer to trial they'll be joined as accessories in the act. They'll find themselves in opposition to the only authority which can help them back to a normal life. There'll be no peace for them until this man is found."

"And this love you bring, Mark? Where does that show itself?"

"We dispense with it," said Hanlon flatly. "Because a one-sided love is barren and bitter. We administer justice. We rule according to the statute books. It's probably wiser in the long run."

"Are you sure that you can dispense with it?"

"I'm sure of it, Father. I have to be."

The old priest stood up and gathered his cloak about him.

His eyes were sombre now and the fire seemed to have died a little behind his drawn face. He said quietly:

"The Bürgermeister told me what you wanted. I've made arrangements for the requiem and the funeral. I wondered, perhaps, if you'd care to serve my Mass. It—it would be like old times."

Some of the coldness melted out of the eyes of Mark Hanlon as he looked at his white-haired mentor and saw how old and tired and frail he was. He hesitated a moment then he told him, kindly enough:

"Better not, Father. I haven't been to the Sacraments for a long time. And, besides, there's a political aspect as well. There are Lutherans as well as Catholics in Bad Quellenberg. The Occupying Power cannot afford to identify itself too closely with either. I'll be at the Mass and the funeral. That's the best I can do."

The old priest looked at him steadily for a long moment, then he drew himself up and said in his deep, firm voice:

"You asked me what made this a madhouse, my son. You yourself have given me the answer. Too much politics and too little love."

He did not offer his hand this time but bowed stiffly and turned to go.

"*Servus*, Major."

"*Auf Wiedersehn*, Father," said Mark Hanlon coolly.

CHAPTER 3

At the highest point on the scenic promenade which encircled Bad Quellenberg, a house had been built. An acre of pines had been cleared and milled for timber, the clearing had been levelled behind a retaining wall of mountain rock, and on the broad, artificial plateau the building had been reared, three storeys of stone and timber, whose windows stared out across the town and the fall of the valley.

A fringe of pines screened it from the road and a grilled gate with an electric lock kept it private from casual visitors. Behind the pines there was a wide expanse of lawn, which in springtime blazed with flowers and blossoming bushes. There was a paved terrace which took the sun, summer and winter, and the mountains screened it from the winds that came searching down the defiles.

The place was called, conventionally enough, Valhalla; but the locals had another name for it—*das Spinnenhaus*, the Spiderhouse. A brass plate on the gatepost named its owner: Doctor Sepp Kunzli, Solicitor.

No one, at first sight, looked less like a spider than this trim, dapper advocate. His sleek dark hair and his olive skin recalled the Romans who had garrisoned the Danube centuries ago. The disciplined grace of his movements made him look younger than his forty-five years.

It was his eyes that gave him away. They were dark and dead like an insect's. They saw at all angles, from a multitude of facets. But there was no light in them—no faintest hint of the thoughts that went on behind them. They were a spider's eyes, calculating, predatory, pitiless.

The truth about Sepp Kunzli was simple but startling: he had been dead for a long time.

Most men die slowly, under the small, daily crucifixions of living. They submit, gratefully enough, to the last drugged decline into old age and forgetfulness. Some, the fortunate, achieve a fuller flowering of the spirit, as their physical life is pruned away.

Sepp Kunzli had died, suddenly and despairingly, one bright summer's day; and the man who walked thereafter, in his shoes, was a cold spectre with a first-class brain—and a splinter of ice where his heart should have been.

In the mid-'thirties he had been a rising young lawyer in Vienna. He had stepped straight from university into his father's practice, an old family firm, with connections in Bavaria and Hungary and Switzerland and all the provinces of Austria. Land was changing hands quickly, long-headed folk were liquidating their holdings and building up foreign funds, so that more and more clients came to the sober, baroque office near the Ringstrasse.

He met and married a young Jewess, daughter of one of the minor merchant bankers, who brought him a handsome dowry. They had no children, but they had been singularly happy, in the last springtime before the Anschluss.

A week after the first German units had rolled into Vienna,

Sepp Kunzli came home to find his wife with her head in the gas oven and a pathetic little note clasped in her hand:

I have loved you too much to be a burden to you now.
Forgive me.

Another man might have shot himself or run crazy, or embarked on a despairing campaign of hate and vengeance. Kunzli did none of these things. He buried his wife quietly, sold his house, settled into bachelor lodgings in another quarter and went about his business with a cold concentration that shocked his family and alienated his friends.

He closed the accounts of old clients and began to build new ones—senior Party officials, members of the new administration, investors from Germany.

He bought property and sold it for them. He advised them on their investments at home and found loopholes for their dealings abroad. He became the confidant of their marriage secrets and the negotiator of their diplomatic divorces. When they pressed him to join the Party he pointed out that he could serve them better by remaining out of it. But he made substantial donations to its funds and travelled freely abroad on a specially endorsed passport.

Finally, he broke with his father's firm and took all his clients with him. He left Vienna and came to Bad Quellenberg —and his clients came too, after he had showed them the advantages of representation so near to the borders of Italy, Yugoslavia and Switzerland, so far from the muddy intrigues of the capital.

What he did not tell them was that this was the final step out of a world he hated, the first move in a cool campaign to exploit the men who had killed his wife and quenched the last spark of love in himself.

He found no joy in it. He was incapable of joy. All that was left was the icy passion of the chessplayer, toppling the pawns from the board, moving relentlessly forward to the final, savourless checkmate.

When he traded for his clients in Switzerland, he charged them exorbitant commissions. When Berlin issued new regulations against foreign trading, he opened cover accounts for them in his own name, using their securities to bolster his private trading, invoking the influence of senior officials to preserve his own immunity. The timid he blackmailed, subtly.

The bold he encouraged to excesses that put them further and further in his debt. He was always ready to guarantee a mortgage or pick up a promissory note. A spendthrift wife could always count on him for a loan—and he was never too anxious to collect it.

When the big men came to Bad Quellenberg he entertained them lavishly. When they were recalled to duty he seduced their wives and their daughters and their mistresses with a calculated passion that left them gasping at first—and afterwards strangely afraid.

In Bad Quellenberg itself he played the same game, easily and with discretion. He held liens on the best building land, notes against the biggest hotels. The contractors were in his pocket and the councillors followed the policies he drew for them.

The web that was spun in the Spiderhouse spread more widely and intricately as the years went on and its threads were anchored in the most unlikely places. There was a man in Zürich named John Winter to whom he had sought an introduction through a close-mouthed Swiss banker. Whenever he came to Switzerland they met by appointment in the banker's private office and Kunzli passed on to him information that ranged from troop movements on the Tauern line, to the latest indiscretions of a Reichsminister's wife. He always refused payments for this information, presenting himself as a patriot who had the interests of his country at heart. The closest scrutiny in London had failed to find any flaws in the information or any suggestion of double dealing by the donor. Kunzli was written down as a safe agent, a man to be remembered in later days.

It was the biggest of his gambles, but without it there could be no triumph. There was no point in ruining an enemy if you too were involved in his downfall. Now the gamble seemed to have paid off. The Allies had won the war. The men who had killed his wife were coming, each in his turn, to their proper end. Out of their fear and greed he had made a fortune. At last the flies were struggling in the web and the spider could sit and smile and eat them at his leisure. . . .

So, on this winter afternoon, while the first snowfall settled on the hills and on the black pines, he sat in his study and pondered his diplomatic approaches to the Occupying Power.

He smiled bleakly when he thought of Holzinger called in like a messenger, and Fischer trounced into activity, and even the Church hauled up for discipline.

Mayer had telephoned him from the Sonnblick with a series of commentaries on their comings and goings. A useful man, Mayer, admirably placed for inside tips on the market. Mayer had been his personal appointee and had covered his salary ten times over with bedroom gossip and indiscretions from the conference room.

The new commander was something of an enigma. He talked perfect German. He acted like a man who knew his own mind. He would need to be approached carefully. Co-operation, on equal terms: that should be the keynote. The occasion would present itself soon enough.

The murder was already the talk of the town. Holzinger and Fischer were in a neat dilemma. If they caught the boy the whole population would be at their throats. If they didn't, they fell foul of the new authority. It would be interesting to know whether the English wanted him caught or whether they would prefer to forget the business after a decent interval. They were a subtle people, with a great respect for law and a singular talent for interpreting it to suit themselves.

He wondered if the killer had been named yet, and whether he came from the hills or from the town. These things were important too. If he belonged to one of the old families, the peasants would hide him for years, fending off all investigations with a blank, animal stubbornness. If he were from the town, one of the immigrant stock from Salzburg or Vienna or Graz, they might be happier to let him go to save themselves trouble. The tribal instinct was still strong in the upland valleys.

One thing was certain. Whatever happened, Sepp Kunzli would make a profit. Both sides would need a mediator. Both would pay, in their own coin, for his skilled services.

He was still chewing on this sweet thought, when the door opened and his niece came into the room.

She was dressed, mountain fashion, in ski trousers and walking boots and a long greatcoat with a fur collar. Her blonde hair was braided and wound into a coronet, and her green Tyrolean hat was tipped at a jaunty angle over a face bright as a porcelain doll's.

She crossed the room quickly and kissed her uncle lightly

on the forehead. He made no response to the gesture but asked her calmly:

"Are you going out?"

"Yes. To the hospital first. There's an hour's therapy with the amputees."

"How are they getting along?"

He had no interest in the answer, but he asked the question with the cool impersonal courtesy which seemed necessary to maintain a comfortable relationship.

"Some of them are doing very well. Young Dietrich starts with his sticks today. And Heinzi Reitlinger can light a cigarette with his artificial hand. I'm quite proud of them."

"I'm glad."

"I—I was wondering. Uncle . . ." She faltered and broke off.

"What were you wondering, Anna?"

"Whether you'd mind if I invited a few of them to the house one evening. The ambulance would bring them and . . ."

"I'm sorry, my dear. I've spent a good deal of money to provide recreation facilities in the town. I see no reason why my privacy should be invaded."

"Just as you say, Uncle." If she was disappointed, she gave no sign of it. Her voice was as calm as his own, but warm still and friendly. "By the way, I shan't be back to tea."

"Why not?"

"Father Albertus telephoned. He's asked for choir practice this evening. The English soldier is to be buried tomorrow. We're to sing the requiem."

For the first time a flicker of interest showed in Kunzli's dark, dead eyes. He said, with mild sarcasm: "We don't have requiems sung for our own boys. I wonder why."

"Perhaps because there are too many of them."

He looked up sharply, but there was nothing in her face but that frank, bewildering innocence which she had brought with her into his house and against which all his ironies blunted themselves. At first it had annoyed him. He thought it the kind of careful insolence which children use on people they dislike. He had tried to goad her out of it, until one day she faced him, a leggy, gangling schoolgirl, and said quite gently: "You mustn't be cruel to me, Uncle; you will only hurt your-self more and make me unhappy. Then we couldn't live together, could we?"

38

It was then he had made his first surrender to an innocence he didn't believe in. He made it again now. He shrugged and said: "Don't be late for dinner."

"I won't; *Auf Wiedersehn*, Uncle."

"*Wiedersehn*, Anna."

She brushed her hand lightly across his hair and was gone. Sepp Kunzli wondered, for the thousandth time, what folly had made him admit her into his life.

She was his brother's child, but after his departure from Vienna he had neither seen nor heard of her until one day she turned up on his doorstep, scared and red eyed, accompanied by a brawny peasant woman from the Burgenland.

The Burgenländerin came with a poor opinion of Sepp and a determination to see justice done to her chick.

In her thick, raw dialect she told him that Anna's father was dead—shot down over England—and that the mother was coughing her heart out in a Vienna sanatorium and likely to die in weeks. The old people were dead and Sepp was the last surviving relative. Was he going to do his duty or wasn't he? How in the name of the seven saints could he live in this big barn of a place while his own kin were left lonely? It didn't matter to her, she'd take the child happily and bring her up in the Burgenland. Come to that, she'd probably be better off with a good God-fearing family. But she had rights didn't she? And if the *feine Mann* didn't want to look after her, he should be ashamed of himself.

Ten minutes of this and Sepp Kunzli was beaten. He took the girl—an awkward fifteen-year-old—into his house and consigned her to the care of his housekeeper and tried to forget her. Both the housekeeper and Anna herself seemed happy to help him do it. When her mother died it was the housekeeper who soothed her out of her grief, while Kunzli took himself off to Switzerland, oblivious of a lonely teenager moping through the big house.

It was the housekeeper who bought her clothes and encouraged her to meet other girls and had Father Albertus introduce her into the choir and the Church Guilds and the Hospital Auxiliary.

One day, with a shock of surprise, Kunzli realised that he had a woman in the house, a young and beautiful woman, with a curious, tolerant affection for him and a critical eye for his calculated follies. He couldn't ignore her any more—nor did he want any longer to dispense with her. She was as familiar as an article of furniture, and as comforting.

When she suggested, quite simply, that he should make her a small allowance to save repeated demands for clothing and feminine necessaries, he agreed without question and doubled what she asked. He was even prepared to commend her common sense. She bought him small, useless gifts for his birthday and for the feasts; and he was forced to return the courtesy. He had never once kissed her, nor taken her in his arms, but she showed no resentment at his lack of love. His barbed humour left her untouched. If she disapproved of his seductions, she said nothing, and she was impervious to the strutting gallantries of his male guests. In a world gone mad she seemed to carry with her the springtime sanity of Eden. But Sepp Kunzli's Eden was so long lost, he lacked the wit to recognise it.

The girl was there. She would probably stay there until some man asked her to marry him—and the sooner one did, the better. Meanwhile she was an uncomfortable reminder that little girls grow up and rich men grow old, and that revenge and money are the dustiest triumphs of all.

The sudden shrilling of the desk phone cut across his reverie. He lifted the receiver and heard an unfamiliar Viennese voice:

"Doktor Kunzli?"

"This is Kunzli. Yes?"

"This is Mark Hanlon, Occupation Commander."

Kunzli was instantly cordial.

"My dear Major Hanlon! Nice of you to ring. I was waiting until you'd settled in before coming to pay respects. I knew you would have much to do and . . ."

"I've had word about you from Klagenfurt," Hanlon cut in crisply. "I'd like to see you as soon as possible."

"Certainly, Major. Perhaps you would care to dine with me tonight; I could send a car . . ."

"I'm sorry. That's not possible. I'd like to see you in my office about five this afternoon. Can you manage that?"

"Well . . . it's somewhat short notice, but . . ."

"Thank you, Doktor. I'll expect you. *Auf Wiedersehn.*"

"*Auf Wiedersehn*, Major," said Sepp Kunzli, but the line was already dead. He replaced the receiver slowly on its cradle and sat back in his chair, cupping his chin on his hand and

40

staring out at the noiseless, tumbling snowflakes and the grey mist gathering in the valley.

As the first day of his command wore itself out, Hanlon lapsed deeper and deeper into a black temper. The visit of Father Albertus had revived memories he preferred to leave buried, and had raised issues, personal and public, which promised new problems in his already complex task. The attitude of the local authority was already defining itself as one of passive resistance and Captain Johnson was showing himself an amiable cynic apt enough for military command but too young to lend either moral support or useful counsel to his senior officer.

Quicker than he had dreamed, Mark Hanlon was coming to the conclusion that sentimental journeys were always a mistake, and that old loves, like old kisses, should be left to fade gracefully in the memory chest. Love was a shared thing. It demanded an equality, a confession of mutual need. When there was one who kissed and another who turned the cheek, love died of quick starvation. He had found that in his private life. It was being thrust upon him now in his public one. If he wanted to lie comfortably in his bed, he must sleep alone, with bayonets at the door and the sword of office always at his hand. And if there came those who talked the language of love and offered a little more than the cold coin of tribute, he must mistrust them. If he made commerce with them it must be the commerce of the bawdy house—money paid for value received. And a pox on the careless who picked the wrong bedfellow!

Which explains why Karl Adalbert Fischer got a poor welcome and the rough edge of the Major's tongue when he came to make his first report. Hanlon kept him standing, like a junior, in front of the desk and questioned him with cool precision.

"The car is wrecked you say?"

"That's right, Major. The roads are icy, as you know. The tyres were worn and the steering has always been slightly defective. A tyre burst and the car skidded off the road and down the embankment. It was lucky my men were not killed."

"Odd that this should have happened only five miles from town."

Fischer shrugged and spread his hands helplessly.

Who can say where an accident will happen? My men's

behaviour was quite exemplary. One of them came back to report to me. The other two went forward on foot to the scene of the crime. By the time they got there, the snow was falling heavily. All tracks had been obliterated. Questions at the nearest farmhouses revealed nothing."

"Very convenient."

"If the Major insinuates . . ." Fischer flushed and wagged his head in comical indignation.

"Save it!" Hanlon cut him off curtly. "How do you propose to function without a car?"

"We can't."

"Then use your private vehicle. Pay yourself petrol and maintenance, and I'll give you one of my men to drive it. He speaks German and will be able to assist you in your investigations."

Fischer gulped and stammered uneasily. "We—we will welcome any assistance you can give us."

"I'm sure you will. You'll be sending out ski parties daily to question the outlying farmers. I have four good skiers among my troops. I'll appoint one to each party."

"Ski parties!" Fischer's eyes widened in surprise. "Does the Major know how many men I have? Six! I still have to maintain order in the town—and you ask me to search the mountains and the valleys with ski parties!"

"There are four Alpine guides and at least ten foresters who are out of work in the winter. Use them to make up your parties. They'll report here each morning for their orders. I'd hate to think that advance information was circulated in the search areas."

"Major, I did not come here to be insulted! I must ask you to . . ."

Hanlon went on with the same unhurried irony: "You will have in the town records a nominal roll of the members of the Quellenberg Regiment. You will also have a casualty list showing those dead and missing, and those already repatriated. We take out the dead—who are the majority—and we have a first list of families who may know something about the soldier with the scar. Does that make sense to you Fischer?"

"No!" said the little policeman, with sudden anger. "I cannot work with a man who mistrusts me."

Hanlon leaned back in his chair and looked at him with sardonic amusement.

"You're mistaken, my friend, I do trust you—to hold up this search in every way possible! I'm not sure that I blame you either. In your place I'd probably do the same. I hope to convince you you'll be making a mistake." He straightened again and opened the folder that lay in front of him. His tone was deceptively mild. "It's in my competence to dismiss you, Fischer; the grounds are: Party associations, incompetence, or unwillingness to co-operate. I could even trump up a case to have you detained for investigation by the War Crimes people. Your salary would stop. You'd lose all pension rights. Your name would be circulated on a black list to other Occupation areas. You'd find it very hard to get another job even as a snow sweeper."

"Why do you want to keep me, then?"

"I'm a practical fellow." Hanlon smiled at him blandly. "I think a town functions better under its normal administrators. This place has a fairly clean record. If it were kept clean, everyone would profit. There'd be a better chance of getting food and coal rations and penicillin for the hospital. There'd be a good case to put up to Klagenfurt for turning it into a rest area for Occupation troops—which would bring revenue into the town and make a beginning for the old tourist trade. We could make a showpiece of it, Fischer, a model for the rest of Austria —if we could co-operate."

"You mean, if I hand you an Austrian soldier for hanging"

"Put it that way if you like."

"How else should I put it, Major?"

"There are two ways," said Hanlon deliberately. "You can call it recognition of common law, a recognition that murder is crime and deserves punishment to protect the community. You can't change that principle because the victim happens to wear a British uniform. If you don't like the taste of that, try this one." He quoted in the old German of the Bible—"It is expedient that one man should die for the people."

"Too many men have died already 'for the people'," said Fischer with surprising bitterness. "The people! The nation! Greater Germany! Millions died for them. And you demand yet another victim."

"I don't want victims," said Hanlon quietly. "I'm trying to point out that you can't live in two worlds. If you want to live by law you've got to accept the codes. If you want to live in the jungle you can do that too, at a price. It's up to you."

"Have you ever killed a man, Major?"

The question took him by surprise. He stared at the little policeman, who stood, stiff and impassive, clothed with a new, curious dignity. He hesitated a moment, then gave him the answer.

"Yes. I've killed several in five years of war."

"Then why do you talk like God Almighty on Judgment Day?"

Hanlon crashed his fist on the desk so that the inkstand jumped and the papers fluttered wildly to the floor.

"Because I've got to! Because somebody's got to play God and bring order in this bloody chaos!"

"Give us a chance and we'd do it ourselves."

A slow smile dawned on the bird-like face of the little policeman. The Major was human after all. There was a fund of anger in him and angry men were apt to indiscretion. It surprised him therefore when Hanlon returned his smile and tossed the argument back to him.

"I'm sure you could organise yourselves, Fischer, but I can't put my head on the block for your mistakes. So either we work together, or you go under guard to Klagenfurt on tonight's train. Which is it?"

"I'll co-operate," said Karl Adalbert Fischer. His long neck drooped, his shoulders sagged and he stood with downcast eyes like a man who has just thrown away the last shreds of honour. In reality he was bubbling with satisfaction. The Englishman was scared, the job was too big for him. He would accept a compromise, even if he wasn't prepared to admit it. Hanlon's next blunt words shattered the brief illusion.

"Good! Now tell me—what's the man's name? And where does he live?"

The comical head snapped back and his mouth gaped open. "I—I don't understand you."

"I think you do. You wouldn't have risked your job for someone you didn't know. Let's have it, Fischer. What's his name?"

"You're mistaken, Major," said Fischer with stiff dignity. "I don't know the man. If I did you'd have had him by now."

"I'll accept your word for it," said Hanlon genially. "But I'll charge you as an accessory if I find you're lying. Now let's get down to business."

For the next thirty minutes he rehearsed the policeman in the strategic details of a man-hunt in the mountains. By the time he had finished, Fischer was sweating under his collar and wondering whether his nephew's neck or his own was more in danger.

Then Hanlon dismissed him and telephoned the Spider-house to summon Sepp Kunzli.

He came, like a man of substance, in his own car, driven by a uniformed chauffeur. His entrance to Headquarters was managed with some care. The chauffeur got out and parleyed with the guard, so that when the Herr Doktor descended he was not kept waiting in the cold like the others but ushered in with ceremony and taken immediately upstairs.

The lounging soldiers looked curiously at his dapper figure, the sober black hat, the coat with the high astrakhan collar, the pigskin gloves, the elegant cane. Mayer and the porter bowed ceremoniously as he passed, but he gave them no more than a cursory nod.

To the surprise of Johnson and the sergeant, Hanlon stood to greet him, shook hands, seated him comfortably and offered cigarettes.

Kunzli accepted the courtesies with grace and a warm inward content. His first fears were groundless, it seemed. The peremptory telephone call meant no more than the brusqueness of a busy man. Hanlon had charm and intelligence. It shouldn't be too difficult to establish an understanding.

The opening gambit was encouraging. Hanlon opened his folder and took out a letter which he unfolded and laid on the desk in front of him. He said cordially:

"Klargenfurt have sent me a letter, Herr Doktor. It came from Zürich via London."

"I'd be interested to hear the contents."

"It's quite short. It says: 'Doktor Sepp Kunzli of Bad Quellenberg has been known to us as a reliable agent since 1943. We recommend that you extend to him the immunities usual in such cases and we suggest that his services may be of some value to your local commander.' It's signed John Winter, Lieutenant-Colonel, British Military Attaché, Geneva, Switzerland."

"I'm flattered. Also I am grateful. The English are men of their word."

45

"We like to remember our friends," said Hanlon casually. "We need some help at this moment. I'd like to know whether you're interested in co-operating."

"Naturally, Herr Major. Anything in my power. These are difficult times—for all of us."

The lips smiled, but the slate-grey eyes were void of expression. The hands were slack and expressionless on the armrests of the chair.

"Good. Tell me, Herr Doktor—how would you assess the strength and political importance of the Nazi Party in Bad Quellenberg?"

"Numerically strong, but of no importance whatsoever, then or now." The answer came out readily and with conviction. "Important people came here, important issues were discussed here, but the local membership was made up of petty functionaries, gauleiters, policemen, schoolteachers whose promotion depended on a good Party record. For the rest . . ." Kunzli shrugged expressively, "you know what these mountain people are—irredentist, isolationist, intolerant of foreigners and officials alike. The Party never penetrated below the surface of their lives."

Hanlon nodded appreciatively. The answer was concise and intelligent. It squared with the information at his disposal, with his own younger experience.

"Was there any sort of persecution of Jews or opposition elements?"

Kunzli shook his head. "None that would come within the scope of your inquiry, Major. There were no crimes of violence. There were no midnight arrests. This province is predominantly Catholic and the Party handled it with more than usual discretion. There was discrimination. There was an exodus of Jews in the early days. But the violence and the terror were no more than a legend in the valley."

"For a man with a tragic history, you're being very fair, Herr Doktor."

Kunzli shrugged and made a small rueful mouth. "New lies will not bring back the dead. New persecutions will not wipe out the memory of the old. These people here—what are they? A small country folk wrapped up in themselves and their tiny problems. We can afford to be generous with them, Major."

The 'we' was carefully placed, neatly timed. It suggested identity of interest without presuming to state it. The English had a taste and a talent for subtleties like that. Hanlon smiled absently and passed on to the next question.

"You, of course, were never a Party member."

"Never."

"But you did considerable business with its members—and on their behalf?"

Kunzli felt a faint uneasy fear, like a knife pricking round his heart, but his eyes were blank and his face composed as he gave the off-hand answer:

"I'm a professional man, Major. If I made religion or politics a condition of service I'd have starved long ago; as would every business man in the world."

"I was making another point," murmured Hanlon apologetically. "Attached to the letter from Switzerland was a memorandum pointing to the scope of your interests, particularly in negotiating property and bonds on behalf of prominent Party members."

"That's every solicitor's bread and butter."

"It is suggested there was jam too—lots of it."

"I made considerable profit, yes. I would have made more if I could. It was part of my revenge on these people for what they had done to my life."

"We're happy in the success of our friends." Hanlon grinned disarmingly. "But a question does arise: how much of this property was originally expropriated—say, from concentration camp victims—and how much of it can be traced and restored to them, or to their heirs?"

So that was it! The blades were pricking closer now. And behind the spider's eyes a careful brain ticked like an adding machine, balancing the odds, weighing the risks against the profits. He hesitated a moment, then answered with easy frankness:

"I can tell you now that a good many expropriated estates passed through my hands at one stage or another. How many, I couldn't guess. Many reached me at third or fourth hand. To make an accurate list would require months of search—years, possibly."

"But you would be prepared to assist us in such a search."

"Naturally."

"You would make available your personal records?"

"Of course."

"Including those held in Swiss banks?"

"Certainly. But I should have to go there myself and with-draw them from the various safe deposits. They are in different names, the procedure is a little too complicated to be dealt with by post."

"I'll arrange your exit papers," said Hanlon with gentle gratitude. "And while you're away no doubt our assessors could begin working on your papers here?"

"I doubt they'd make any sense of them." A faint irritation coloured his tone. "You must remember, Major, I was running a risky business and like your diverting Mr Pepys I kept many of my records in a code decipherable only by myself."

"In that case I'll make your exit papers valid for seven days only. Naturally you'll want to get back as soon as possible."

"Of course."

"How soon can you leave?"

"That depends on you, Major," said Kunzli tartly. "Natur-ally I shall need a specific list of instructions. Then I shall have to check this list against my files here, to see what additional material is required from Switzerland. . . ."

"I'll send you the instructions tomorrow," said Hanlon. "Might we say a week from then?"

He flipped over the pages of his date pad, and waited, pencil poised for the confirmation.

"A week will be enough."

"Good." He made a swift notation on the pad. "Your exit papers will be ready the day before you leave. I'll have them sent round to you."

"As you wish, Major."

"Then I don't need to detain you any longer, Herr Doktor. Thank you so much for coming. *Auf Wiedersehn.*"

He stood up and offered his hand. Kunzli took it limply and turned away. His back was straight and his face was composed, but behind the metallic eyes a bitter thought was framing itself. For the first time in many long years, he had misjudged the market. It was only a matter of time before the bottom dropped out of it completely. He'd better start selling, and selling fast!

CHAPTER 4

WHEN SEPP Kunzli had left, Hanlon changed into ski clothes and walked out alone to look at the town. His first day in Bad Quellenberg was nearly over and he needed time and privacy to ponder the experience.

The snow was still falling heavily, filling the air like blown feathers, softening the harsh contours, icing the bleak trees, coating the town from road to rooftop, deadening the footfalls of the homing burghers. The mountains were hidden by a mist that swirled in from the southern defiles and drooped in ragged streamers over the pines. Yellow lights pricked out round the amphitheatre of buildings, and already the dusk was darkening into night.

From the entrance to the Sonnblick, the road wound downwards through buildings of diminishing importance, towards the centre of the old town, where the waterfall ran under the roadway, a silent ice-bound torrent, writhing fantastically from the steep crags to the valley floor.

When Hanlon moved out from the lighted doorway, the cold hit him like a knife and he twitched the hood of his parka up over his head and walked briskly down the slope. Behind him he heard the frosty tinkle of bells and he stepped aside to watch the passing of a peasant sleigh piled high with firewood and driven by an old man with Bismarck whiskers and a high green hat. The horse stepped awkwardly on its high-toed shoes and its breath made little cloud puffs among the fluttering snowflakes. Hanlon followed the silver music of the harness down the road.

The first buildings he passed were high and dark, their windows were shuttered and their balconies covered with board frames to protect them from the snow. Their doors were locked and the snow was piled high on the deserted steps.

These were the big hotels, pride of the town, source of its boom-time revenue. Now they were white elephants, eating their heads off, the interest piling up on their mortgages, the snow ruining the roof covers, the water freezing in the pipes, the dank cold of winter seeping through their corridors.

'This,' thought Hanlon moodily, 'is the way towns die, and empires too. Not by the sporadic cataclysms—war, earthquake, fire and flood—but by the slow recession of life from the members towards the small pumping heart, whose ventricles are the market, the shops, the beerhouse, the church. After a while the heart stops too, because when the members are dead the body is inert and useless, and life is a fruitless repetition of pulse beats—lost energy, motion that leads nowhere!'

Then he remembered that this was the purpose of his own coming: to jolt new life into the fading heart, to set the blood moving outwards again to the cold extremities, to give them warmth and articulation and a new direction. Instead he had wasted a whole day on a cynical display of power, as if one frightened a dying man back to life, instead of coaxing him slowly to desire it first, then fight for it.

Thinking of death, he remembered Sergeant Willis, who was now being laid in his little pine box and who tomorrow would be buried in the churchyard of St Julian. A man of no importance during his life, his death had made him important to many people. A bachelor, without relatives, he might have died of a coronary occlusion and dropped out of time without a ripple of significance. But because he had been killed a little after the legal season, a whole town lay under the threat of an interdict as fearful as that which the old Popes visited on faithless cities. And he, Mark Hanlon, who had sat, a stripling novice, at the feet of Father Albertus, was the sinister Eminence who could nail the damnation on the locked doors of the church and mete out a rigorous justice instead of a life-giving mercy.

But interdicts were out of fashion. Even the Church had dropped them long since. No matter how many sacks of ashes you tipped on a man's head, you couldn't bend his will to repentance. The folk of Bad Quellenberg regretted the crime—there was no doubt of that. The rub was that they would not assume the guilt of the murderer or the responsibility for hunting him down. Morally—and Mark Hanlon had a nice moral judgment—they were right. A man was answerable for his own sins, but not for those of his neighbour.

Which brought him to the core of a very sour apple. He had put off the cassock long ago. His hands had never been anointed for shriving in the tribunal of the spirit. He wore a new uniform now. He carried a commission to administer a new and sinister legality: collective guilt.

'There is not one criminal,' said the jurists of the New Order, 'there are many. There is not only the man behind the gun, but all the others before him and after him: the father who begot him, the mother who suckled him, the woman who married him, and the priest who baptised him. All of them had a part in his making, all of them must share his guilt and his punishment.'

So Major Hanlon came at one stride to a blank wall of frustration, and to the lighted entrance of the last big hotel on the promenade.

Unlike its neighbours on the high ground, this one was set back from the road and reached by a gravelled arc of driveway. It was flanked by a parking apron where three battered ambulances stood, grey and forlorn, with the snow piling up on the radiators and canopies, and making small drifts around the hub caps.

The stucco was peeling off the pediment and the proud Gothic 'Hotel Kaiserhof' was half hidden by a white pine board with the inscription '121. Allgemeines Feldlazarett'. A pale yellow light shone behind the glass doors, and Hanlon saw an elderly corporal, with his jacket unbuttoned, picking his teeth behind the reception desk.

Beyond him was a sparse passage of people—an orderly wheeling a trolley of food, a nurse in a drab uniform, a shuffling convalescent with a military tunic over a pair of striped pyjama trousers, a lumpish woman in a long green coat with a pigtailed child at her side.

It came to him with a faint shock of surprise that this place too, and its inmates, were part of his charge. The charge, like the name, had a sinister sound to it. Lazarett—the house of the beggars, the dwelling of the maimed, the defeated, the abode of all poor devils who fought for lost causes and hopeless creeds, and who must now lick their sores at the gates of the New Princes.

He must come to see them, inspect their quarters, examine the problems of restoring them to normal life. His skin crawled at the thought of the shame to them and to himself, when he walked down the rows of beds in the uniform of the victor. What would they think? How would they feel? What words could he find to mend their broken dignity?

Every fighting man had that right at least—they stripped him of all others when he put on his uniform, even the right to question the cause for which he died. But how did you make him feel you understood and respected him, when you walked by with crowns up and polished buttons, while he sat on a bedpan or lay with tubes in his belly or a raw stump where his hand should be?

Then he remembered he wasn't in uniform. He was dressed like any mountain man, in ski clothes and hooded parka. Now was the time to get it over and done with. He pushed open the door and walked into the foyer.

The elderly corporal looked up and questioned him with hostile indifference.

"Well? Who are you? What do you want?"

Hanlon fought down his irritation and answered, mildly enough: "I'd like to see the Chief Medical Officer."

"Got an appointment?"

"I don't need one."

"What's your name?"

"You wouldn't be able to spell it if I told you." Hanlon grinned at him with sour humour. "Now be a good chap and tell me where I can find him."

The corporal shook his head stubbornly.

"Regulations, friend. We sign all visitors in and sign 'em out. We don't disturb the medical staff unless it's urgent. They're overworked, they say. Now let's have your name, eh?"

"Hanlon, H-A-N-L-O-N," he spelt it out slowly, German fashion, while the orderly licked his pencil stub and copied it slowly on a printed form.

"Business?"

"Personal."

The pencil stayed poised in mid-air and the corporal grumbled impatiently.

"Oh no! Not again! We get 'em all shapes and at all hours. They want to know how their Heinzi's getting on with his bellyache or whether Gerhardt's going to be any good to his wife when he comes out. You'll have to do better than that. Now, why do you want to see the Chief?"

'To hell with you!' thought Hanlon irritably. 'I try to do you a kindness and you want to put me through the hoops like a performing monkey!'

Aloud he said: "My business is personal with the Chief Medical Officer. It has nothing to do with any individual patient. Please telephone my name and ask him to see me."

"Sorry, friend. That's the regulation; I'm here to see it's carried out. You tell me your business and I'll see what I can do."

"You've got my name," snapped Hanlon. "My rank is Major. I'm the British Occupation Commander for the Quellenberg Area. Now, do I see the Chief Medical Officer or not?"

The corporal leapt up as though he had been stuck with a pin. He stood rigidly at attention and stammered apologies. Hanlon cut him off in mid-period.

"Where do I find him?"

"Upstairs, Major. First floor, room twenty. I—I'll take you up." He buttoned his tunic hastily and came out from behind his desk. Hanlon followed him up the carpetless stairs to room twenty.

The man who stood to greet him was something of a surprise. He was more than six feet tall, broad as a tree trunk, with blond hair and ruddy cheeks and ice-blue eyes and fists like small hams. He had a ready smile and a deep voice that still retained a trace of the Tyrolese burr. His name, he told Hanlon, was Reinhardt Huber. He carried Colonel's rank and Doctorates from Vienna and Padua.

His blunt good humour and his shrewd peasant wit were a tonic to Hanlon's flagging spirits. The first courtesies over, he plunged straight into discussion.

"So we both have problems, Major. You help me to solve mine; maybe I can show you some answers in return."

"Let's hear yours first, Herr Doktor."

"I give them to you in one packet, my friend. I have four hundred men in this place, two hundred serious cases—everything from amputations to paraplegia. How do I cure them with starvation rations, poor equipment, no drugs and the last litres of anæsthetics? Faith healing? But even that's no good when they have lost faith in the past and can see no hope for the future."

"I can improve the rations, I think," said Hanlon calmly. "We can co-ordinate local supplies and shipments from other provinces. We can organise the market so that you get a better share for the sick. Drugs? I doubt it. All available supplies are being rushed to concentration-camp victims. I can't get any of these. We might do better with surgical anæsthetics. I'll try anyway."

Huber's face clouded. He looked down at the backs of his large, spatulate hands.

"The time of the hecatombs! The day of the genocides! The world will remember them for a thousand years."

"I doubt it," said Hanlon dryly. "One dead man makes a tragedy, a million make a compost heap. Plant the graveyards with pines and they'll disappear in twenty years. Give the journalists their heads for the same time—and they'll bury the truth under a mountain of newsprint. That's why nobody learns the lessons of history. There's no history left—only broken pillars and scattered shards. The rest is commentary and partisan opinion."

Huber looked up sharply, scanning the quirky Celtic face for any sign of mockery. Then, surprisingly, he chuckled softly.

"My God! Maybe we have one at last—an honest man with a sense of proportion. We can use both. So, no drugs, possibly some anæsthetic, better food. It's a beginning."

"What else do you need?"

"Clothing, new bedding and surgical instruments."

Hanlon shook his head. "All hopeless until the priorities have been met—which won't be for a long time yet. What else?"

"Information. What happens to the boys when I discharge them?"

"You clear them with me and I'll arrange a rail warrant, inter-zone passes and enough rations to see them back to their home towns. After that they come under the jurisdiction of local authorities. If there are cases of special hardship, let me know and I'll deal with them as best I can."

The big Tyrolean nodded. He leaned back in his chair, stretched his long legs and clasped his hands behind his head.

"We are better off than I expected, Major. I'm grateful. Now tell me—is there anything I can do for you?"

"You can give me some advice," said Hanlon quietly.

Huber threw back his head and laughed gustily. Hanlon looked at him with faint irritation.

"Something amusing, Herr Doktor?"

"No, no! Something unexpected and rather wonderful. A

man who sits where you sit and asks advice of the defeated. The best I can promise you is an honest answer."

"It's all I want."

Then, without quite knowing why—unless it were by that sudden act of faith that makes one man sometimes trust another—he told him all that had happened since his coming to Quellenberg, and all the questions it had raised in his own mind. Huber heard him out with growing seriousness, and when the story was done he leaned forward across the desk, gesturing with his large, strong hands.

"First, there is yourself. I do not see that you can take any other view, or any other action than you have done. This is a crime—it demands pursuit and legal process. You have a right to insist on the co-operation of the local authorities. If they don't give it to you, they must take the consequences. But there are other things you should remember. Understand me!" he waved a deprecating hand. "I have no local loyalties. I do not belong here. I am a surgeon, which gives a man a certain detachment and a respect for the scalpel. First, you should think of the killer himself—and the reason for this motiveless murder."

"That's the point." Hanlon leaned forward earnestly. "Why? Why?"

"I'm guessing," said Huber in his deep, grave voice. "But it is a guess based on my daily experience in this place. There is a limit to what the human body and the human mind can bear. A man may die of surgical shock. A man may go mad with terror or grief or the sudden impact of the evil of the world. These are the extremes. But there are a thousand steps downward to the valley of death or the caverns of insanity. The smallest wound leaves a scar in the tissue. The smallest shock makes a striation in the memory. Sometimes the faculties are permanently impaired. I can patch up a cripple, but I cannot make him walk straight. Still less can I make a crippled mind think straight. You have been a soldier. You know what war can do to the most normal man. How one will run screaming at the thunder of the barrage, and another will sit drooling and dumb as a cataleptic. How one goes into a rut like a beast at the smell of blood and another sweats with terror in a closed carriage. . . ."

Hanlon nodded thoughtfully. It was a new thought and vaguely comforting. Huber went on:

"From what you tell me of this killing, its suddenness, its blank unreason. I guess that it was done by a man who is temporarily or permanently deranged."

"All the more reason for bringing him in," said Hanlon sharply, "before it happens again."

"I agree."

"Then why this closing of the ranks? Why this attempt to turn me into a hangman, and the other fellow into a hunted hero?"

"That's a different matter altogether." Huber grinned and relaxed again. "If—if you were to offer me a cigarette, Major, I wouldn't refuse it."

"Of course. I'm sorry." He took out his cigarette case and then lit up for both of them. The Doktor leaned back and inhaled long and gratefully. Then he took up the thread of his argument.

"First you must try to understand these people—the way they live, the way they think."

"I thought I did understand them," said Hanlon wryly. "I lived among them long enough."

"Where? When?"

"Years ago—before the war. I was a Jesuit novice in Graz. Four years."

"That explains it."

"What?"

"The perfect accent. The—the fact that you are *sympathisch*, and more liberal than I expected."

"To you perhaps, but not to them."

"Give them time, my friend, give them time. They too are suffering from shock." He heaved his big frame out of the chair and began to pace the floor, piecing out his thoughts slowly at first, then with more emphatic eloquence. "These people—my own folk in the Tyrol—are centuries away from the plainsmen and from the city dwellers. It is the mountains, you see. They make a barrier to change, a frontier behind which retreat the best and the worst of the old customs. Cross one ridge and you must learn a new language. Push into the farther valleys, and you are back with the tribes—Celts, Alemanni, Cimbrians, Goths and Vandals. Examine their beliefs and you find that they worship the Christus in the shadow of the old gods. They are moody and suspicious. A man from the next valley is a stranger. An Ausländer like yourself is a man from another planet. I might stay in Quellenberg till the end of my days but they would still call me an immigrant—as they do these hoteliers and shopkeepers. Look at their land and you will learn something more about them, perhaps the most important thing of all. The meadows cling precariously to the hillsides, small and sparse for all their summer green. The last mowing must feed their stock all through the winter. So there are few beasts and each one is precious. If they cut down too many pines the avalanches come and sweep everything down into the valley. When they kill a pig, it is a big event, and they live on black bread and salted pork and the milk from one cow. If they fish out the streams there is no food for Fridays. When a son dies it is one hand less to the axes and the mowing. When a child is born it is one more mouth to feed, but one more assurance of continuity. Their life is harsh, you see, and their hold on it is insecure, so they treasure it, in all its forms— the strong son, the weanling heifer, the woman who breeds well and makes good milk. In Carinthia and in the Tyrol it is an old joke that the girls can't say no and that half the babes are begotten on the wrong side of the blanket. Yet even this is a sort of homage to life. A barren girl is a burden to her husband. A couple without children go hungry in their old age. Better then that they begin to breed before they marry." He broke off and faced Hanlon with a wry, apologetic smile. "I don't know how much sense this makes to you, but . . ."

"It makes sense. But it doesn't make my job any easier."

"Agreed. But it might save some wear on your temper."

Hanlon stood up and held out his hand.

"I'll remember that, Doktor. And thank you."

Huber's big fist closed over his own.

"It was nothing. I hope it helps a little. You are already helping me a great deal. Would you like to see the rest of the place?"

"No, thanks. Another time. I've had a big day."

"Let me walk down with you."

As they walked out of the door, Hanlon cannoned against the girl who was hurrying down the corridor. He murmured an apology and stepped aside, but Huber caught the girl by the arm and brought her back.

"Not so fast, Fräulein. This is someone you should meet." He made the introduction with a humorous flourish: "Fräulein Anna Kunzli, Major Hanlon, British Occupation Commander.

Fräulein Kunzli is one of our voluntary aides. She helps to exercise the amputees with their new limbs."

"Happy to meet you, Fräulein. Er—you did say Kunzli?"

"That's right." Huber gave him a quick, shrewd glance. "Herr Doktor Kunzli is one of our prominent citizens."

"I met him this afternoon," said Hanlon carefully.

"This young lady is his niece."

"Oh."

Huber was quick to cover the awkward hiatus.

"How were your patients this afternoon, Anna?"

"Good—very good. They only need some encouragement and they try very hard. But they get tired so quickly."

"Thanks to Major Hanlon, we may soon be able to feed them better. Then they won't tire so easily."

"That would be wonderful, truly wonderful." Her pleasure was so genuine, her smile so frank, that Hanlon looked at her with faint surprise. He was old enough to have a salutary cynicism about women, and the fresh innocence of this one was all the more startling. He smiled gently and said:

"It will take a little time, but we'll get something moving."

"Where are you going now, Anna?" asked Huber.

"Down to the church. We're practising for the requiem to-morrow. That—that was a terrible thing, Major. We're all very upset about it. That's why we're making a special effort. The whole choir will be there, and . . ."

"Perhaps I could walk down with you. I'm going that way." The words came out unbidden, and hastily, as if he were faintly ashamed of them, but the girl accepted simply.

"Thank you. I'd like that."

They made their farewells, and Huber stood at his door watching them walk side by side down the corridor. He wondered idly what was the connection between Hanlon and Sepp Kunzli, and what might come of this chance meeting with Kunzli's niece. The girl wore her innocence like an armour and Hanlon was preoccupied with the devious manipulation of power. But given time they would both come to bed, together or with others, it made small matter, so long as new blood came into this old land whose young sires had been killed off, or were lying, restless and impotent, in every room of the 121. Allgemeines Feldlazarett.

Hanlon's own thoughts were never further from bed or the breeding of new Quellenbergers.

As he stepped out of the hospital with the girl at his side he was suddenly angry with himself. His small, eager courtesy was a diplomatic error. It established a personal element in a relationship which, to be successful, must remain impersonal.

The girl was a link, however tenuous, between himself and Sepp Kunzli. Through her he could be subjected to the small demands of politeness. Her innocence might set a limit to his dealings with a man who, like himself, was far from innocent. He could ignore politeness, of course, and break down the barriers, but that would entail a certain blame, and this too he was unwilling to shoulder.

He pulled his hood farther round his face and hoped that no one would recognise him as they passed the lighted shop fronts farther down the road. That would make a gossip in the town. It would range him with the immigrant and the exploiter, a thing he could ill afford.

Unconsciously he began to hurry and the girl had to double her step to keep pace with him. She made no complaint, but after a few moments she slid on a patch of loose snow and would have fallen had he not thrown out an arm to steady her. In the brief moment when he held her to him and felt the young warmth of her, he realised that he was making a fool of himself. He was a man doing a courtesy to a girl ten years his junior. To hell with the gossip. To hell with the diplomacies. He apologised warmly.

"I'm sorry. I didn't realise I was walking so fast. Will you take my arm?"

"Thank you."

They fell into step and walked leisurely along the arched colonnade with its quaint shop signs and its shabby naked windows. No new goods had come into Quellenberg for a long time now and the merchants were hoarding their last stocks under the counter. They passed one man putting up his shutters, a grey stooping woman trotting a dachshund on a frayed leash, a pair of peasants talking in a dark alcove. No one paid any attention to them. After a moment the girl said in her clear, untroubled voice:

"This is a sad town now."

"War is a sad business," said Mark Hanlon.

"It's not the war. It's the end of it. Everything seems suddenly pointless."

"To you too?"

"Oh no, not to me."

"What's the difference?" Her frankness disarmed him and piqued his curiosity.

"I suppose because I've got nothing to lose." She said it so simply that it took his breath away. "My father was killed—flying a plane over England. My mother died in Vienna. So I came to live with Uncle Sepp. I love him, but he's not very fond of me. So I'm not afraid of losing him. I'm young and I don't seem to want very much—so I'm lucky, I suppose."

"Luckier than you know." But privately he wondered how long that luck would last, and what would happen when desire awoke and the hunger for the unattainable.

Her next question left him momentarily speechless.

"Are you a Catholic, Major?"

"Well . . . yes. Why do you ask?"

"Father Albertus said we'd be lucky if we got a Catholic here. He said Catholics all over the world have the same belief, so they are better able to understand one another—and be kind to each other."

He was glad that his face was hooded so that she could not see the irony in his smile. He told her gently:

"It doesn't always follow, my dear. It's one thing to believe. It's quite another to put your belief into practice. Catholics can be just as brutal to one another as Buddhists or Lutherans. They can lie and cheat just as well as those of other faiths. It was a Catholic who broke Father Albertus's hands for him."

"I've never been able to understand that."

"It takes a long time," said Hanlon softly.

They walked the rest of the way in silence, and when they came to the churchyard gate he stopped. The girl hesitated a moment, then thanked him and held out her hand.

"I—I hope you'll come to visit us some time, Major. I know my uncle will be glad to see you."

"Later, perhaps. When we're all more settled."

"*Auf Wiedersehn*, Major."

"*Auf Wiedersehn*, Fräulein."

He watched her walk down the path through the silent forest of headboards, and a few moments later he heard the first plangent notes of the organ, and the sound of young voices, clear as bells in the mountain air. He stood a long time, listening, while the snowflakes settled on his head and on his shoulders, and the cold crept into his blood like a slow death.

CHAPTER 5

WHEN THE *Mädchen* had cleared away the last of the dinner dishes, Bürgermeister Max Holzinger exploded into dyspeptic anger.

"The man is a cold intriguer—the worst possible choice for us here! He has a charm that might beguile you into trusting him. Then at the last moment he is smiling coldly and twisting the knife in your ribs. I have never been so disappointed, or so humiliated!"

His wife and daughter watched him as he strode unevenly up and down the carpet, pouring out on them the shame and puzzlement of his first encounter with the Occupying Power. He had come home silent and depressed. He had picked sourly at his dinner and drunk twice as much wine as usual. He had snapped at the maid and hustled her weeping from the room as soon as the meal was done. Then, private at last and a little drunk, he had given full vent to his helpless fury.

". . . His attitude to the funeral ceremony was quite cold-blooded, a showpiece not to honour the dead but to shame the people and let them feel the new power in the land. He's organising a manhunt. As if we had not had enough of them all these years! I wonder he doesn't call for bloodhounds as well. I had a long talk with Fischer and we're both quite decided he'll get no co-operation from us. We'll teach him a . . ."

"You're a fool, Max!" said Liesl Holzinger, and the venom in her voice stopped him like a bullet. He gaped at her.

"Wha—what did you say?"

"You're a fool to join yourself with Fischer—and a bigger one to set yourself in opposition to the *Engländer*! He can crush you at one blow!"

He was vaguely afraid of the new woman looking out from her eyes and speaking with her lips. Like all his countrymen he was accustomed to submission from his women and a soothing audience for his outbursts. He answered her tartly:

"You don't understand, Liesl. This is politics—men's business. Unless we begin with strength we shall end with a heavier yoke round our necks. I tell you, Liesl . . ."

"I tell you, Max!" She stood up, eyes blazing, mouth tight and angry, facing him. Her daughter saw with some surprise how her big, full figure dwarfed her husband, and how uncertain he seemed in the face of her attack. "Once you could tell me what was my business, and what wasn't. Now it's changed. I tell you! Why? Because my life is at stake, and Traudl's and the lives of all women like us. If you fight this man he will destroy you—and us with you. You've done it before—you and your dreamers. You killed my son . . ."

"Liesl, I beg of you . . ."

"No, Max! It's too late now. The war's finished. You lost it. We've got peace now—and we're not going to let you lose that too."

"Liesl, you don't understand what he wants. He wants us to hand a boy over to him—like common informers, like—like——"

"Then hand him over!" she blazed at him. "Hand him over and let us have some quiet in our lives. You handed over our son, didn't you? You didn't plot with Fischer to keep him from the Army. Why this one?"

"Because . . ." he stumbled and stammered, knowing how much of it was hurt pride, and how little was reasoned argument. "It's hard to explain, but . . ."

"Then let me explain something, Max." Her voice was quiet now, but cold and loveless. "If you persist in this, I leave you. We both do. We go to the *Engländer* and explain our position. We tell him what you've done about the house. We tell him we want no part of plots and politics—only to be left quiet to re-make our lives. I think he will listen. I don't think he'd let us starve."

"You wouldn't dare!"

"I would—and so would Traudl."

Holzinger looked at his daughter, lounging as she always did in the chair, smoking placidly, watching them both with the cool irony of disappointed youth.

"Is it true, Traudl?"

"Quite true, Father." And she smiled as she said it. "Life's

62

been a one-sided bargain for a long time. I agree with Mother. It's time we changed it."

He was beaten and he knew it. A man can fight all enemies but those of his own household. For a long moment he looked from one to the other, then his face sagged and his shoulders drooped so that he looked like a man become suddenly old. Then he turned away and walked to the window and stood there, hands clasped behind his back, his fingers lacing and unlacing nervously. When he spoke again his voice was low and hesitant:

"I . . . I don't know what you expect me to do."

It shocked him to hear his daughter's voice answer him, deliberate and merciless:

"Make friends with him, Father. Co-operate. Play games with Fischer if you want, but remember always where the real power lies. After a while the Englishman will be lonely. All men get lonely away from their own countries and their own women. Pay him courtesies. When a moment offers, invite him here."

"And then?"

"Mother and I will do the rest."

For a good half minute he did not answer, then the full import of her words seemed to strike him. He swung round and faced them again. His voice was almost a whisper.

"Do you know what you're saying? It's . . . it's almost obscene."

"Is it, Father?" Her full lips twisted into a small bitter smile. "It seems to me all life is a sort of obscenity—the way children are bred and born, the way they die, spilling their brains out on the ground, their bellies bursting open with bullets, the way women breed them again, because their husbands come home and want to be warmed and feel like men. It's the way the world rolls. I don't see what you have to complain about."

"I won't have my daughter made a harlot."

"It's a risk you take—with wives and daughters," said Liesl Holzinger coldly. "But, with any luck, we might get her married to the Englishman."

As he looked from one to the other—at the blonde Teuton strength of the mother and the dark changeling beauty of the daughter—an old doubt began to stir like an aching tooth. And Max Holzinger asked himself whether history might not be repeating itself in the mountain house of Bad Quellenberg.

Karl Adalbert Fischer had troubles of a different kind.

The sagging telephone lines that led from Quellenberg to the high villages were coated with ice and conversation was carried on through a constant sizzle of static that sounded like frying bacon. So he was obliged to shout to make any sense at all—and his brother-in-law Franz Wikivill was an obstinate fellow who needed constant repetition to beat sense into his head.

"Listen, Franz, for God's sake! I don't want arguments, I want facts. Is the boy home yet?"

"He's home, yes. But . . ."

"How is he? Does he know what he's done?"

"I can't get any sense out of him at all. He was raving when he came in. Now he just lies on the bed staring at the ceiling."

"Did you get his guns?"

"What's that?"

"I said, did you get his guns?"

"How can I? He won't let them out of his reach."

"*Gott im Himmel!* What sort of children do I deal with? All right. Now listen carefully. I want you to get him out of the house now and take him up to the ski hut on the Gamsfeld."

"It's late, Max. It's still snowing. You know that's a bad trip even in daylight."

"Get him up there tonight if you don't want him in gaol tomorrow!" Fischer was almost sobbing with anger and frustration. "The English will be combing the hills, and the Gamsfeld is the safest place for a while. I'll try to get up and see him myself tomorrow."

"But you don't understand, Karl. He won't stay there. He won't stay anywhere. For a while he's quite normal, then his black mood comes on him and we can do nothing with him. The only one who can reach him at all is his sister. Even she . . ."

"Then for God's sake send her up to the hut with him. She's young and healthy. She can make the trip. Have them take food and wine. There's fuel enough to keep them going."

"We can't go on like this, Karl." Even with the distance and the static his brother-in-law's voice was fretful and panicky. "Can't you get him out into another zone?"

"What zone, for God's sake? The French and Americans will be notified that he's wanted. If they take him they'll send him back under guard. If the Russians get him they'll send him to Siberia—if they don't shoot him out of hand. Our only hope is to keep him moving about the hills."

"But can't you give him new papers?"

"Yes. But I can't give him a new face! If I could, everything would be . . ." He broke off and stood staring at the receiver. A new and startling idea had come to him. He watched it flower, swiftly and suddenly like a conjuror's tree. If he could bring it to fruit it would be the sweetest triumph of all. The faint voice crackled petulantly in his ear.

"Karl! . . . Karl! . . . Are you still there?"

"Yes. But I'm going now. I've just got a thought."

"I can't hear you!"

"It doesn't matter. Get the boy up to the Gamsfeld tonight. Without fail."

"I tell you, Karl . . ."

"Get him there! If you don't I wash my hands of the whole business and the boy will hang. *Auf Wiedersehn*, Franz."

He slammed down the receiver and stood there, a small triumphant smile playing about his lips.

A new face! Give the boy a new face and you had a new man, safe from pursuit and punishment. Hanlon's description of the murderer was now a matter of record—a lean, vulpine fellow with a scar on his right cheek. Remove the scar, let a plastic surgeon rebuild the face and the case broke down on the first process—identification.

With a new face and new papers he could move his nephew quietly into the American zone and let him fend for himself. There were friends in Salzburg who would be happy to give him a start. The more he thought about it, the more he liked it.

He crossed to the filing cabinet, unlocked it and took out the leather-bound folio. He carried it to the table, laid it open and began to leaf carefully through the last pages until he came to the name he wanted. Then slowly, but with deepening satisfaction, he began to read the very private history of Rudi Winkler.

In the palmy days of the town he had been a frequent visitor—a little roly-poly Bavarian with a dimpling face and soft hands and a gossipy humour. He had bought a small building plot on one of the less favoured promenades and built himself a log chalet which he had decorated in rustic fashion and which was kept for him by a bony widow with a trap mouth and a bitter tongue.

During the summer holidays he filled the place with blond young men who did the less arduous climbs, swam naked in the mountain pools and drank wine and sang sentimental *Lieder* till the small hours of the morning.

The upper circles of visiting society knew nothing about him and the locals knew little more, because he was an amiable fellow who took his pleasures with discretion and because his housekeeper kept her knowledge and her disapproval to herself. His documents gave small information. He was a doctor, it seemed, medical officer to an obscure SS unit in Bavaria. For a transient record it was enough, but, once Winkler became a property owner in Quellenberg, Fischer could not be content until he had burrowed deeper into his past and built up a more satisfactory dossier.

It took time and patience, but in the end he got it.

Winkler had been a surgeon in Munich, a rising man with a fashionable practice in the new plastic surgery: women wanted their breasts lifted and the wrinkles smoothed out and their noses trimmed to the new Nordic fashion of beauty. There had been a scandal—one of Winkler's boys and the son of a Party official. The boy had been beaten up after a drinking party and had died of his injuries. The scandal had been hushed up quickly and Winkler had found it convenient to close his practice and find a new job. The SS unit turned out to be a concentration camp where Winkler was engaged on plastic experiments with the inmates.

All of it—names, dates, places—was studiously entered in the leather-bound folio.

Just after the Allied breakthrough, Winkler had turned up again, for good. Austria was still the Third Reich, he was living in his own house, he carried a valid-looking discharge paper: his legal status was beyond question. Fischer had been happy to let him keep it. He was happier still now that he saw some profit forthcoming.

He closed the big folio, wrapped it carefully in brown paper, stowed it in his battered briefcase and locked the catch. He took a last look round the dusty disordered office, then switched off the lights and walked out, closing the door behind him.

It was late and he had not eaten, but he was confident that Rudi Winkler would be only too happy to feed him.

He was surprised to find the little Bavarian a genial host and his trap-faced housekeeper an excellent cook. They dined in comradely fashion on buttered trout and a well-mixed salad. They approached the proposition as coolly as if it were a business contract, as indeed it was.

They drank a litre of *Gumpoldskirchner* and finished with an *Apfelstrudel*, light as an angel's wing. Fischer was wiping the last crumbs of it from his mouth when Winkler smiled happily and said in his amiable voice:

"You know, my friend, I like the idea very much."

Fischer stared at him, incredulous. The roly-poly fellow wasn't frightened at all. He was treating the matter as a joke; which from one point of view was encouraging, and from another strange and slightly sinister. Fischer challenged him curtly:

"It's no joke, Winkler, believe me. If you make a slip, it's the end for you." He slashed the edge of his hand across his throat in the hangman gesture. "*Kaputt!* Just like that."

"*Kaputt* for both of us," chuckled Rudi Winkler.

"Don't be so sure of that," growled Fischer. "I've got mitigating circumstances. The boy's my relative. You've got none—and a dirty history besides."

Winkler was still laughing. His eyes had the vacant innocence of a child's. His light girlish voice might have been retailing boudoir gossip.

"We're going to bury my past tonight. We're never going to think of it or refer to it again. You're going to tear my record from your dossier. You're going to give me new papers and a new past and a new future. And I'm going to give your nephew a new face."

"Do you think you can do it?"

"Sure of it, my dear man. Whether it will be better or worse than the old one is a moot point, depending on my nerves, and how creative I feel. But it will be a new one. Oh yes."

"Where will you do the job?"

"Here of course, private and comfortable. I hope your nephew is an agreeable fellow. I'm lonely. I crave company."

"He's all right when he's normal," said Fischer irritably. "He's a doctor, like you. Very intelligent—which is a wonder, considering the damn fool my sister married. But when he gets these violent spells . . ." A new thought struck him and sent him off at a tangent. "How will you be able to handle him?"

"Sedatives," said Winkler cheerfully, "which of course you'll have to rake up for me. I'll be giving you a list of the anæsthetics, drugs and other stuff I'll need. God knows where you'll get them, but we can't start until they're available."

"I'll get 'em. Anything else?"

"I'll need an assistant for the operations. A trained nurse or medical orderly would be ideal. If not, then someone intelligent and trustworthy."

"I'll think about it. I don't like trusting anybody these days."

"You're scared, aren't you?" Winkler giggled with girlish malice.

"I am," said Fischer bluntly. "I find it keeps me careful."

"I'm not."

"I've been wondering why."

The dumpling face creased into a good-humoured smile. His childish eyes sparkled. The soft hands fluttered like white moths in delicate gesture.

"I'm an epicure, my dear Fischer. I have tasted all the pleasures—even the subtlest, which is that of watching a man die, slowly, under my own meticulous hands. Thanks to you, I hope to prolong my enjoyment in modest comfort. If, however, it is necessary to curtail it, I shall not be too unhappy, because the term will be set not by another but by myself." He put a hand into his breast pocket and brought out a small gelatine capsule which he held up to the light. "There it is, my friend. Death in my own two fingers. I can accept or reject it at a whim. Why should I be afraid—of you or anyone else? I am beyond the reach of any man, and even my going will be a kind of pleasure. Does that answer your question?"

Fischer nodded but did not answer. He shivered, involuntarily, as if a goose had walked over his gravestone. He had heard his quota of tales about the concentration camps, and had shrugged them off as an Englishman might shrug off some story of provincial bedlam, or an American might dismiss a rumour of third degree in the precinct cellars.

There were trash in every country and you had to make places to dump them. It was the system. You had to administer it. You couldn't argue with it. In a place like Quellenberg you were able to forget it. Now for the first time he saw the kind of fellow who flourished on the rubbish heap and how little like a man he really was. With a shock of horror he realised that he had just made a partner of him.

In the warm comfort of the Spiderhouse, Sepp Kunzli savoured his brandy and listened with careful disinterest to his niece's story of her meeting with Mark Hanlon. The narrative excited her—a new man, an *Ausländer*, an officer of the Occupation forces, had walked unbidden into the small ambit of her life. She remembered all the details: his dress, his voice, his face. She gave a literal transcript of his few, laconic remarks.

Kunzli nodded and smiled in his distant fashion, but behind the dead, metallic eyes every item was shuffled and indexed and filed for future reference; the sum of trivial facts was added to his own experience. The final tally was disturbing. A subtle man himself, Kunzli was quick to sense the talent in others, quicker still to see the danger of it.

He questioned the girl with elaborate unconcern:

"I wonder what he was doing at the hospital."

"I told you, Uncle. He was seeing Doktor Huber. He's promised to arrange better food for the patients."

"Rash of him," said Kunzli mildly, "considering it's winter and food stocks are low, and the black market gets most of it before it leaves the cities."

"But he would know, wouldn't he? He wouldn't promise if he couldn't do it."

"Probably not. He struck me as a careful man. You left him at the church, you say?"

"Yes, why?"

"I wondered why he didn't go in. You tell me he's a Catholic. It seems strange."

"I—I was going to ask him in—to hear the singing. Then I didn't like to." And she added the innocent rider, "Men aren't usually very interested in such things, are they?"

"Not usually," said her uncle dryly. "By the way . . ."

"Yes, Uncle?"

"I haven't told you, but Major Hanlon has asked me to make a visit to Switzerland."

"That's wonderful. Why?"

"He wants me to dig up some information on the estates of concentration-camp victims—and other persons. I'll be gone about a week. If you cared to invite the Major to the house during that time I'm sure he'd appreciate it."

"Do you think so, Uncle? Do you think I should—with you away?"

"Why not? You have Martha to chaperone you, and prepare the place. The Major himself would certainly be grateful. A new man in a foreign town—it would be only courteous."

"How . . . how should I ask him?"

"A note, of course. Quite short and formal. Fräulein Anna Kunzli requests the pleasure of Major Hanlon and his officers —don't forget that, ask his officers as well. It's only politeness. Dinner is the best invitation. Gives you time to relax and know one another."

"Yes, Uncle. Tell me . . ." She stumbled a little and flushed as she put the question. "What do you think of the Major, Uncle?"

"Charming," said Sepp Kunzli softly. "An exceptionally clever man."

"He must think very highly of you too, Uncle. Otherwise he wouldn't ask you to go to Switzerland."

"He hasn't told me what he thinks, my dear. I'd give a great deal to know."

He smiled as he said it, knowing that the irony would be lost on her. But the smile died quickly when he looked down and saw in her eyes a light he had never thought to find there.

Green sickness, he told himself irritably. The first late flowering of interest in a man. It should bloom briefly and die as soon. But if it did not? A new doubt pricked at him, a new irony of which he himself was the butt. He shrugged it away hastily. What could possibly grow between this innocent and a man twice her age who sat in the shadow of the eagles and the victor's axe?

In the ornate suite at the Sonnblick, which had once housed the ornate bulk of Reichsmarschall Göring, Major Mark Hanlon was preparing himself for bed. He had dined late with Captain Johnson and over the wine and the brandy they had rehearsed the day's doings, the programme of the funeral, the lines of the policy they would follow for the first weeks of the Occupation.

Then, at one stride, fatigue had overtaken him. His eyes burned, his head felt as though it were stuffed with cotton-wool, his limbs were heavy and languid.

He had hustled Johnson off to finish his drinking with the sergeants, and had rung for the maid to draw a bath and lay out his night things.

Now he lay steaming in the big marble tub, feeling his tiredness soak out of his bones, while the sharp mountain water toned his skin and relaxed his muscles. It was a historic luxury, this of the bath, and years of campaign living had given it a new edge of pleasure for him.

A daily baptism in hot water gave a man the illusion, if not of renewed innocence, at least of renewed competence in his traffic with the world. Scrubby genius was always at a discount. The biggest killings were made by men with fresh collars and clean hands.

Soap and water worked miracles for a man's self esteem, and the perfumed vapour clouds softened the harsh outlines of reality. Which was probably the reason why the old patricians had sat comfortably in the steam rooms while the Huns were battering on the gates of the Empire, and why Mark Hanlon forgot for a while the dead man being screwed into his coffin in the basement, and the scar-faced killer skulking somewhere between the pines and the white peaks.

He smiled wryly at the tag end of the thought and hoisted himself reluctantly from the water. His towel lay warm and crisp on the heated rail and as he rubbed himself briskly a new thought came to him.

All this profusion of wine and food and service was the perquisite of the conqueror. Children were whimpering with hunger in the cellars of Berlin. Girls were selling themselves in Vienna for a tin of American coffee. Families were shivering over a dish of smouldering twigs in a hundred ruins. And all over Europe men like himself were sitting like Cæsars, with full bellies and warm bodies and stewards to serve them and women to solace them at a finger click.

Some would grasp the luxury avidly and gorge themselves into sickness of body and soul. Some would accept it with thoughtless arrogance as the natural coin of tribute. Others, like himself, would have the grace to be ashamed of themselves. But they would all enjoy it and none of them would have the courage to deny themselves in order to keep their dignity among the dispossessed. It was the beginning of the slow corruption of conquest which would end with victor and vanquished lying together in the stink of common defeat, in the despairing repetition of ancient sins.

He finished his toilet, put on his pyjamas and climbed into the huge bed under the billowing mountain of eiderdown.

It was the time he always dreaded, this last lonely hour of the day, when memory stirred and conscience itched and desire woke, warm and fruitless in his loins. There was much to remember, much that he wished forgotten, more that he wanted but knew that he could never have.

The thing that plagued him was the inevitability of it all.

There was the illusion of choice, the illusion of determining one's road. But the lines were cast by others and when you came to the crossroads the decision was already made for you. You looked back and thought, 'If I had done this . . . if I had chosen thus and thus . . .' But this was hindsight and historic fallacy. In spite of the signposts there was only one road—and you were already predisposed to walk it.

Father Albertus preached that there was a grace sufficient to every moment. But even he added the rider that some moments needed an extraordinary grace and this a man must petition with prayer and fasting, if it were not to pass him by.

'Drop it, man! Drop it! For this one night forget that you're a spoiled priest and a husband whose wife doesn't love him and a celibate by temporary circumstance and not by choice.

'You're the Occupying Power, the consul on his couch with guards at the door and servants within call. Tomorrow you bury the dead and begin to rule the living. Who knows? History tells strange stories. Kings have coupled happily with serving maids. Prefects have been known to enjoy their wine. And some Cæsars have slept quietly—if only for a little while.'

He reached out, switched off the light and turned over on his side. Five minutes later he was asleep and that night he did not dream at all.

CHAPTER 6

THE FUNERAL is man's oldest theatre. The only time he looks larger than life is when he is dead. All his debts are paid. He has no detractors, only friends. Even for the least loved, there is the pantomime of graveside affection. The humblest oaf commands respect when he lies under the pall.

The funeral of Sergeant Willis was a beautifully mounted performance.

At eight in the morning the coffin was brought up from the cellars and laid on trestles in the foyer of the Sonnblick. A Union Jack was draped over it and a sergeant and four men mounted the death watch.

At eight-thirty the Bürgermeister arrived with the five senior councillors of Bad Quellenberg. They were dressed in the costume of the province: light grey trousers and jackets, faced and piped with mountain green, their lapels decorated with carved bone ornaments—stags' heads, edelweiss, wolf jowls. They wore long cloaks and green hats, each crested with a tuft of chamois hair.

After them came Father Albertus, in stole and surplice, accompanied by a cross bearer and acolytes with wax tapers.

They stood talking and shuffling uneasily for nearly half an hour, because Major Hanlon was busy giving the final briefing to the ski patrols who were to make the first search of the mountain farms. They watched Captain Johnson assembling the cortège guard and those who understood English gathered that he was telling them how to keep step and formation on the steep, icy roadway.

At nine o'clock Hanlon himself came down, in battledress and greatcoat, carrying his gloves and his swaggerstick like a symbol of office. He greeted them coolly and gave the order for the procession to begin.

The troops formed up in the roadway, the acolytes paired off with the cross bearer in front and Father Albertus behind, the councillors hoisted the coffin on to their ageing shoulders, and, at a command from Captain Johnson, the cortège moved off, with Johnson and Hanlon bringing up the rear.

It had stopped snowing, but the sky was still overcast and the flames of the tapers wavered uncertainly in the chill air. The only sounds were the muffled tread of the marchers and the deep voice of Father Albertus reciting the antiphon and the shrill boy chorus answering him.

The familiar Latin cadences brought back a rush of memories to Hanlon and for a moment he thought that he was back in the monastic serenity of Graz, taking part in the comforting ceremonies of dismissal when one of the older brethren had died. The sight of Johnson, pacing it out self-consciously beside him, recalled him to reality.

Then he saw that the street was lined with people.

They were all there, ankledeep in the snow—the very young, the very old, the walking cripples from the Lazarett, the gnarled grey foresters with the dignity of the mountains still on their bent shoulders. Peasant mothers with scrubbed shiny faces held firmly to the shoulders of their children who stood huddling back against their skirts. The shopkeepers stood stiffly outside their shuttered windows. The nurses and medical staff were lined outside the portico of the hospital, whose upper windows were crowded with patients wiping the mist from the glass to get a better view.

They were silent and stony faced, but, as the cortège passed, some of the women bent their heads and wept silently, re-membering their own dead ones. Husbands put their arms protectively round the shoulders of their wives. Fathers patted their daughters' arms in self-conscious sympathy. After his first hurried glance, Hanlon stared straight ahead, march-ing slowly and carefully on the treacherous surface.

When they reached the flat ground which was the last approach to the church, the bells began to toll, slowly and mournfully. The mountains took up the sound and soon the valley and the town were full of the echoing threnody.

As if by common instinct, the townsfolk stepped out into the roadway and formed into a long straggling procession behind the coffin. Hanlon could hear their shuffling tread like a counterpoint to the melody of the bells.

At the lych gate the procession halted. The troops re-formed themselves into a guard of honour so that the acolytes and the priest and the following townsfolk could pass between them into the building. Johnson remained outside, but Hanlon went into the church, where a verger led him to a pew in the front row. He saw the bearers lay the coffin on the big brass stand in front of the sanctuary, then to his amazement the vergers came and stacked it about with wreaths of pine and holly and snow flowers and hot-house blooms that must have come from a dozen private homes—cyclamen, orchids, liliums and azaleas.

A lump came into his throat and he buried his face in an attitude of prayer. When he raised his head the church was full of the rustle of people, the guard was mounted on the coffin and Father Albertus was robing himself in the black chasuble to begin the Mass. When he came to the foot of the altar the first notes of the organ pealed sombrely under the lofty groining of the roof.

"*Requiem aeternam dona eis, Domine.*" The young voices of the choir rose in urgent supplication. "*Et lux perpetua luceat eis.*"

"A hymn is due to Thee, O God, in Sion. A vow shall be paid to Thee in Jerusalem. Hear my prayer. All flesh shall come to Thee . . ."

The chant swept over him in plangent waves as he watched the frail figure of the priest moving stiffly in the heavy Gothic vestments through the preparatory rituals of the sacrifice.

The prayer for the departed: "O God, whose property is mercy and forgiveness, we pray Thee on behalf of the soul of Thy servant . . ."

The letter of Paul to the Corinthians: "Behold, I show you a mystery. . . . We shall all be changed. . . . This corruptible must put on incorruption, and this mortal must put on immortality . . ."

Then the choir again, the long minatory chant of the *Dies Irae*. It was sung as he had not heard it before, the first line of each verse taken as solo, the following couplet sung with full voice by the choir.

> *Dies Irae, dies illa,*
> *Solvet saeclum in favilla,*
> *Teste David cum Sybilla . . .*

The clear impassioned voice of the singer was familiar to him—Anna Kunzli, the girl who lived without love in the Spiderhouse.

When the hymn was finished Father Albertus crossed the altar and after ritual responses began to read in his deep, throbbing voice the gospel for the day of decease:

". . . I am the resurrection and the life. He that believeth in me, though he were dead, yet shall he live: and whosoever liveth and believeth in me shall never die . . ."

Every line and every cadence was familiar to Hanlon, yet in spite of himself he was caught by its perennial majesty and swept backward to a vision of the lost paradise, before he had eaten the fruit of the tree of knowledge and begun his long progress as a citizen of the world.

He belonged here, as did all the others. He had been born into the Church as into a family. He needed it, as a plant needs contact with the soil from which it sprang, as a branch needs sap from its own tap root. Yet by a series of decisions, by repeated concessions to circumstance, he had withdrawn himself from it, so that the life spring was cut off and the sap no longer flowed. The hunger was deep in him, but he could not yet bend himself to confess it. He was still the prodigal, welcome whenever he cared to come, but no longer a sharer in the intimate strengthening life around the hearthstone.

This was what the theologians meant when they talked of sin as a truncation and a kind of death. This was the meaning of mercy and man's need of it . . . a light in the darkness, a hand stretched out to lead the wanderer on new paths, unguessed, undreamed of, in so much perplexity.

The silver bells sounded for the Consecration and the Elevation and he bent his head, though he could not bend his will.

When, at long last, the Mass was over, Father Albertus took off his chasuble and with only the black stole round his neck came down to bless the coffin. The acolytes formed up, the bearers came forward again and they carried Sergeant Willis out into the churchyard, to the black hole that gaped in the snow at the foot of the Christus.

The troops were drawn up in front of the grave, their arms and battledress incongruous among the bleak headboards and the limp figure of the Crucified. The flag was stripped off the coffin and it was lowered slowly into the hole while Father Albertus recited the prayers of dismissal and the responses ran like a small ripple of wind through the crowd.

When the prayers were finished the gravedigger handed Hanlon a clod of earth, frozen and hard as stone. He took it gingerly, and tossed it into the open grave and heard it thud hollowly on the coffin lid. Somewhere in the crowd a woman sobbed and a rustle of pity stirred them all.

As the gravedigger began shovelling the earth, Father Albertus's strong voice led them into the recitation of the rosary and Hanlon heard his own voice making the repetitive response: "Holy Mary, Mother of God, pray for us sinners now and at the hour of our death. Amen."

When the earth was piled into a little mound, the digger covered it with clean snow and the men came forward to pile the wreaths and the flowers on top of it. The sergeant gave a series of sharp commands and the volley rang out, clattering from hill to hill.

It was over. Sergeant Willis was committed to an alien earth. The troops marched away and the people stood aside to let them pass, then they too began to drift away, silent and constrained, while Hanlon still stood, bowed and numb beside the wooden Christus.

An old grandmother pushed a tiny child towards him. She held up a bunch of snow roses and said in her piping voice:

"*Für den Toten*. For the dead one."

Hanlon took the flowers, and bent to lay them with the others. Then the pity and shame of it took hold of him and for the first time in many years he found himself weeping. The last townsfolk turned away discreetly, and after a while he felt Father Albertus's hand on his shoulder and heard his voice, soft and strangely comforting:

"When a man can weep, there is still hope for him. Go home, my son, and I will pray for you."

As he walked out of the churchyard he saw Anna Kunzli standing under the pines and feeding the birds that came fluttering down to take the crumbs from her hands. He passed her by without a word, but her eyes followed him, full of the soft pity of youth and innocence.

CHAPTER 7

ONE OF the few Quellenbergers who did not attend the funeral was Karl Adalbert Fischer.

This morning he had his own fish to fry and, with the town closed and the citizens involved in a longish ceremony, he counted on being private for the cookery.

He rose early, shaved and dressed himself in ski clothes, over which he put his long cloak in case any of the citizens should remark on the curious appearance of their police chief. When his housekeeper offered him coffee, he refused curtly and told her he would breakfast later at the office. Then he went out, hurrying to reach the town before the citizens were astir.

His first call was Frau Gretl Metzger, the plump young matron with a breast like a pouter pigeon, who kept the tobacco shop. Long ago he had had a placid but pleasant affair with her, which had ended, with mutual goodwill, when he had found a younger girl friend. She had married a works-foreman on one of the building projects—a vacuous youth who talked too much and drank more than he earned. When he had been called to the colours, Gretl came to Fischer for advice and he had recommended her for a tobacco licence under the state monopoly. Since then he had always been sure of a smoke—and a bed during the intermissions of his love life.

But this morning's visit had nothing to do with love. Gretl's husband was home again—halfway home, at least. He was a patient in the Feldlazarett. On the retreat from Russia he had walked into a grenade blast. They had brought him back, wretched but alive, to the pointless purgatory of the Lazarett. Gretl visited him dutifully every evening, and every second evening she walked back home with a strapping young orderly from the hospital. This fact, like all others, had been entered in Fischer's big folio. Now he intended to make use of it.

Gretl met him at the door with her hair in curlers and her plump body wrapped in a loose dressing-gown that gaped a little wider when she greeted him. Fischer grinned with satisfaction and patted the nearer curves as he moved past her into the apartment.

She giggled with pleasure, kissed him roundly and drew him into the small sitting-room, where she sat beside him on the settee.

"Karl! This is a nice surprise. What brings you here so early?" She bridled girlishly. "Don't tell me you . . ."

"No, *Liebchen*," he assured her genially. "Much as I'd like to, I'm a busy man and I've got a hard day ahead of me. I'll have to save my strength. I want you to do something for me."

"Anything you want, Karl, you know that." She drew the dressing-gown over her plump chest. There was no point in getting cold if there was no pleasure at the end of it.

"Good. This boy friend of yours, Gretl . . ."

She pouted prettily and tossed her curl papers.

"That one! He's nothing. He talks too much and does too little. Sometimes I think he's half a you-know-what. But what's a girl to do? All the good ones are dead or damaged."

"It's a hard world," agreed Karl Adalbert Fischer. "Is he fond of you?"

"Raves about me," said Gretl emphatically. "There's never

been a woman like me. If my husband were dead he'd marry me. Probably because I remind him of his mother."

"That's good too. I want you to get him to do something for me, privately, you understand. No names, no questions."

"What is it, Karl?"

He handed her the list of drugs that Rudi Winkler had written for him.

"This lot—all of them should be available in the hospital. Your boy friend should be able to lay his hands on them easily enough. Get him to bring them to you, a little at a time if he has to. But I must have them quickly."

She stared at him in surprise.

"You mean, steal them?"

"Acquire them," said Fischer with a gentle smile. "If he asks any questions tell him there's money in it. I'll pay for them."

"But if he refuses?"

"You told me he was crazy about you, *Liebchen*. If he did refuse . . ." He shrugged away the threat. "It might be hard to recommend your tobacco licence when it comes up for review."

"You wouldn't do it, Karl!"

He patted her breast with a reassuring hand.

"Of course I wouldn't, Gretl. I just want you to understand that it's important. That's all."

"I—I understand, Karl." She bent towards him, so that the gown fell open again. "Couldn't you stay a while . . . a little while?"

"Long enough for a cup of coffee," said Fischer briskly. "Then I must go. Another time, eh?"

Half an hour later he was knocking on the door of the small cabin that stood at the foot of the Gondelbahn, the long aerial cable that swung the shining gondolas up the slope to the summit of the Grauglockner. The man who opened it to him was the engineer who ran the machinery and maintained it in the off-season. Fischer gave him his instructions bluntly and briefly.

"This is police business. No one must know that I've been here. Fit me with skis and a pair of sticks. Then start the engine and hoist me to the top. If anybody wants to know why the *Gondel* is running, tell them you're testing the motors. I'll be gone a couple of hours. When I'm ready to come down I'll telephone you from the peak. You'll tell me whether the coast is clear before you bring me down. Is that clear?"

It was clear. The engineer was a canny fellow who knew when weather was blowing up. He brought out his own skis and shifted the clamps with a screwdriver so that they fitted snugly on the small feet of the policeman. He gave him a pair of women's stocks, because he was a small man. Then he led him over to one of the small aluminium gondolas and closed him inside.

Three minutes later, Fischer was swaying out over the pine tops on the first stage of his journey to the Gamsfeld hut.

When he got out of the gondola, lugging the skis and sticks after him, an icy wind struck him, whipping at his cloak, searing his eyes and his nostrils. He cursed savagely and struggled into the shelter of the small log hut. He should have known better. He was too old for this sort of thing. He shed his cloak, folded it neatly on the wooden bench and laid his uniform cap on top of it.

He pulled on a skier's cap, laced it under his chin and pulled up the hood of his jacket. Then he bent down to lock his boots into the skis and shuffled out into the snow, keeping in the shelter of the log walls. Then he looked about him.

He was ringed by mountains—a tumult of waves in a petrified sea. Their troughs were dark with the pine belts and the nestling of villages. Their peaks were bright with snow spume, spilling downwards in a continuous flow broken only by black tors and knife-edge spurs, jagged and sinister. The desolation dwarfed him. The cold wind shook the props of his small courage. He had to make an effort of will to thrust out from the shelter of the wall for the long, transverse run down to the Gamsfeld.

His goal was a small log hut, about five hundred feet from the saddle on the opposite side of the range from Bad Quellenberg. In the old days it had been the first stage of a half-day run for the novices—down to the Gamsfeld, two miles more down to the Hunge valley, up by the chair lift and then a long, steady run home to Quellenberg. Fischer had done it a hundred times in his youth—now it was a middle-aged folly, forced on him by the ties of blood and family. Besides, he couldn't afford time for the Hungetal run. He would have to climb back to the saddle and take the *Gondel*.

He could see the hut clearly from his take-off point—a low

stone building crouching like a big animal under its snowy roof. A thin spiral of smoke rose from the squat chimney and was blown away down the valley by the driving wind. They were there, then. His journey had not been in vain. He pushed himself off, uncertainly at first, but when he felt the blades bite in for purchase and the wind whipping his cheeks, he began to relax. His slack muscles responded to old memories, and for the first time in years Karl Fischer began to enjoy himself.

Like most pleasures, this one ended all too quickly.

The door of the hut faced downward over the valley. His approach brought him to the blind side of the building. He slipped off his skis and walked carefully round it, bending low as he passed under the window. If his nephew were in one of his crazy fits, there was no knowing how he might be welcomed.

When he reached the door he stood to one side of it, flattening himself against the wall. Then he reached over and knocked firmly. There was no answer, but he heard a small rustle of movement inside the hut. He called loudly:

"Martha! Johann! It's me, Uncle Karl. Open up!"

There was a pause, then a man's voice, harsh and strained, challenged him:

"If you're not, I'll blow your head off."

"Nonsense, boy! Look, I'll step back so that you can see me from the window. For God's sake try to talk sense to him, Martha."

He heard her chiding her brother angrily:

"Don't be silly, Johann. I'll go. Nobody will harm me; besides, that's Uncle's voice."

Fischer stepped back into the snow and, a moment later, the curtain was drawn aside from the window and his niece's face looked out at him. Then the door opened and, half laughing, half crying, she drew him into the hut.

The first thing he saw was his nephew crouched in a corner of the bunk, his pistol aimed at the doorway. Fischer grinned at him cheerfully. "Put it away, lad, for God's sake! You'll hurt someone."

Johann stared at him for a moment with sullen mistrust, then slowly lowered the pistol and put it down on the bunk, still within reach. Fischer peeled off gloves and cap and moved over to the old round-bellied stove to warm himself. The girl followed, questioning him anxiously:

"What is it, Uncle? What's going on? What will happen to Johann—all of us?"

"Nothing," he told them breezily. "Nothing at all. Uncle Karl has fixed everything. I'll tell you about it later. Now I'm cold and hungry. Can you fix me something?"

"Of course. Oh, Uncle, that's the best news we could have."

She threw her arms round his neck and kissed him, then bustled away, rummaging in the knapsacks for bread and cheese, spooning black ersatz coffee into a saucepan of snow-water. Fischer took out his cigarette case and held it out to his nephew.

"Like one?"

"Throw it to me."

"Just as you like."

He took out a cigarette for himself, lit it, then tossed the case and the lighter to his nephew, who took out three cigarettes. One he put in his mouth, the other two he laid down on the shelf at the side of the bunk. He lit up and began to smoke avidly.

"You can have the lot, if you like," said Fischer mildly.

"Thanks."

He emptied the case and tossed it back to Fischer with the lighter. The lighter fell short and Fischer moved across the floor to pick it up. Johann raised the gun and kept it trained on him until he had retrieved the lighter and moved back to his place beside the stove. Fischer said nothing, but smoked placidly, watching him through the smoke drift.

'Like a wolf,' he thought. 'Scarred, hungry, run down to the rib case, but he'd snap your throat out before you could say God's mercy. Not so long ago he was a child, with a bright pink face and his mother's eyes. I used to dandle him on my knee and feed him with sugar plums. Then he was a student, feckless as most, but with a charm to him. And afterwards the big thing—Universität—when he'd come home sober and serious at term's end, with his mouth full of big words and his head full of dreams about saving the world with a scalpel and a bottle of dill water. Now look at him. What did the war do to him that he hasn't told us? Or is it simply that if you hunt a man long enough and keep him running far enough, you turn him into a wolf? And what do we do with you now, boy? How do we coax you out of your corner and begin to make you a man again?'

Suddenly his nephew began to speak, and Fischer felt the hairs bristling on his nape. The voice had changed completely, although the man himself still sat tense and crouching, with staring bloodshot eyes, the fingers of his free hand still lying on the gun butt. It was a calm voice, measured, mild, almost academic in its dryness, as if another man were speaking out of the distorted wolf's face. It said:

"I'm sorry to be a worry to you, but you must try to understand. There's a name for this trouble of mine—a doctor would know it—trauma. It's as if I were cut in two, with the best part of me on one side and the worst on the other, and the good beyond my reach. If you tried to take my gun now I'd shoot you, I know that. I'd know I shouldn't, but I couldn't help myself. Instinct, instead of reason. The control mechanism doesn't function. The family told me I killed a man. I—I remember it vaguely. I saw them driving up the road. I thought they were Russkis coming after me again. I was tired of running. I wanted to get down and fight it out, once for all. I know I should give myself up. But I can't. I'd go screaming crazy, without hope of recovery. I'm a good enough doctor to know that. Maybe if I could rest a while, stop running, have a good doctor to help me, I could get better. But that's not possible now, is it?"

As he spoke the wild look died slowly from his eyes, which became glazed and dead, and when he had finished, two large tears squeezed themselves out of the inflamed ducts and rolled slowly down his lean, stubbled cheeks.

His sister watched him spellbound, the saucepan suspended in mid-air, but Fischer went on smoking casually. After a while he said, very quietly:

"That's what I came to talk to you about. I've found a doctor for you, and a place where you can be treated in quiet and safety."

"I won't go. I can't." The wild light came back into his eyes. His fingers closed convulsively round the pistol.

"It's up to you," said the little policeman calmly. "The English have patrols out, searching the valleys and the heights. They'll do it for months if they have to. Which means I'll have to keep shifting you round from hut to hut. A few weeks of that and you'll be dead. The only other alternative is the one I've given you. Take your pick."

"Where is this place? Who's the doctor?"

"His name is Winkler. He's on the run like yourself. I've offered him new identity papers if he'll take you in, nurse you a while, then do a plastic on your face so that we can get you out into the American zone when you're well again."

"Where does he live?"

"Quellenberg. He's got a chalet tucked away in the trees at the wrong end of the Mozart promenade." He chuckled amiably. "His housekeeper's got a face like an axe, but she cooks like an angel. I dined with them last night. Winkler's got a good cellar too. You could live like a king—and thumb your nose at the world. Think it over anyway, while we have some coffee."

The girl took the hint and turned back to her preparations. Fischer sat down on the opposite bunk and began leafing through a four-year-old copy of the *Wiener Zeitung* full of smiling Party men and marching heroes. He felt like tossing it into the stove, but it gave him something to do and left the boy free to sort out his tangled thoughts. After a while he spoke again, and for the first time a note of uncertainty made itself heard:

"How—how would you get me down to town without being seen?"

His uncle looked up from his newspaper and answered easily:

"That one worried me at first, but I think I've got the answer."

"What?"

"It means staying up here another day or two, of course. But that's nothing so long as we can steer the Englishmen away. I might start a rumour or two to take them to the other side of the valley. Toss me another cigarette, will you?" Without thinking, his nephew reached out and threw one of the cigarettes from the pile at his elbow. Fischer felt a small flutter of hope. He lit the cigarette and went on: "December the sixth is St Nicholas's Day. The saint visits all the houses with his page and with the Krampus following behind to scare the naughty children. There'll be twenty or thirty Krampuses coming into town on that night; if we dress you in goatskins and put a Krampus mask on your head, who's to tell what you are?"

"Uncle!" The girl swung round excitedly, almost overturning the coffee pot. "That's brilliant. It couldn't fail. You know yourself, Johann, you've never been able to guess who it was under the goat masks. Say you'll agree, say it, please!"

She went to him swiftly and sat on the bunk beside him, and for the first time his hands reached not for the gun but for her. He buried his face in her shoulder and said wearily: "I wish I could believe it, Martha."

Fischer turned studiously back to his paper, while she coaxed and pleaded with him until the coffee boiled over on the stove and she had to leap up to rescue it. There were only two cups, so she gave one to each of the men together with a round of black bread and a large slice of cheese. It was rough fare and Fischer felt himself choking on it, but his nephew ate and drank ravenously as if afraid it might be snatched from him.

When it was all gone he put down the cup and wiped his mouth with the back of his hand. Then he lit a cigarette and stretched out on the bunk, smoking and staring up at the timbers of the roof. Without turning his head he asked cautiously:

"Are you sure we can do this, Uncle?"

"I'm risking my own neck," said Fischer with a show of irritation. "If I'm caught, I'll have a harder time than you. Any lawyer could get you mitigation—a good one might save you altogether. For me there's no defence. You're not even my son!"

"I'll do it, then." He said it in a voice so near to normal that they both stared at him. Then Fischer told him bluntly:

"There's a condition."

"What?"

His nephew slewed round sharply to face him.

"I want you to give me your guns."

"No!" Instantly, he was an animal again, tense, staring, his lips drawn back in a rictus of fear.

"When you go into town," said Fischer calmly, "you will be afraid. If you carry your guns, you will kill someone else as you killed the Englishman. You must know that. If you don't give them to me now, I wash my hands of you. You can go your own way, running and running till you die in your tracks or somebody puts a bullet in your head. I'm risking my whole career on you, lad. The one thing I won't risk is another killing. That's final!"

There was a long silence. The girl and her uncle looked warily at the haggard face and the wild eyes, hoping for some sign that reason had penetrated to the still functioning intelligence. They could see the eyes glazing again, the mouth slackening, after the first impact of panic. Then a new question was tossed at them:

"I—I trust you, Uncle. But what about the others? You know what the town is like for talk. Sooner or later they'll know where I am, and who I am. What then?"

"It's a fair question, boy. I'll give you a straight answer." Fischer stuck his thumbs in his belt and rocked gently back and forth on his heels, grinning cheerfully. "I know the people better than you do. First, they've got too many worries of their own to stick their noses into my business. Second, they know that there'd be no profit if they did, I know too much about 'em. Third—and this may surprise you, but it's true—they don't want you caught. They need you safe and well. So many of the boys are gone, the ones that are left are doubly precious. Once we've patched you up you'll have so many offers of marriage you'll have to beat 'em off with sticks."

"Marriage!" The word burst out of him in a wild shout of laughter. "Marriage! That's a good one! That's the funniest joke I've heard in years. Laugh, why don't you, laugh!"

"It isn't funny," said Fischer.

"Isn't it?" He was halfway off the bunk, shouting wildly. "Then try this, Uncle! Twice the Russkis took me, and twice I escaped. The Chetniks got me too in Yugoslavia, but they let me go. You know why? Because they said I was no good to them any more. I was no good to anyone any more. . . ."

His voice rose to a high scream that cut off suddenly as he pitched to the floor in a dead faint. The girl ran to him and knelt down, cradling his head on her lap, crooning to him in a low desperate voice. Fischer stood looking down at him like a man turned to stone.

"You poor bastard," he said softly, "you poor, poor bastard."

He walked to the bunk, picked up the pistol and the rifle and turned towards the door. The girl's voice stopped him:

"You're not leaving us, Uncle?"

"Better I do," said Fischer sombrely. "When he comes round put him to bed and keep him warm. Tomorrow I'll send your father up with the costume and instructions for getting him down to the town. Can you control him till then?"

The girl looked down at the shabby, shrunken figure on the floor, then up again at her uncle.

"There's not much left to control, is there?"

"Nothing at all," said Karl Adalbert Fischer.

Then he went out, closing the door softly behind him.

CHAPTER 8

HALF AN hour after the funeral, Mark Hanlon was back at his desk in the Sonnblick. The crisis of emotion had passed quickly, leaving him, as tears and passion do, purged for a while of anger, regret and indecision, and ready for the work in hand.

There was a mountain of it waiting for him: supply arrangements for his troops and for the town, a survey of local economic resources, a security check to screen war criminals and Party fanatics, an examination of the town records and the impounding of relevant documents, a search for expropriate estates, the repatriation of Austrian troops, border liaison with the American zone, road and rail traffic control, democratic reform of local education, a search for arms dumps and privately held weapons. . . .

Johnson and he worked through the stacks of memoranda till their heads were buzzing and the mimeographed type danced crazily in front of their eyes. Their lunch was a plate of sandwiches and a pot of coffee and at three in the afternoon they were still wrestling with the primary problem: how to set up a complete system of local government with a handful of tired troops and a set of officials all of whom were suspect on one count or another.

"It can't be done," said Johnson wearily. He canted his chair at a perilous angle, put his feet on the table and lit a cigarette. "Ten into one won't go. That's all there is to it."

"Try telling that to Klagenfurt, laddy. You'll get a flea in your ear and a quick discharge . . . services no longer required."

"Not such a bad idea. It's been a damn long war."

"All wasted if we ball up the peace."

"It's balled up already," said Johnson with youthful wisdom. "Always has been. Always will be. The minute the guns stop, the politicians are in, carving up the bodies. Look at Yalta. We went to war to save Poland, so we said. Now we've handed it to the Russkis on a platter—and half Europe as well. Why worry over all this!" He waved an impatient hand at the stacks of typescript. "Why not flush it down the toilet and let the politicos have their heads? It comes to the same thing in the end."

"Because there aren't any politicians in Quellenberg," said Hanlon quietly.

"The place is crawling with 'em," said Johnson emphatically. "We've had 'em here in this room—Holzinger, Kunzli, the little bobby—and all the others we haven't met yet."

"At the moment, they've got no authority. We've got it. I want to see if it can't be used properly, to build something permanent."

"Like what?"

"Read all about it!" said Hanlon with a grin. He tossed a stack of memoranda into Johnson's lap so that he overbalanced and toppled backward to the floor.

"You haven't answered my question," said Johnson as he picked himself up and kicked the scattered papers into a heap. "I don't think you can."

"There is an answer, you know, Johnny." Hanlon was suddenly serious again. "And it's a damn sight simpler than all that rubbish in the memos. We've got to get things organised so that the men can get working and the kids can start eating properly and so that everybody gets a fair share. We've got to weed out any murderers and rapists and professional torturers who've tried to slip back to Quellenberg to live as honest citizens. We've got to restore stolen property to its rightful owners—if they're alive and can be found. We've got to kick out the official exploiters and find honest men to replace 'em so that people get a fair deal in business life and justice in the courts."

"Better buy yourself a lantern and live in a tub," said Johnson perkily. "You can't even get your own mess sergeant to stay honest."

Hanlon shrugged it off.

"That's the nature of the beast."

"Does it change, just because he speaks German?"

Hanlon was silent for a while, chewing the cud of the question; then he leaned forward across the table, gesturing in careful exposition.

"Let's get something straight, Johnny, right from the start. I'm a good deal older than you and I've got a lot more reason to be dubious about the good that's in people. But I've learnt something that I think is important. Whatever good there is in this cockeyed world started small and stayed small for a long time. When it grew, it grew slowly, like a tree, so that folk hardly noticed it, until one day it was big and its branches sheltered a lot of poor devils like you and me. That's what I hope for from this job—to start a small good growing. If I didn't believe it possible I'd be quite happy to whore my way through it and line my pockets at the same time—or blow my brains out! I'm not sure which."

"Better make up your mind, Major," said Johnson with a lopsided grin. "You might come to it sooner than you think."

"To hell with you, Johnny!" said Hanlon irritably. "Let's get back to work."

Together they bent over a verbose instruction on 'The Status of Dependents of Persons Under Remand as Suspected War Criminals'.

Late in the afternoon, when the early dark was already down on the mountains, the leaders of the ski parties came in to make their reports. All of them tallied with that presented by a hatchet-faced corporal. He had been a schoolteacher and his German was good, if pedantic. His intelligence was much higher than his opinion of the Army and those who ran it. For Hanlon he had a grudging respect, which he expressed by an emphatic bluntness of utterance.

"He's around, sir. We all got the same feeling. The farmers are covering up. The police know it and they're covering up too."

"What makes you say that?"

"First, they say they don't understand our German—which is a lie. The police understand it, so do they. They refuse to speak anything but dialect. That's a pose, too. They lay it on like stage Irish."

Hanlon nodded thoughtfully. It was an old trick to embarrass the visitor. They played the dumb ox when it suited them, but when their pockets were hit they squawked loudly enough. And in Hochdeutsch too!

"What else, Corporal?"

"The atmosphere, sir: like kids in a classroom. You know there's mischief, by the way they look at you, the elaborate innocence they put on. And you can't get the truth—even if you beat their silly heads against the wall."

"If we lean on 'em hard enough, they'll crack," said Hanlon.

"No, sir."

"Why not?"

"Because they're ready for us. They can see us coming miles away, from those mountain farms. Even if we knew the man was hiding in one of 'em he'd have a two-mile start before we reached the place. We're climbing *up*, remember, on skis. You know how slow that is. To get to the back valleys we've got to go up first, then down—unless we're going to trudge through the drifts in the passes. Even then any lookout would spot us. They've only got to send their visitor out into the pine belts and we've lost him."

"Are the police co-operative?"

"Very," said the corporal dryly. "They stand around and wait for us to tell 'em what to do. They forget where the tracks are and they find it hard to read a map reference, and they travel slowly even on the best slopes—but you couldn't pin a charge on 'em. We'll never get our man this way. I'll lay odds on it."

"We're going to keep it up all the same," said Hanlon with a grin.

"Do you mind saying why, sir?"

"How do you feel, Corporal?"

He got the answer in one expressive word.

"Fine. Now put yourself in the position of the killer. If we have parties out every day, each in a different sector, what happens? He's got to keep moving. If, as I suspect, he's a sick man, sooner or later he's got to stop moving. Then what?"

"They'll hide him."

"Where? You know what these mountain farms are like. One big building to house the family and the animals and the winter hay. You could turn one upside down in half an hour."

"They'll shift him down to the town."

"Then we get him," said Mark Hanlon with flat finality.

And even the doubting corporal was half convinced he would do it.

When the conference broke up, Johnson raised the question of exit papers for Sepp Kunzli.

"I don't see where you're heading on this one, Mark. We had a good report on him. Yet you're starting to put him on the jumps. Why?"

"Stolen property, Johnny. He's a high-class fence. I'd hate him to get away with it, though he probably will."

"How does that tie up with the report?"

"London said he was a good agent, in war time. All that means is that he was a good gambler—laying off the risks."

"Then why let him out of the country?"

"I've got to," said Hanlon wryly. "The way the Swiss banks work, I haven't a hope of getting access to his papers unless he brings them to me himself."

"Do you think he will?"

"Some of them."

"How do you know he won't skip?"

"He's got too much property inside Austria—and a niece as well. It's my guess he'll decide to sit out his hand and rely on lawyer's tricks to hold most of his property intact. As I say, he'll probably do it. But we'll prise some of it out of him—and a lot of other information as well."

Captain Johnson cocked a jaundiced eye at his Commanding Officer. "You're a devious blighter, aren't you?"

Hanlon made a gesture of weary distaste.

"How else do you deal with a devious operator? He sets out to avenge his wife by plucking the Party men, and somewhere along the line the taste for revenge changes to a taste for money. But he still goes on justifying himself as a sort of Monte Cristo. He's nothing of the kind. He's an exploiter, profiting from plundered estates."

"And his niece sings in the choir," said Johnson with apparent irrelevance. "Pretty wench too—in a virginal sort of way."

"I hadn't noticed," said Hanlon coolly.

"You're getting old, Mark," chuckled Johnson with genial cruelty. "I notice all the girls, all the time."

Hanlon rounded on him angrily.

"You keep your hands on your change and your mind on

the job—and do your leching away from the office! Is that clear?"

Johnson stared at him, surprised at the outburst.

"I'm sorry. It was only a joke. Dammit all . . ."

There was a knock at the door and, in answer to Hanlon's summons, Sergeant Jennings came in with a large red-sealed envelope.

"Just arrived, sir. Safe hand from Klagenfurt."

"Thanks, Jennings."

The sergeant saluted and went out. Hanlon broke the seals and found inside two more envelopes similarly marked. The innermost one contained a long memorandum. He conned it swiftly and then threw back his head and laughed and laughed till the tears ran down his face. Johnson watched him with growing puzzlement until finally curiosity got the better of him.

"Well, what's it about? What's so funny?

Hanlon recovered himself at last and told him with sardonic deliberation:

"Life's little ironies, Johnny. Just as we're getting ourselves organised they dump this in our lap. By arrangement with the US Command at Salzburg, three hundred displaced persons from three concentration camps will be billeted on us for Christmas and indefinitely thereafter. The International Red Cross will supply medical services and supplies. Accommodation and all other services will be arranged by us. They arrive a week from today."

"God Almighty!" Johnson swore softly. "There's a packet of trouble."

"Bigger than you know." Hanlon laughed again, humourlessly. "I wonder what Holzinger will say when I tell him."

By the time they had got through dinner, Hanlon was sick of his own company and that of his junior. It wasn't the boy's fault. He was agreeable and intelligent; he had a sense of humour and a mordant wit. If he took the world and himself less than seriously, he was to be envied, not blamed. If his commander had a bellyache or a heartache, that was no reason why his own wine should go sour.

But tonight Hanlon was restless. The ornate room stifled him. The mountain of work on his desk appalled him. The exchanges of the dinner-table were stale to him—old tales, familiar and wearisome, new speculations, profitless and impertinent. He wanted to get out for a while.

Where to go? There were no clubs. The bars were closed for want of custom. He had no friends in this alien town. It was unwise for him to drink with the NCOs or the men. He had no taste for solitary tipple.

Huber would be glad to see him at the hospital, but tonight he shrank from the atmosphere of ether and antiseptics, the uncomfortable evidence of suffering and mortality. Father Albertus would welcome him too; but what would they talk of but memories or metaphysics? Uncomfortable subjects, both.

Then he thought of Holzinger. There was business to talk with him, and no valid reason why it shouldn't be talked in comfort. Holzinger had put on a good show at the funeral, he had earned a courtesy. Why not call on him, tender an official thanks, and let him digest the new pill in privacy? If excuse were needed, there it was to hand. He would go.

He checked the position of Holzinger's house on the area map, and went out.

The clouds had cleared away now. The sky was clear and bright with diamond points. The freeze was beginning and the cold cut into him like a razor. The snow shone, ghostly in the starlight, and the crystals crackled under his feet as he strode briskly through the town and on to the wooded promenade that led to the Bürgermeister's house.

He found himself thinking out his entrance like an actor, planning the words, rehearsing the gestures. 'I will say this, and he will answer me so and so. I will smile to show him that there is no enmity. I will apologise for the intrusion, so that he will understand that I respect his privacy. I will come quickly to the compliment to give him confidence. I must uphold his dignity in the presence of his family. And before the evening is done I must reaffirm my own authority, gently, lest he think that hospitality gives him a hold over me.'

It was a weakness and he knew it. He needed company, diversion, comfort against the bleak loneliness of power. But the lapse was small and easily repaired. The chastest of men leans to the comfort of women, even if he has no intention to bed with her. He smiled sourly to himself at the thought of all this careful moralising over a simple act. It were a monastic habit and he had never lost it, though he had often succeeded in forgetting it.

A maid in a black dress and a white starched apron opened the door to him. She gaped at his uniform, then stammered an apology and left him standing in the hall while she went to fetch Holzinger. The Bürgermeister was obviously rattled, but he recovered himself quickly and held out his hand in greeting.

"Good evening, Major. This is a pleasant surprise."

Hanlon smiled and took the offered hand.

"I hope I'm not intruding."

"Not at all. There is only my family at home. They will be happy to see you."

Now the compliment, carefully phrased, sedulously rehearsed.

"I was touched by the arrangements you made for the funeral. I wanted to tell you personally . . . informally."

Holzinger bowed stiffly, and his face softened into a smile of gratitude.

"That was kind, Major."

"A small courtesy," murmured Hanlon. "We have enough unpleasant business to transact in the daytime, without sleeping on it as well."

Now it was done, decently and in order: the apology, the compliment, the subtle caution. Dignity was assured on both sides. Holzinger took his arm and led him into the bright drawing-room.

The first thing he saw was the two women, tense in their chairs, staring at him. The expression in the mother's eyes was a strange mixture of surprise, puzzlement, fear. The daughter's was cool, appraising, and then suddenly interested.

Holzinger made the introductions and they both looked a little startled when he bent over their hands, continental fashion, and greeted them in his pure colloquial German.

Holzinger led him to a chair.

"Sit down, Major. Make yourself comfortable. A drink? Schnapps? Sliwowitz?"

"Anything you have."

In the small hiatus that followed, while Holzinger poured the drinks and the two women searched for an opening gambit, he took stock of the room: solid Biedermeier comfort, good pictures, deep carpet, brocaded curtains, Viennese porcelain, Lipizzaner horses, a grand piano, twinkling lustres, an old carved marriage chest from Land Salzburg. On the mantel a photograph of a young man in Alpenjäger uniform, the son probably. . . .

"Where did you learn German, Major?" Liesl Holzinger's voice surprised him, as it did all strangers, with its depth and smoothness.

"I was a student in Graz years ago."

"Then you know our country well, and understand the people."

"I like to think so." Hanlon smiled in careful deprecation. "Much has changed of course, since I was here."

"Most Englishmen never speak as well as you."

"I'm half Irish, perhaps that explains it."

"Perhaps."

He had the feeling that she was weighing him, measuring his reactions, listening for the undertones in his voice, watching for any significance of gesture. The women were the strength in this house, he decided, the shrewdness too. He wondered vaguely whether Holzinger was happy with his dark-eyed daughter and his blonde Valkyrie of a wife.

The drinks were brought and they toasted each other.

"*Prost!*" said Mark Hanlon.

"*Prost!*" said Max Holzinger.

"To peace," said his wife.

The dark girl said nothing at all.

Holzinger laid down his glass and began to talk.

"The Major was telling me, Liesl, that he was very touched by our burial service this morning." He said it eagerly, almost defensively, as if anxious to affirm his good standing with the Occupying Power.

"It was the least we could do," said his wife emphatically. "A thing like that involves us all, even those who were not involved before. Have you found the murderer yet, Major?"

"No. It will take time."

"The sooner the better," said Traudl casually. "Then we can all start living normally."

Holzinger and Liesl looked at her sharply, but her eyes and her smile were innocent of malice. Hanlon grinned and said gently:

"There's no reason why you shouldn't begin now, Fräulein. The war's over. After a while the rhythm of life will start to pick up again. It always does, you know."

95

"Easy to say—for the winner," said the girl bluntly.

"Traudl!" Her mother turned on her with a sharp exclamation of anger.

"It's all right," said Hanlon with a smile. "It's fair comment. It's the young ones who inherit the mess." He turned back to the girl. "Don't get the wrong idea about us, Fräulein. The only reason I'm here is to keep order and try to start life moving again. After that I go home—I'd like to be there now."

"Then why is everybody afraid of you?"

"Are they?"

"You know they are!" She tossed it to him in smiling challenge. "Everybody, including Father here."

Holzinger flushed and began to protest, but Hanlon cut him short with a gesture, and answered the girl with sober gentleness:

"We're all a little afraid of strangers. Nobody likes a policeman camped on his doorstep. You get used to them in time, then you forget them, and after a while they go home."

He got up, walked over to the piano and sat down. As the others watched him, curious and vaguely worried, he began to play, stiffly at first, then with fluid grace, the 'Kärnter Heimatlied', which is the tenderest of all songs of the motherland province of Austria.

The music seemed to take possession of him, smoothing the lines from his face, relaxing the stiffness in him, so that the drab uniform seemed to sit oddly on his shoulders. The melody flowed from his hands, supple and golden, singing of snow-peak and waterfall, of blossom trees and green meadows, of birdsong and the sparkle of mayflies, and the hunger of an exile for the good land that nurtured him. Its pathos tugged their heartstrings so that they left their chairs and came to him, moving quietly, lest the tenuous magic break. Hanlon neither saw nor heard them. He had surrendered to the memories that flowed out from his fingertips, old folk tunes, snatches of Schubertlieder, wisps of Mozart and Haydn, a monastery chant, a Tyrolese yodel—scraps and shreds of forgotten happiness stitched into a bright patchwork of melody. Somewhere between the monk and the soldier there had been a musician too, a fellow with a song in his heart and talent in his hands, but he had been thrust into the background, to emerge at this unlikely moment.

Holzinger stood in the background, fighting down a small rush of emotion, but the women stood close to Hanlon, so that the warmth of their bodies went out to him and their perfume was all about him, heady as the music. When his playing faltered, they prompted him, taking up the melody with soft voices, their faces bent to him, their white hands fluttering to the beat. He closed his eyes and played on, surrendering himself to the sound and perfume and the rhythm of his stirring blood.

Then slowly the pleasure spent itself and the music died in a low minor cadence that lingered a long while in the quiet room. The women moved away, reluctantly, and Hanlon swung round on the stool to face them. His mouth was puckered into a self-conscious grin and he made a little diffident gesture of apology.

"That's all, I'm afraid."

"*Wunderschön!*" said Liesl Holzinger softly.

"A great kindness," said Holzinger awkwardly. "We all appreciate it." The girl said nothing. She had already turned away to light a cigarette, but her body was alive with the music and with desire for the man who had played it.

"You see," said Hanlon, mocking her lightly. "We're not all monsters, Fräulein. Some of us are quite *sympathisch* when you get to know us."

Even as he said it he remembered that Franck had played Chopin in the butchery of Warsaw, and fiddlers had played Brahms outside the doors of the gas chambers. But Irmtraud Holzinger was unconscious of such ironies. She raised her head, so that he saw the passion in her eyes and the frank invitation.

"I'll remember it now, Major. I hope you'll play for us again."

"I hope you'll ask me," murmured Hanlon, and cursed himself for the easy gallantry.

"You are welcome at any time, Major," Holzinger assured him with formal courtesy.

"The Major is a busy man. We must not make demands on him," said Liesl Holzinger, who was still the wisest of them all.

A little while later he took his leave. The women stood in the porch to watch him go, but Holzinger walked down the steps with him to the garden gate. He held out his hand and said in his sincere, uneasy voice:

"I'm glad you came, Major. I hope this may be the beginning of an understanding between us."

"I hope so too," said Hanlon politely. "I'd like you to call on me in the morning. There's a lot to discuss."

"No more trouble, I hope?" asked Holzinger unhappily.

"No more than usual. Don't let it spoil your rest, Herr Bürgermeister. Goodnight. And thank you for the hospitality."

"Goodnight, Major. Come safely home."

He stood a long time at the gate, watching the shadowy figure striding out along the promenade, then he too turned away and walked back to the house, where his women were discussing an important question: whether Mark Hanlon was married or single.

CHAPTER 9

WHEN HOLZINGER presented himself at the Sonnblick at nine-thirty the following morning, he found to his surprise that Fischer and Father Albertus were already there. The three of them sat uneasily in the big room, under the unfriendly eye of Captain Johnson, each wondering why the others had been summoned. Hanlon, it seemed, was busy with the briefing of the search parties and Johnson was content to let them wait and wonder.

Twenty minutes later Hanlon arrived, made a brief apology and plunged straight into business. Cool, detached, he sat behind the big desk with its mountains of paper and read them the official directive on the arrival and reception of displaced persons from the concentration camps. When he had finished he laid down the manuscript and looked at the three faces in front of him. He said calmly:

"There it is, gentlemen. I'd like your comments. You may speak as freely as you want."

There was a long pause. The three men looked at each other, then back at the official mask of the man behind the desk.

"It's—it's a surprise," said Holzinger carefully. "I can't pretend it's a pleasant one."

"There'll be trouble," said Fischer bluntly. "As there has

been in other places. Disorder, attempts at rape and murder. I have not the staff to handle them. The Occupying Power must assume the responsibility."

Hanlon said nothing. He looked down at the backs of his hands and waited. Then Father Albertus spoke. His deep voice was full of conviction.

"We have a debt to these people. Whatever we do will be too little to repay it. Whatever trouble we have is not too much."

Hanlon looked up. A small sardonic smile twitched the corners of his mouth.

"Well, gentlemen?"

Holzinger shrugged helplessly.

"We—we can't quarrel with the principle. We shall do what we can."

"I do quarrel with it," said Fischer stubbornly.

Hanlon answered him, mildly enough:

"I'd like your view, Fischer."

The small head jerked forward on the long neck. The bird-like eyes were bright with anger. The hands made jerky, emphatic gestures.

"There is a debt—we admit it. There is a problem of rehabilitation—we admit that too. But we do not solve the problem by dumping these people in the middle of a small community like this one which has no protection against . . ."

"Against what?" Hanlon shot the question at him.

"Hate," said Fischer bluntly. "And revenge! Don't tell me they don't want it. You know what happened when the camps were thrown open—bloody murder! Not only of guards and executioners, but of local villagers. These people know they're protected. Put a DP in the dock against a German or an Austrian. Who wins? Who must win? How do you keep order in a situation like that? Don't mistake me. I know what was done in the camps. I know what happens when you brutalise a man so much that you turn him into a beast. But they weren't all martyrs. There were rapists and perverts as well as Jews and politicals. Do you let those loose on us—our women and children? I can't look at the big issues. I've lived and worked here all my life. Why dump all this—this corruption on us?"

"Because all of us had our part in it, Karl," said Father Albertus sombrely. "All of us co-operated by silence, by

99

cowardice, by eating the fruits that were manured by millions of dead. You say you know what went on. You could never know, unless you had been there and endured the horror in your own body. You talk of vengeance, murder, rape. Wait till you see these people. They have no heart left for hate—or love either. In many of them even the will to live is dead. You are afraid of them, you say? What is to be feared from a skeleton? You fear for our women. Is there lust in a starving body, whose strength is consumed by the feeblest motion? I will tell you what you are afraid of—what we're all afraid of—our own guilt staring at us from dead eyes, our own shame stalking in the sunlight of this town!"

There was a long silence in the ornate room, so that each man was conscious of his own pulsebeat, the small, crepitant rustle of his clothing against his body. Even Hanlon, who had brought the old priest for this very reason, was awed by his eloquent condemnation. After a while he said very quietly:

"It seems we're all agreed on the main issue, gentlemen. There are some practical matters I'd like to discuss with you. First is the requisition of a suitable building. I'd like your recommendations, Holzinger. Then we'll inspect it together before I make the order."

"I'll let you have them tomorrow morning, Major."

"Good. Next is the question of staffing. The medical nucleus will be supplied by International Red Cross—doctors, nurses, trained orderlies. We'll need wardmaids, cleaners, staff for the laundry, the kitchen, the boiler room, clerical assistants . . . How do we raise them?"

"You'll have to conscript them," said Fischer sourly. "Nobody in his right senses would volunteer for work in such a place."

"You underrate our people, Karl," said the old priest calmly. "They have at bottom a Christian conscience. If this proposal is presented to them in the right fashion, they will respond—many of them anyway. I shall preach about it on Sunday. If those in authority give the example . . ." He shot a quick, quizzical glance at Holzinger, ". . . if their families offer voluntary service, the others will follow. We have time to prepare them. We should make use of it properly."

"If you can do that," said Hanlon, without emphasis, "you'll make it easier for me and for yourselves."

Holzinger nodded, but said nothing. He was wondering what Liesl would say, and his daughter, when he asked them to take the lead, for an example to the citizens.

The first ground gained, Hanlon led them carefully through a discussion of details: rates of payment, the provision of transport from the station to the hospital, entertainment, recruiting methods. The tension slackened gradually, and at the end of an hour he ordered coffee to be sent up and passed round cigarettes. The morning was going well and he wanted to take advantage of it.

The next question was a ticklish one: the status of Party members and the sequestration of their estates. He saw Fischer and Holzinger tense suddenly when he raised it.

"Understand me, gentlemen. I have a certain latitude in time and action on this matter. I am as anxious as you are to avoid injustice, which profits nobody. The only true balance will be achieved when the first free elections are held and the wish of the people is made known. However, you must understand that I am under the general pressure of policy. I must be able to justify to higher authority my action—or my delay in taking action. Do I make myself clear?"

Holzinger and Fischer nodded. The priest watched him with gentle, perceptive eyes. He went on:

"The first thing I propose is the impounding of documents —city records, Party lists, police files, electoral rolls, registers of births, deaths, marriages; all papers relating to property in the Quellenberg area. Captain Johnson and his men will take possession of these immediately and issue appropriate receipts. The documents will be returned to you after scrutiny and collation."

Holzinger shifted uneasily and the chair creaked loudly. He flushed and mopped his face. Fischer sat bolt upright, his eyes filmed over like a bird's, unwinking, inscrutable.

"It will be necessary for me to issue a proclamation, which I have already drafted," he tapped the manila folder at his side, "making it clear to all citizens that they are free to apply to me with any information of previous misconduct or misappropriation by Party officials. Information may be submitted in the form of charges or as simple requests for inquiry. Its source will be kept secret and a full investigation will be made before legal action is taken. I'm sure you will understand the need for this free access. Many people have lived in fear for a long time.

The course of justice has been perverted for many years. I'm sure you are all anxious to redress the balance."

"You won't do it this way," said Fischer in his bald emphatic fashion. "Most of us are condemned out of hand."

"By opinion perhaps," snapped Hanlon, "but not by the law. For the present I am the law. The fact that you are still in office is proof of my impartiality."

Father Albertus permitted himself a smile behind his broken hand. His old pupil was showing up well. Holzinger said awkwardly:

"Many of the records were destroyed before the surrender."

"We expected that," said Hanlon easily. "We'll make do with what is left. Military records, especially those relating to arms and ammunition dumps, are specially important. It will make your job easier, Fischer, if these can be found."

Fischer nodded and said irritably:

"You'd better issue a new order on the surrender of fire-arms. It's like prising out teeth to get 'em now."

"I'll do that," said Hanlon. He relaxed and leaned back in his chair, smiling at them amiably. "That's enough for today, gentlemen. We've covered a lot of ground. We'll get round to the rest of it in time. Any questions before we break up?"

"One," said Fischer. "It's small enough, but the people would like to know. The feasts are coming on—St Nicholas the day after tomorrow, Christmas, New Year, the Three Kings. There are the old customs—St Nicholas and Krampus visit the children, you know how it goes. Do you want them stopped, or do I let them go on?"

"Let them go on. We want to interfere as little as possible with the local life. We thought that . . . if the people cared . . . we'd invite the children here to the Sonnblick for a Christmas party. We'll supply the food and the presents."

"It would be a good thought," said Father Albertus. "They haven't eaten well for a long time."

"Leave it to me, then." Hanlon stood up. "Thank you, gentlemen. Captain Johnson will go with you to arrange about the documents. I'll telephone you before our next meeting."

They rose, bowed stiffly and walked from the room, Johnson first, then Holzinger and Fischer, with Father Albertus bringing up the rear. At the door the old man stopped and looked back. His transparent face was lit with a gentle smile:

"Authority sits well on you, Brother Mark. I believe you will do good for us here."

The door closed on him and Mark Hanlon was left alone chewing the butt of a new, disturbing thought . . .

Fischer had started it—the small furtive doubt that lurked behind an apparently simple statement.

'The feasts are coming on . . . The people will want to know.' Fischer was not a man to be interested in feasts or in the people. The question was irrelevant, yet strangely obtrusive among all the big issues they had discussed. Who cared, now, about Father Christmas and his attendant devil? The answer was simple. Fischer cared. But why?

He puzzled about it for an hour before he found the answer.

On the sixth of December the goatmen came down from the mountains. They wore huge, grotesque wooden masks carved by forgotten craftsmen. They had six horns and jagged teeth and twisted mouths and leering eyes, lit sometimes by torch-batteries so that they winked horribly in the darkness. From neck to ankle they were clothed in goatskins. Their cinctures were rattling chains and on their backs they wore great balls of hollow iron that rattled and drummed as they walked. They came shouting and howling in a curious reverberant chant that filled the valleys and echoed dully against the mountain-sides.

When they came to the town they split up into threes and fours to attend the various impersonations of St Nicholas, who went from house to house with gifts for the children. The people called them 'Krampus', which is the name of the attendant devil of St Nicholas who frightens off the robbers and carries the switch to beat naughty boys. But they were much older than Krampus—they were in fact one of the faces of Freya, the wife of Woden, King of the old, bloody Valhalla.

While the Saint went into the houses to distribute his gifts they stayed outside, drumming and howling, peering in at the windows, because the children were afraid of them and often cried. The adults were afraid too, however much they laughed, because this was a memory old in the blood, a memory of twisted horrors dancing in the firelight between the rock tors and in the clearings of the pine wood.

After the giving of gifts, the Krampuses left the Saint and went down to the town, drunk from the wine they had been given at the doors. They paraded the streets, then stood in doors and alleys to catch the girls and bind them with the chains and make them pay a forfeit for their release.

The girls were afraid, but excited too, because this was another memory: the smell of sweat and rough hide, the harsh kisses from under a lifted mask, the hide lifted too sometimes, and the thrust of urgent loins.

Hanlon remembered it all as he paced the room, searching for the significant term that was the key to Fischer's interest. Finally he found it.

All the goat-costumes belonged to old, mountain families, by whom the custom was kept alive. Dress a man in the mask and the hide and his own mother would not know him.

The answer lay before him, pat and final.

On St Nicholas's Day the killer would be brought down to hide in the town, and the man behind the plan was Karl Adalbert Fischer.

"We'll get him, Johnny!" said Hanlon eagerly. "Given an ounce of luck, we'll get him."

It was late afternoon, the curtains were drawn and the room was bathed in bright yellow light from the chandeliers. They were bent over the map, tracing on its mica cover the ways by which the goatmen might be expected to converge on the town. Johnson nodded approvingly. This was the sort of thing he understood best, a tactical operation, aimed at a limited objective. His questions were brisk and pertinent.

"You want us to wait, Mark. Why not take them as they come in?"

"Because they straggle in," said Hanlon. "They come from a dozen different points all over the hills. They use the back paths and mountain tracks. We'd dissipate our forces and reduce our chances of a full check."

"Fair enough. You want them all to come into town, is that right?"

"Yes. Then we seal off the approaches and let the troops operate in a central area. There's another advantage—most of the Krampuses will be drunk by then. They get a glass of wine at every house."

"Makes it easier," said Johnson with a grin. "But we might have a fight or two on our hands."

"I doubt it."

"What's the timing on this, Mark?"

"After dark. They don't start their rounds of the houses until about five-thirty. There's a small ceremony at each home, so they won't start to concentrate down here till about eight. Say nine, to be on the safe side. The housemaids and the nurses won't be free till after that, so we don't stand any risk of losing them."

Johnson shot him a quick admiring glance.

"You've got this well taped, Mark."

"I've been here before, remember," said Hanlon with a grin. "But it's not quite as watertight as it looks. The first gamble is that our man may not be brought right into town at all. He may be taken to one of the outer homes and left there, before the main business of the evening begins."

"How do you cover that one?"

"It's a lucky dip. You pays your money and you takes your chance. I'm going to leave the big operation of the evening to you, Johnny. I'm going to dress in ski clothes and coast around the other areas from nightfall onwards. I may be wasting my time. I may be lucky."

"What's the next problem?"

"Surprise," Hanlon told him crisply. "How do we filter the best part of a company of troops into the town—all armed—without signalling the punches?"

"We can't," said Johnson thoughtfully. "We might lessen the shock a bit, though."

"How?"

"Day after tomorrow is the big event, right?"

"Right."

"That gives us tonight and tomorrow night. Why not call Sergeant Jennings up here and talk to him? Tell him the story and have him send the troops out for an airing, both nights. Keep the drunks home and let the others have a drink or two in the *Stüberls*. Let 'em wear sidearms, to get the natives used to the look of those too. A couple of nights of that and they'll be halfway conditioned to having us around."

"Good." Hanlon nodded thoughtfully. "It might work. Let's get Jennings up and give him the drill."

"Before you do, Mark . . ."

"Yes?"

"What about Fischer?"

"Leave Fischer to me." Hanlon's tone was bleak. "Just

now I need him where he is; that's why I'm giving him rope. Later I'll hang him with it."

In his shabby office, under the wine-splashed map of defeats, Karl Adalbert Fischer was planning his own campaign.

He was doing it in characteristic fashion, with his feet on the table, a bottle of schnapps at his elbow, the telephone in one hand and one of Gretl Metzger's cigars in the other. He was talking to Rudi Winkler.

"I have a present for you, my friend."

"Charming! Charming!" Winkler's high skittish laugh crackled over the wire. "I love presents. When do I get it?"

"Day after tomorrow. St Nicholas is calling on you, and Krampus too, of course."

"To beat me? I'd enjoy that, you know." He laughed immoderately at the insinuation and Fischer, waiting, frowned till he was calm again.

"You know the ceremony, of course. You give the Saint and his attendants a drink and a small present, then push 'em off. One of the Krampuses will stay behind."

"Clever!" said Winkler softly. "I like that. Did you get the —er, sweetmeats I ordered?"

"They're coming. I've placed the order."

"Good! . . ." He leaned significantly on the next words. "And you were going to replace some documents for me."

"That's done too," said Fischer, grinning to himself. "I'll bring them round the day after St Nicholas."

"Careful fellow," said Winkler petulantly.

Now it was Fischer's turn to chuckle.

"We live in troubled times, my friend. One can never be too careful. *Auf Wiedersehn*."

"*Auf Wiedersehn*."

Fischer put down the receiver then lifted it again and began dialling another number. This time it was the widow Metzger who answered, but her voice was strained and off-key. He questioned her quickly.

"Gretl, this is Karl. Are you alone?"

"No."

"Is it the boy friend?"

"Yes."

"Has he brought the stuff?"

"Some."

"What about the rest?"

"Later."

"Are you sure of that?"

"Yes."

"Does he know who it's for?"

"Of course not!" She dropped her voice to a whisper. "He wants to know how much."

"I'll name the price when I see the goods," said Fischer curtly. "Keep him happy, *Liebchen*—and you'll keep your licence. *Servus*, little one."

"*Servus*," said Gretl limply.

Once again he put down the receiver and poured himself a glass of schnapps. He tossed it off at a gulp and he felt it slide down slowly to glow like a warm coal at the pit of his belly.

It was one of the most enduring satisfactions of his life to sit here in this drab room and jerk the strings that made the puppets dance. He enjoyed good liquor but abstinence never irked him. Abstinence from women troubled him more, but he never had been forced to abstain for very long. Now that he was getting older the need was less and the moment required a certain preparation. But the exercise of power was a continuing pleasure. Age only sharpened it, and practice never diminished it. Only one thing could curtail it—the whim of the Occupying Power.

The risk was there, would be there for a long time. He could do nothing but prepare himself for the worst, and hope it never came. Meanwhile, he found a keen delight in this battle to circumvent Hanlon and save this poor maimed devil who was his sister's son. If he succeeded it would be spittle in the Major's eye and a sweet salve to his own pride.

He smoked slowly through the rest of his cigar, then heaved himself out of the chair and picked up the large suitcase that stood in the corner of the room. He laid it on the table, unlocked it and took out its contents—a complete Krampus costume, which until two hours ago had lain, dusty and neglected, in a glass case in the tiny municipal museum.

It was, according to the record, the oldest known costume in the province, dating back four hundred years. The skin was lank and rubbed bare in many places. The chains and iron rattles were hand-forged in some old mountain smithy. The horns were cracked and brittle but the wooden mask was a carver's masterpiece—an evil grotesque, its patina soft as silk under the hand.

Fischer held it up by the horns and stared into the big agate eyes and the gap-toothed mouth. Childhood memories stirred and a sudden shiver of fear shook him. This was the old evil that lurked still in the mountains and in the black forests. This was the grafting of beast and man which had haunted the nightmares of his ancestors and which had sprung up to walk and breed again in the last decade of Europe.

He wondered if this were the face that Father Albertus had seen in the torture rooms of Mauthausen—which he himself might soon see, tormented and terrible, in the frosty sunlight of Bad Quellenberg.

Hastily he thrust the mask back into the suitcase, covered it with the goatskin and piled the chains on top of it. Then he locked the case and carried it out to his car.

Five minutes later he was driving slowly out of town towards the mountain village where his sister and her husband lived. The snow was shining in the starlight, but there was black night between the colonnades of pines. Every shadow was a leaping demon and every tree bole sheltered a grinning monster with stony malevolent eyes.

CHAPTER 10

By five-thirty on St Nicholas's Day all the children of Bad Quellenberg were scrubbed and dressed in their Sunday clothes. They sat, excited but uneasy, in kitchens and parlours, whispering to one another, listening for the howls and the drumming that heralded the coming of the Saint, with his sackful of gifts. Their parents bustled about, laying out the wine and the sugarcakes and the small money with which the visitors must be welcomed, and if the children stirred too much they warned them: "Practise your prayers. The Saint will want to hear you recite them. If you fail, the Krampus will take you and beat you with the chains and leave you tied in the snow."

All of them, parents and children, were touched by the faint panic fear of the goatmen. This one day was a symbol of their whole lives. There were gifts—but the gifts had to be earned. Behind the smiling giver, with his crown of flowers, stood the twisted demons ready to seize the forgetful and the defaulters.

The houses were lit, but they were small islands of security in the darkness of the mountains. The Advent candles burnt comfortably on the pine wreaths, a symbol of the coming of the Christ-child. But, outside, the baleful eyes of the Krampuses winked horribly and their distorted faces pressed against the windowpanes. Childish voices were raised in the *Pater* and *Ave* which the Saint demanded, but they could not wholly exorcise the terror of the old gods.

Mark Hanlon felt it too, as he strode out, muffled and hooded, to work his way round the outer approaches, while Johnson and his non-coms made their final plans for the picketing of the town itself.

The house lights were sparse among the trees, the promenades were deserted and the echoing howl of the goatmen was borne to him faintly, mixed with the sound of running water and the creak of the pines bending under weight of snow.

He plunged his hands into the pockets of his parka and felt the butt of his pistol, hard and comforting.

The air was very still. He could hear his own heart beat and the scuff of his boots on the white path. A branch sagged above him, and snow broke over his hood and shoulders. A bat flew out and startled him, and he followed its dipping, uncertain flight back into the forest shadows.

When he reached the high ground, he looked back and saw the town nestling in the neck of the valley, dwarfed to doll size by the peaks, its lights pale and uncertain against the star-blaze and the high shining snowfield. The first excitement of his adventure died in him quickly. This too was a small thing —sordid, meaningless. There was no dignity in a manhunt, no triumph in a hanging.

The chant of the goatmen was nearer now and, as he looked up the path, he saw through the trees the approach of the first small procession: two boys, dressed as pages, each carrying a sack on his back, the Saint, with high headdress of paper flowers, and behind them three Krampuses, prancing and howling.

He stepped back into the shadows and waited for them to come.

He took the pistol out of his pocket and released the safety-catch. He threw back his hood and felt the cold strike at his face and neck. They had left the trees now and were advancing down the straight stretch of path towards him. When they came abreast he stepped out and called sharply: "Wait there!"

They froze in their tracks, their faces turned towards him— the soft faces of the boys, a girl's face, incongruous under the cottonwool whiskers of the Saint, the distorted faces of the attendant devils. All of them were watching the gun in his hand. He identified himself curtly:

"My name is Hanlon, Occupation Commander. Identity check. Take off your masks."

They hesitated, looking at one another in doubt and puzzlement.

"Take them off."

Slowly the Krampus figures raised their hands and lifted the heavy wooden masks from their heads. The change was so comical that he almost laughed aloud. Three doltish faces looked at him, scared and gaping. Their eyes were vacant and hostile. Their cheeks were stubbled but unscarred. None of them was the man he wanted.

"That's all. You can put them on now."

They settled the masks again and stood there, not understanding what was expected of them. Hanlon grinned and waved them away with his pistol.

"You can go. It's just a formality. *Güte Reise.*"

None of them answered his greeting. The girl saint prodded the pages furtively and they moved off. But the howling had stopped and the drumming and the dancing. They looked just what they were, a bunch of scrubby mummers playing an old farce, crude and senseless.

Hanlon put his gun back in his pocket and leaned back against the rough bark of a pine tree. He took out cigarettes and lit one, but the sharp mountain air made him cough and he tossed away the cigarette and trod it into a snowdrift. He felt faintly ridiculous. He wondered how many more times this would happen to him before the evening was out.

Four times was the count; and each time he felt more uncomfortable and more irritated at having committed himself to the chancy venture. The cold was beginning to eat into him and there was no warmth in these repeated failures. He looked at his watch. Seven-thirty. An hour and a half before Johnson and his men started operations in the town. He decided to work his way round to the other side of the valley along the big path that traversed the neck and linked the two opposing walls of mountains.

He stepped out briskly, head thrust forward, shoulders humped, hands thrust deep into his pockets. He had walked for about ten minutes when he saw something that stopped him in his tracks. Twenty yards ahead was a high stone wall, broken by a big iron gate. Behind it, high among the trees, were the lights of a large house.

Outside the gate were three Krampus figures. Their backs were towards him, and they were talking earnestly among themselves, so that they neither saw nor heard him. The oddity was that they were alone. There was no sign of the Saint or his attendant pages. Unless, of course, they had finished their rounds and were waiting to go down to the town. In any case, they had to be identified.

Hanlon took out his pistol and walked briskly towards them. They turned sharply at his footfall, but he was already upon them and at the sight of the gun they backed carefully against the wall. Hanlon looked at them a moment, noticing with a flicker of interest that one of the costumes was older than the rest, the hide worn and bedraggled, the mask more fantastic and ornate. He told them, as he had told all the previous parties:

"Identity check. Take off your masks."

A thick voice answered him in dialect.

"Why should we? Can't we even have our feast days in private?"

"It's an order," said Hanlon mildly. "Let's get it over and you can go about your business. Take 'em off."

None of the figures moved. Their agate eyes stared at him, expressionless. The saw-tooth mouths leered at him. 'They're drunk,' thought Hanlon. 'Drunk and stubborn.' He reasoned with them carefully:

"You don't want trouble. Neither do I. But I can make it for you if you play the fool. Take off your masks. Let me have a look at you. Then you can all go down and finish your drinking in town."

"And if we don't?" The thick voice was truculent now.

"A wise man doesn't argue with a gun," said Hanlon sharply.

Then another voice spoke, from behind the oldest mask. An educated voice, he noticed, free of the raw peasant accent.

"Do as he says. We don't want trouble."

"But listen . . .!"

"Do as he says."

Slowly, the first man raised his hands and began to lift his mask. Hanlon's attention wavered for a moment so that he missed the swift movement as the second man flicked up his chain belt and swung it against the side of his head.

There was a crack like splitting timber and Hanlon went down, spreadeagled in the roadway, his face buried in a drift. A slow spreading of blood stained into the snow and quickly froze. The feet of the goatmen trampled him savagely as they hurried off into the darkness of the trees.

His wakening was a slow nightmare of pain and blindness and nausea and stifling perplexity. He was smothered by darkness and the darkness was a stone roof against which he battered himself till his head seemed ready to burst. It was a black liquid forced down his throat by faceless torturers. It was fire scalding his face and his hands. It was a horror that enveloped him like the stink of a charnelhouse. It was a sea on which he floated, a whirlpool in which he spun dizzily, a swamp in which he gasped helplessly against drowning.

There were leaden pennies on his eyes and when he tried to move them he realised that his hands were bound in cerecloths and his face was swathed like a mummy's. He was choked with sickness, and his tongue fell backward into his gullet when he tried to shout. He heard voices that babbled without meaning and names that he had once known but were now alien symbols. He was alive in a world too small for movement. He was adrift in a space without limits.

Then the nightmare passed and a small comforting death took hold of him. The resurrection came slowly. He understood that he was in a bed. He was alive and warm. And if he moved there was pain.

The first thing he saw was the broad, ruddy face of Doktor Huber. It was blurred at first and wavering. Then slowly it came into focus. There was a band around his forehead with a mirror in the centre of it. He held a pencil torch close to Hanlon's eyes and his big fingers were holding up one eyelid and forcing down the lower conjunctiva.

Hanlon blinked and the fingers released their grip. Huber gave a small exclamation of satisfaction and stepped back. Behind him Hanlon saw the tense white face of Captain Johnson and the blonde head of Anna Kunzli. He tried to turn his head to take in the details of the room, but a stab of pain checked him. He closed his eyes and struggled to hold on to consciousness.

When he opened them again, Doktor Huber was smiling at him. He tried to speak, but his voice seemed to come from another man, small and far away.

"What are you doing here, Huber? Where am I? What happened?"

Huber smiled gravely and shook his head.

"It's a long question, Major. Let's leave it awhile. I want to have another look at your eyes. Can you see me quite clearly?"

"Yes."

"Good."

Huber bent over him again, peering into the pupils with his tiny light, angling it carefully into the dark lens of the eyeball, searching for any sign of hæmorrhage or clotting in the intricate network of blood vessels. Then he straightened up and put the torch back in his pocket.

"You're a very lucky man, Major. You could have been killed. You might have been blinded or deafened."

"What happened to me?" asked Hanlon weakly.

"Give me a mirror," said Huber to the girl. She turned away and a moment later she was back with a small hand mirror. Huber held it up in front of Hanlon's face and he stared at the image that confronted him.

His head was bound with swathes of bandage, bloody on the left side. His face was covered with lint held in place by adhesive plaster. When he tried to lift his hands to touch it, he saw that they too were bandaged. He looked at Huber's grave face.

"I—I don't understand."

"Herr Kunzli's housekeeper found you lying in the snow outside the gate. Your head was laid open by a massive blow. How it didn't crack your skull or give you a brain hæmorrhage, I don't know. Your face and hands are badly frostbitten. If you'd lain there much longer you'd be dead. She called Herr Kunzli and Anna here and they brought you up to the house, then sent for me. I called Captain Johnson."

"How long have I been here?"

"Thirty-six hours," said Huber soberly. "You've had me very worried."

"Thirty-six hours?" He could feel the nausea coming back, his hold on the world weakening again. He struggled to tell them. "I—I met the Krampus . . . our man . . . hit me with . . . with . . . chain . . ." Darkness closed over him again. His eyes drooped and his head lolled slackly on the pillow.

Huber stood looking down at him a moment, then turned back to Johnson.

"Did that mean anything to you, Captain?"

"Attempted murder," said Johnson curtly.

Huber nodded.

"I understand. He spoke to me about this business. It might easily have been murder. It—it could still be . . ."

Johnson stared at him, shocked.

"But I thought you said . . ."

"I can't find any sign of hæmorrhage. There may be one, none the less. We can only wait and see how he progresses over the next few days.

"Shouldn't we get him back to the Sonnblick?"

"No!" Huber was emphatic about it. "I cannot have him moved in any circumstances. Fräulein Anna here can look after him. You can come to see him whenever you want. I'll visit him twice a day until we are sure there are no complications."

"I'm—very grateful," said Johnson awkwardly in German. Then for the first time the girl spoke:

"We're happy to do what we can, Captain. I promise you I'll give him every care. What should I expect, Doktor? What should I do?"

"He'll be like this for a day or two, drifting between consciousness and unconsciousness. The conscious periods should become longer as he progresses. Feed him a little broth when he can take it. You know how to take a pulse count and a temperature; call me if there is any perceptible slackening, or if there is fever. He may vomit today—let me know if it is severe, or if the unconsciousness lasts too long. I'll change the dressings when I come. No visitors, except the Captain. Even from you, Captain, no long talk until he begins to mend properly."

Johnson nodded.

"I understand, Doktor."

"Fräulein?"

"I understand too."

"If you want medicine, drugs . . ." said Johnson uncertainly.

"I'll call on you," Huber answered him with a ghost of a smile. Then a new thought struck him and his broad face clouded again. "There's a murderer in the town, Captain. What do you propose to do about it?"

Johnson told him savagely: "I'm going to take the town apart, house by house. Why?"

"Advice from a friend," said Huber slowly. "Leave it a day or two, until the Major can talk to us. You will lose nothing, I promise you. On the other hand you may gain much."

"I'll think about it."

"Do that, Captain. Come, Anna, there are more instructions for you." He turned and led the girl out of the room.

Johnson stood a long time looking down at the slack figure on the bed, at the frostbitten hands and the ravaged face and the bandaged head lolling against the white pillow.

Whenever he woke, the girl was there. Sometimes there was sunlight behind her, so that her hair shone like a golden coronet. When he woke, babbling in the dark or moaning with the pain of his burnt face and hands, she would be bending over him, her hair in plaits, her body ethereal in a white gown with lace at the throat and at the wrists. Her hands soothed him and her voice calmed him, and the fragrance of her perfume lingered with him. When he lapsed again it was as if she followed him past the borders of sleep and into the blackness beyond.

He fought his way out of nightmares, shouting her name: "Anna! Anna!" and she was with him even before he knew it. He submitted without humiliation to be washed and cleansed by her, and, when the dressings were stripped off his wounds and he gasped with the pain, her arms were there to support him. She fed him like a child, spooning the food over his swollen, blistered lips.

He understood now that he was sleeping in her room, and in her bed, and that she had moved to a small cubbyhole across the hall to be within sound of his voice, day and night.

She sat with him through the day, reading, knitting, mending, dozing sometimes because her night had been broken. If he tried to talk she answered once or twice, then hushed him, so that he lay relaxed in a healing doze until the next pains shook him and she came running to his side.

Because he was a man who had been disappointed in one woman he was all the more surprised by the solicitude of this one. Because he was sick he accepted it without question, but gratitude deepened in him as consciousness established itself.

For the first forty-eight hours he tossed uneasily between the brief crests of waking and the long deep troughs of darkness. Then slowly the rhythm changed. There was more day than night; less sleep, more pain; more comfort in the hands and the voice and the young, attentive face under the coronet of corn-gold hair.

One morning when she had finished washing him and smoothing the sheets, she sat down on the end of the bed. He reached out his bandaged hands and laid them on hers. He said languidly:

"You're very good to me, Anna."

"I like doing it, Mark," she told him with gentle gravity. His name was a habit with her now, after the watchful hours and their struggle together.

"Why? Sickness is never pleasant, least of all for the nurse."

"All my life people have cared for me," she told him simply. "Now, for the first time, there is someone I can care for; I like that."

He nodded agreement. It was a thing he understood; something he had once believed in before he had put on cynicism like an armour against the disappointments of passion. Now he was sick and he wore no armour—and who could mistrust such patent innocence? He asked her again:

"Have I been hard to manage?"

She smiled at him.

"Not really. Sometimes you were afraid—and I was afraid too. Sometimes in your sleep you cursed and swore. But men always do that when they're hurt, don't they?"

He tried to smile at her, but his lips were cracked and painful, so that the smile was only in his eyes.

"I'm afraid we do. Was it very bad?"

"Most of it was in English, so I didn't understand it. The German was bad enough." She was silent a moment, watching his face—the stubble growing up around the dressings, the blue sunken skin under the eyes, the prominent bones of the jaw and the lines etched around the mouth by pain and experience. She reached forward with an oddly intimate gesture and brushed away a wisp of cotton trailing towards his lips. Then she asked him quietly:

"Mark, who is Lynn?"

The smile went out of his eyes. His voice was no longer languid, but tight and strained. "Where did you hear that name?"

"You were calling it in your nightmare, over and over again."

"What did I say?"

"I didn't understand. You were talking in English."

"Oh."

He relaxed again, closing his eyes and feeling his body limp under the sheets. Anna's voice seemed to come from a long way off:

"I'm sorry. Perhaps I shouldn't have asked. I—I didn't mean to pry. It seemed to trouble you, that's all."

"It does sometimes."

He opened his eyes and tried to smile at her again, but when he saw how troubled she was, he drew her a little closer with his maimed hands and said gently:

"It's an old story. Old and unhappy. Lynn is my wife."

She was not looking at him now, but down at his hands, muffled and shapeless in the bandages, and at her own, clasped over them gently.

"You don't have to talk about it. Unless you want to."

For the first time in years he did want to talk about it. Here, in the privacy of the sick room, in the sexless intimacy of the first healing day, he could do it without shame. The patient has no pride when the nurse strips him down and bathes him like a babe. Why should he have it when she asks him about his nightmares and he has so much need to purge them out of his soul? So, he told her:

"I was very young, very hungry for love. I had been in a monastery, you see, where passion is suppressed by discipline and love is supposed to be transfigured into a love of God, which the divines call Charity. It is sometimes, when a man is old and the urges of youth have been boned out of him. Sometimes, too, when a man is young—but then only by a special intervention of the Almighty, who wants a saint or two in each century. Me? I should never have been there in the first place; so I was out of both classes."

"How did you come there?"

"By accident." He grinned at her disarmingly. "My father died when I was young. He was a Liverpool Irishman who stayed in Germany after the First War to garrison Hamburg."

"Just like you, Mark."

"Just like me. The week before he was due home, he was killed by a runaway car. We were left to fend for ourselves. I was the youngest and a drain on the family. I was lonely too, and I didn't know where I was going or why, so when the good Father came around with his sermon on vocations and his little handful of leaflets, I was in—body, soul and reach-me-down breeches."

"And you were unhappy?" The wide innocent eyes were fixed on his face.

"Not at first. Not for a long while. But I wasn't happy either. And it's a big truth, Anna——" he leaned on it sombrely—"we're meant to be happy—in monasteries, in marriage, even the Christus on the cross. If we're not, there's something amiss with ourselves, or the folk we live with: generally it's both. So, after a few years, I left. Father Albertus tapped me on the head and gave me his blessing and sent me back to the big wide world I knew nothing about, except that there were girls in it, and I hoped one day one of 'em might love me . . ."

"Father Albertus!" She stared at him, unbelieving. "You were with him, here? In Austria?"

He nodded, amused at her shock.

"In Graz. He was Novice Master then."

She shook her head vaguely as if trying to clear it of some confusion. Her eyes stared past him to some secret speculation of her own.

"So strange, Mark . . . so very strange."

"What?"

"That you should both be here now and that you should be—what you are."

"Not so strange, Anna."

"Why?"

"I wanted to come back. I pulled all the strings I knew to arrange it."

"What made you want it so much?"

"That's the end of the story," he told her lightly. "The riddle you guess at when you have the clues. Three months out of the monastery, I met Lynn. I fell in love with her. Three months after that we were married."

"Did you really love her?"

"Desperately."

"What happened then?"

"Nothing."

"I don't understand you, Mark."

"Nothing happened, *Liebchen*, nothing at all. We were married. We had two children, who write to me sometimes. Then we didn't have any more because Lynn refused to have them—or me either. It took me a long time to understand that she didn't love me. I was necessary to her, but not as a lover, not as a husband. I thought time might bring love, or patience and tenderness, but I was wrong. I thought passion might bring it, but there was no passion in her—not for me. Then one day I understood something else. Love can die too. It sickens like a plant and wilts slowly, and one day it is dead. Nothing can resurrect it—nothing."

"You are still married?"

"Yes."

"Why?"

"For the children's sake—for religion's sake. But there's nothing left in it. I'm here, she's in England, neither of us missing the other."

"Yet you cry for her in your sleep."

"Not for her, Anna; for love, yes. The love I spent for no return. The love I pleaded for but never had."

"One should never plead for love," said the girl gravely. "I found that with Uncle Sepp. It is there or it is not there. If it is not, one can never waken it."

"That," said Mark Hanlon wryly, "is one lesson Father Albertus never taught me. I must remind him of it sometime."

It was out now, and the last of his small strength seemed to have gone with it. He closed his eyes and lay back on the pillow, feeling the drowsiness lap over him in soft, grateful waves. It seemed to him then that Anna Kunzli came and bent over him and touched her lips to his forehead. Illusion? A sweet inconsequent reality? He did not know, and by then he was too tired to care.

CHAPTER 11

As soon as Hanlon was able to sustain a coherent conversation, Johnson was there with his list of problems. The young captain was willing enough to accept responsibility, but wise enough to know his limitations. Huber's counsel had left him dubious about precipitate action and he knew Hanlon would disapprove of a hasty application to Klagenfurt. Somewhat to his surprise, Hanlon disagreed with Huber.

"Let's have action, Johnny, by all means. It won't catch our man but it'll worry hell out of Fischer."

"What do you want, Mark?"

"House searches first, Johnny, simultaneously, all over the town. Keep the areas as widely separated as possible and stagger the times and places so that there's no apparent pattern. Four men to each search: one to the back door, one to the front, two to work the place over from ceiling to cellar."

"Do you want him dead or alive?" asked Johnson with a grin. His good humour was returning now that Hanlon was in the saddle again.

"Alive," said Hanlon definitely. "But let's not take crazy risks."

"Like you, for instance?"

"Like me."

"Any other ideas?"

"I'd like to tap Fischer's telephone and keep a tail on him twenty-four hours a day. But the town's too small and we haven't the men for it. He'd know in ten minutes."

"What are you going to do about him, then?"

"Let him sweat. You can lay odds he's doing it now. Very soon I think he'll decide to call on me. Then we'll see what he has to say for himself."

"What's his connection with the killer, Mark?"

Hanlon frowned and shook his head. He was beginning to tire again and his temples were throbbing.

"I haven't had time to think about it properly, Johnny. But there's a link that will slip into place soon. Leave it to me."

"Only too happy," said Johnson with a grin. "How long do you expect to stay here?"

"I'll be out as soon as Huber agrees, if not before."

"Why rush it?" asked Johnson with plaintive envy. "Home was never like this." He cast an eye approvingly round the room and sniffed the air for the lingering traces of perfume. "Maybe we could both function from here?"

"To hell with you, Johnny." Hanlon laughed in spite of himself.

"Before I go, there's one more question."

"What's that?"

"What do I tell Klagenfurt about this?"

"Nothing," said Hanlon flatly. "I'll write my own report in due course. If they think I'm out of commission they'll have a new commander and half a dozen clodhopping investigators up here in twenty-four hours."

Johnson looked relieved.

"Just thought I'd mention it for the record. And talking of records . . ."

"Yes?"

"The way the paper's pouring in we're going to need a battery of typists to handle it. It's not only what they're sending in but the stuff they want back—reams of it morning and afternoon."

"Leave it," said Hanlon wearily. "Put the urgent stuff through and stack the rest in a corner. I'll look at the staff position when I'm out of this bed."

"At least pick 'em beautiful," pleaded Johnson mockingly. "I'm too young for this celibate life."

"Take long walks in the snow, boy. Take one now. My head's buzzing like a hive, and this frostbite hurts like hell."

"There's a price tag on everything," chuckled Johnson. "Even on pretty nurses. See you later, Mark."

When he had gone, Hanlon closed his eyes and lay back on the pillow, waiting till the pain should pass and he could think clearly again. He could count on Johnson to keep the situation controlled for a while at least; the important thing was to restore his own strength before Klagenfurt got wind of the trouble and sent in a new man and a new team. The search for the man behind the gun had assumed a new, personal significance. He wanted to finish it himself.

In the evening Huber came again for the painful ritual of dressing his wounds. The first moments were the worst, but Anna was there too with soft hands and steadying voice. When he had removed the bandages, Huber handed him a mirror to see for the first time the extent of the damage.

He was shocked by the first sight of the blotched and crusted frostburn which covered more than half his face, but Huber reassured him:

"That will clear up quickly enough. We have arrested the infection and now the new skin begins to grow. This"—he traced the long open scar that ran from the tip of Hanlon's ear, across his temple and down to the cheekbone—"this is another matter. The chain opened you up like a melon skin. The scar will be ugly."

"That makes two of us," said Hanlon thoughtfully. "He was scarred too. The scores are even."

Huber was not impressed. He was examining the raw edges of the wound, cleansing them carefully with a swab.

"Later, we will do a little more work on it. A small plastic will repair the worst of the damage. But you will always be . . ."

"Say that again!"

"Say what?"

"A small plastic . . . was that it?"

Huber and the girl looked at him in surprise.

"That's right," said Huber. "Why do you ask?"

Hanlon looked from one to the other, debating whether to trust them. His eyes were bright with interest and his head was clear of pain and puzzlement. After a moment he said slowly:

"I'd like a promise from you both. What I have to say must be private to the three of us."

"As you wish," said Huber gravely.

Anna Kunzli nodded and said: "Of course, Mark."

Then he gave it to them.

"The man who killed Willis and did this to me is scarred too. We know that he has been brought down to the town. I know—or at least I believe—that Fischer is involved in it somewhere."

"Fischer!" they said it together, on the same rising inflection of surprise.

Hanlon nodded. "It's a long story. It doesn't matter for the moment. What does matter is this: Fischer has enough experience to know that he can't keep his man here indefinitely. Therefore he must have something else in mind. You gave me a feasible idea. A plastic . . . a new face. That means my identification breaks down. That means the killer, whoever he is, could either stay here or be moved into the US zone without fear of discovery."

Huber thought about it for a moment. Then he said quietly:

"It could be. But even that would take time."

"How long?"

"I could not possibly say without seeing the man. Given a fairly easy case, a necessary minimum of skill in the surgeon, and some luck as well, three months. It might be much longer."

"Take the surgeon first," Hanlon quizzed him bluntly. "Who in Quellenberg could do it?"

"I could," Huber told him. "And one other member of my staff."

"Is he likely to be involved with Fischer?"

Huber shook his head.

"I doubt it. Like myself he is a foreigner—a Viennese. He has a wife and children in the British sector. I think he would not risk participation in a thing like this. In any case his movements and contacts would be easy to check."

"Do you know anybody else—a resident?"

"Nobody. The man who could tell you would be Holzinger —and, of course, Fischer himself."

Hanlon's puffed mouth twisted into a painful grin.

"Their information mightn't be quite reliable."

"The town records might help."

"We'll check 'em, line by line."

Huber nodded gravely and bent again to the task of cleansing the raw flesh and laying on the new dressing. Anna Kunzli helped him with deft hands. Quite unexpectedly she said:

"Why don't you ask Father Albertus? He knows everybody in Bad Quellenberg."

Huber looked up from his work and answered in his deep, quiet voice: "It wouldn't do, little one. A priest is like a doctor; he must preserve the secrets of his flock. To ask him would be an indiscretion."

Hanlon tried to nod his agreement, but the new antiseptic burned his face and he winced sharply. Instinctively the girl reached out her hand to quiet him. Huber's quick eye caught the movement but he said nothing.

When the dressings were finished and he was settled again, Hanlon turned to Anna and said gently:

"Would you give the doctor a cigarette, Anna, then leave us for a few moments?"

"Of course."

She rummaged in the drawer of the bedside table, brought out Hanlon's cigarettes, handed one to Huber and put another in Hanlon's mouth. Then she went out, closing the door behind her. Huber lit up for Hanlon and himself, and the two men smoked a few moments in silence. Huber said dryly:

"With training she'd be a very good nurse. She has gentle hands and a warm heart."

Hanlon ignored the hint and said simply:

"I'm in an awkward position, Huber."

"How?"

"Sepp Kunzli. I may have to put him through the wringer. Yet I'm a guest in his house."

Huber eyed him shrewdly through the smokedrifts.

"Has he said anything to you?"

"I haven't seen him. He sends his compliments through Anna, and asks if there's anything I need, but that's all."

"He's discreet," said Huber placidly. "He understands the situation as well as you do. He prefers to keep it impersonal. It's your own fault if you involve yourself."

"Meaning?"

Huber jerked his cigarette significantly towards the door.

"The girl. She's more than half in love with you."

"Nonsense," said Hanlon curtly.

Huber shrugged and spread his hands eloquently.

"It starts as a nonsense. Afterwards . . . it gets serious."

"When can I move out?"

Huber smoked for a few minutes, considering the question.

"I'd like to keep you here another week, just for safety. But, as things are . . ." He paused. "I'll send an ambulance and a couple of orderlies tomorrow to move you back to the hotel. You'll have to stay in bed though and stick to the treatment. Otherwise you're in for trouble."

"I can cope with that sort," said Hanlon with a grin.

"Better if you can avoid it altogether," said Huber. "What else did you want to talk to me about?"

"The killer."

"What about him?"

"I've met him now," said Hanlon. "I think we should revise our opinion."

"Why?"

"Your first thought was that he was deranged. A shock case . . . something like that."

"Yes?"

"When I met him, he was with two other men. He was under no restraint. When he spoke his voice was educated and full of authority. He was obeyed. He acted swiftly and with decision."

"Some of the craziest killers in history have been the most normal in appearance," said Huber coolly. "Besides, there's a flaw in your logic."

"What's that?"

"The man who struck you may not have been the killer at all. It could have been any one of twenty men with a grudge or a bellyful of liquor. It could even have been Fischer himself. There's more than half a chance you're right, but so far it's guesswork."

"As we're placed now I can't do anything but guess. And eliminate the improbables one by one."

"I'm puzzled by your attitude in this matter, Major."

Hanlon looked up, surprised at the blunt challenge.

"What puzzles you, Doktor?"

"The importance you attach to him, the extent of your personal involvement."

Hanlon gave him a crooked smile and put one muffled hand up to his head.

"Doesn't this explain it?"

Huber shook his head. "No, you are too intelligent for that. You are too subtle for crude revenge. You would find no pleasure in it. You know better than I how much is to be done here and how secondary is this question of a capture. You will get him in the end. If Fischer is involved, Fischer will do everything he can to keep him under cover so that he is not a danger to anyone else. But you have this—this psychotic drive to get him."

"Call it a symbol if you want," said Hanlon casually.

"Of what?"

"Of the things we fought against, the things we came here to stamp out—violence, lawlessness, protected murder."

"The trouble with symbols," said Huber calmly, "is that they mean different things to different people. What one man worships, another draws on a lavatory wall."

"We have a common interest," said Hanlon irritably. "Unless the people see that, there is no profit for either of us."

"Then find a common symbol," said Huber with a slow, grave smile.

"What, for instance?"

"Christmas is coming," said the big Tyrolese, with studied irrelevance. "There is a child lying in straw and a homeless pair stabled with the cows. There will be millions of them this year, all over Europe. Think about it, Major—for your own sake, and for ours!"

Two hours after Hanlon's return to the Sonnblick, Karl Adalbert Fischer came to see him. He brought with him a large suitcase and a tubby soft-faced fellow whom he introduced as Herr Rudolf Winkler, a retired bookseller from Munich.

Both of them were politely shocked when they saw Hanlon bandaged to the eyes and propped in the ornate bed. He heard them out in sardonic silence, and Captain Johnson watched them with pale unfriendly eyes.

Fischer had a story to tell and he had brought Winkler to corroborate it. He told it carefully and well.

"It seems we both had the same idea, Major: that an attempt might be made to bring the murderer down to the town on St Nicholas's night. You will remember that I raised the question at our last meeting."

"I remember you made a vague reference."

"I—I did not pursue it, since to one who did not know our customs it might have seemed laughable. I apologise for underrating your experience."

"That's always a mistake," Hanlon told him dryly.

"I realised that when I heard of your accident and when I saw the preparations you had made in the town. It was a clever move, Major. It nearly succeeded."

"Go on."

"When the news got around the town Herr Winkler here telephoned me with some information which he thought might be valuable. I think he should tell you about it himself. Then I have my own comments to add."

The tubby fellow puffed out his smooth cheeks and launched into his story. His voice was high-pitched and faintly effeminate and his soft hands made small fluttering gestures of emphasis.

The time he judged to be about nine o'clock on St Nicholas's night, a little before, or a little after, he could not be certain. At the time it had had no significance. He was at home in his small house at the end of the Mozartstrasse, quiet, withdrawn from the main life of the town. He was not rich. He had to buy modestly and live quietly. However, about this time he heard voices quarrelling outside his gate, men's voices talking in the dialect of the mountains. He was a Bavarian himself and he found them difficult to understand, more so as they seemed to be drunk. He went to the door and looked out. He saw that there were three men dressed in Krampus costumes. Two seemed to be quarrelling with the third. He shouted to them to be quiet and move off. One of them shouted a drunken insult. Then they split up: two of them wandered off towards the town, staggering, the third hurried off up one of the tracks that led through the pinewoods. That was all. It was only after the news of the attack on the Major that he attached any significance to the incident. The Major would understand how it was. He was something of a stranger. There was always drinking at provincial feasts . . .

Then Fischer took up the tale:

"After Herr Winkler's telephone call, I went out immediately to interview him. I followed the track which the third man had taken. About half a mile up the slope there is a wood-cutter's hut—a storehouse for wedges and tools. Inside, stuffed behind some boxes, I found this . . "

He snapped open the suitcase and brought out the Krampus costume which Hanlon had seen on his assailant. Johnson and he stared at it in amazement.

"Do you recognise it, Major?"

"I do."

Fischer nodded with professional gravity.

"There is a special interest in this costume. It is the oldest known example in the area. It was stolen from a showcase in our museum."

Johnson and Hanlon looked at each other. The story was so circumstantial it might be true. Even if it weren't, Fischer must be sure it couldn't be broken. The little policeman went on:

"The mask and the showcase and the metal have been wiped clean of fingerprints. So we understand that we are dealing with intelligent people, who are also very familiar with the town."

"I'd thought of that myself," said Hanlon.

"I thought it would be wise therefore, if we co-operated on an immediate search of the area, beginning at Herr Winkler's house and extending in a circular sector back towards the hills."

"We'll arrange it immediately," Hanlon told him. "Captain Johnson will have a detachment ready to move off in ten minutes."

Fischer nodded approval.

"I wish you to understand, Major, how much we all regret this business, and your own personal misfortune. I promise you our fullest co-operation."

"Thank you, Fischer. And you too, Herr Winkler. Captain Johnson will go with you and will keep in constant touch until I am on my feet again. *Auf Wiedersehn*."

"*Güten Tag*, Major."

They went out; Johnson led them into the corridor and handed them over to Sergeant Jennings. Then he came back to Hanlon.

"Well, Mark? What do you think of it?"

Hanlon shrugged impatiently.

"Fischer's a policeman. He knows a good alibi when he's got it. We'll have to investigate, of course. But I'd take long odds our man is miles away from where Fischer wants us to look."

"That's my feeling, too. What about Winkler?"

"Either an innocent bystander or an accessory. We'll check his papers, but, knowing Fischer, they'll be in order too. Follow it up, Johnny, but don't expect too much."

"You want me to go straight away?"

"Yes. Send Jennings up to look after the office."

"Will do. How are you feeling?"

"Like hell," said Hanlon unhappily. "Fischer's made me look a fool and I can't wait to take it out of his hide."

How big a fool, he could hardly guess.

Forty minutes later Johnson and his non-coms were standing in Winkler's lounge, while the man they were hunting lay, drugged and gagged, under a boxbed, in the room of the trap-mouthed housekeeper.

As soon as Sergeant Jennings arrived, Hanlon dictated a note of thanks to Sepp Kunzli. He enclosed with it a set of travel papers and a detailed list of instructions for the visit to Zürich.

There was a letter for Anna, too, longer, more personal, which the despatch rider was to deliver into her hands.

For the rest of the afternoon he worked steadily through the mass of directives and memoranda that had piled up during his absence.

The amount and complexity of the paper work staggered him at first. Then slowly he began to understand: this was more than half the business of government. The modern world was founded on paper. Without it, chaos would come again.

Policy came first—the broad, deceptively simple statement of ends and means, a document, a manifesto—paper.

Then followed legislation, whose prelude was debate, recorded in sheaves and sheaves of pages, shelves of volumes, millions of words, whose end was more paper—the law: an invocation of authority, a definition of terms, a succession of clauses, a schedule of instructions and of sanctions for offenders, a signature and a seal.

The law was the shortest document of all. But this too began to spawn more words, more pages, more volumes: annotation, glossary, concordance and interpretation.

After the law and the interpretation came the directives handed down from echelon to echelon of administrators through the hands of clerks and typists and messengers, until they came finally to the man who must apply them—the local official.

He need ask no questions. Everything was written for him—on paper. No matter that it might take him a lifetime to find the relevant sheet, it was there, written. Ignorance was no excuse. Every case was covered. Every variant was noted, somewhere.

Then Hanlon began to understand other things, too: how the machinery of government became clogged with paper; how roguery was hidden under a web of words; how administrators hid themselves behind ramparts of books and leaders were insulated from the truth by piles of foolscap; how the voices of reformers were stifled under a vast rubbish of print.

It could happen to him now. He could sit twelve hours a day, reading every word that landed on his desk, replying to them with more words, so that his superiors would name him a careful fellow who kept the record straight—even though men were workless and children were hungry and the hopes of a better life were deferred from year-end to year-end.

There was only one answer. Go back to the policy; see the facts first; apply the remedies on the spot. Here in Bad Quellenberg he could. There was a risk, of course.

The man who dispensed with paper got things done. He also dispensed with protection, and if he made a mistake, he lost his head . . .

By five-thirty his own head was spinning and the nausea was back with him again. He dismissed Jennings, made his way painfully to the bathroom, then crawled back between the sheets and dozed off.

When he woke, Captain Johnson was back with a negative report, and the news that Max Holzinger was waiting to see him.

The Bürgermeister was shocked by Hanlon's appearance, and there was a ring of sincerity in his apology and in his expression of concern. Hanlon was touched and tried to spare him embarrassment. He could not know—and Holzinger could not tell him—that there had been a long and heated argument with Fischer, which had ended in a deadlock, since Fischer was not prepared to hand over his nephew and Holzinger was afraid of the revelation of his own duplicity.

Both men were glad when the awkward preliminaries were over and they began to discuss the preparations for the coming of the displaced persons.

The building Holzinger recommended was the Bella Vista, a large, reasonably modern hotel, halfway between the railway station and the church. It was owned by a wealthy Viennese who had not been heard of since the occupation of Vienna. The lease was held by a Swiss syndicate, and the mortgage was in the hands of Sepp Kunzli. The routine of requisition kept them talking for half an hour.

They discussed staffing arrangements, food, fuel, linen, blankets, cutlery, the call-up of private cars to transport the arrivals from the station. At the end of it Holzinger told him with some eagerness:

"You can leave it all to me, Major. Believe me, I am only too happy to take some of the weight off your shoulders, to make some amends for this—this outrage."

"Forget it," said Hanlon with a smile. "It's an occupational hazard. I'm lucky it wasn't worse."

"We all are," said Holzinger fervently.

He shifted uneasily in his chair, coughed and stammered over the next gambit.

"My—my wife and daughter are downstairs . . ."

"Good God!" Hanlon stared at him in surprise. "Why didn't you tell me? They've been waiting an age."

"It is nothing," Holzinger assured him awkwardly. "They insisted on coming. We—that is, I myself—had a talk with Doktor Huber. He told me you were still in need of attention. Now I have seen it myself. My family would like to take over your care. Huber himself is a busy man and this is, after all, a woman's business."

Hanlon flushed with embarrassment. The offer was patently sincere and singularly attractive as against the cruder minis-trations of an Army orderly. But there was the old problem. It set up an obligation, a personal relationship, which might later become embarrassing. He decided to be frank about it.

"I'm very grateful, Herr Bürgermeister. Believe that. I'd like nothing better than to accept." He grinned disarmingly. "I like my comfort, and I'm a long way from home. But, don't you see, it could be awkward for both of us. Placed as I am, I may have to enter into dispute with you. Don't misunderstand this, but I may even have to remove you from office. If I am under an obligation to you or to your family . . ."

He broke off and let the sentence hang in mid-air. Holzinger nodded and smiled and then bent forward eagerly.

"I'm glad that you told me, Major. Even if you hadn't I should have known it was in your mind. Understand this first —there are no obligations. Business is business. We both know it. But we are not always in business. We are human too. We like to feel that we can do a kindness and repair a wrong. If only for our dignity, we need that. You would do us a favour, if you would accept."

Hanlon was beaten and he knew it. A man couldn't play the cynic all the time. If one believed in human kindness one could not for ever choke back its impulses in others. There was no profit in that for either party. Why deny oneself a comfort that pleased the giver as well? He had made his point. He was practising no deception on Holzinger—though he might be deceiving himself. The old monastic itch again! He brushed it away impatiently. A man could scratch himself raw and have no joy at the end of it.

Holzinger was watching him anxiously, trying to interpret his hesitation. Hanlon's cracked lips parted in a rueful smile. He held up his muffled hands.

"You take me at a disadvantage, Herr Bürgermeister. So long as you and I understand each other, I'll be glad to accept."

A few minutes later Liesl Holzinger and her daughter came up to bathe him and change his dressings. The first breach had been made. The women were moving in to the citadel of the conqueror.

CHAPTER 12

THREE DAYS later the first trainload of concentration camp victims arrived in Bad Quellenberg.

The townsfolk heard them coming a long way off, because the sound of the locomotive was like thunder between the hills, and the high scream of the whistle leapt from peak to peak along the winding defile.

They looked at each other, dubious and half afraid. They remembered the sermon that Father Albertus had preached at the Sunday Masses. They saw his broken hands outflung, and they heard the deep tolling of his voice, challenging them to repentance for a common sin, to restitution for a common injustice, to pity for misery too long ignored.

They remembered, and they were ashamed. They looked away from each other, then reached for coats and hats and began to move, slowly and unwillingly, towards the station.

Soon the approaches and the marshalling yards were jammed and the troops had to clear a passage for the ambulances and the cars and the miscellaneous transport which would carry the sick down to the hospital. On the platform the senior citizens were assembled—the Bürgermeister, the councillors, Karl Adalbert Fischer, Father Albertus. Sepp Kunzli was not there. He was already halfway through the Arlberg, heading for Zürich.

Down by the tracks the troops were drawn up, unarmed and

standing easy, with the stretcher bearers and the drivers waiting behind them. Hanlon and Captain Johnson stood a little apart, watching the final preparations, stamping their feet in the powdery snow, their faces half turned towards the defile, where the scream and the thunder rang louder as the minutes ticked by.

Hanlon was still in bandages. His face was muffled in a thick scarf and his hands were thrust into a fur muff that gave him a faintly comical appearance. But there was no one to laugh at the comedy. This was the last act of a long-drawn tragedy, the final purging moment of pity and of terror.

Then the train came in, hauled by a squat green engine with grotesque antennæ, the snow tossing up in little clouds from under the wheels. It stopped with a rattle and a jerk and the crowd strained forward to catch a glimpse of the occupants; but the windows were misted over and they could see nothing.

The door of the first carriage opened and a tall fellow stepped out. He had a thin hawk face, a scrawny neck, a prominent chin and grey hair. He wore snow boots and baggy trousers and a windbreaker of American pattern with a Red Cross brassard stitched to the sleeve. When Hanlon stepped forward to greet him he introduced himself in a flat Mid-Western drawl:

"I'm Miller, Chief Medical Officer."

"Hanlon, Occupation Commander. We're happy to have you."

"Thanks, Major." Miller shot a quick glance at the silent crowd and at the little group on the platform. "Quite a reception."

"You'd better meet 'em," said Hanlon. "They've tried to be helpful."

He led Miller over to the platform and made the introductions; to Holzinger first, then to Fischer and the councillors. Miller did not offer his hand but nodded curtly and Hanlon was embarrassed by his obvious coldness. He turned away and presented the priest.

"This is Father Albertus, the parish priest. He is himself a camp victim."

Miller's lined face brightened immediately, and he held out his hand. "Glad to know you, Father. You'll be able to help us a great deal."

"Don't misjudge our people, Doctor Miller," said the priest

in his mild, direct fashion. "They are anxious to help you as much as possible."

"I wonder if they'll still be as anxious when they see what I've brought them?" He jerked his thumb significantly towards the train. "Three hundred men, women and children. You'll be burying half of 'em over the next month or two."

Father Albertus nodded gravely but said nothing. Miller turned away. "Come on, Major, let's get going!"

They walked back towards the train and, at a signal from Johnson, the troops and the stretcher bearers followed them, and after a moment they all disappeared inside the train. The people waited, tense and expectant, wondering what monsters might be hidden behind the grey misted windows.

When the first stretcher cases were brought out, a low moan of horror shook the crowd. They were wrapped in blankets and their heads were covered with woollen caps, so that only their faces were visible: but these were yellow as parchment and shrunken back to the bone. Their eyes were sunk in dark sockets, their lips were thin and bloodless, drawn back in a rictus of pain, so that they looked more like corpses than living men. The stretcher bearers carried them lightly, because there was no weight in their bodies. Then the stretchers were stacked, one above the other on the ambulance racks, the doors were closed and the vehicles moved off, lurching through the snow, the wheelchairs rattling strangely in the silence.

After a while there were no more stretchers, and the bearers stepped out, carrying limp bodies in their arms, so that the crowd saw their skeleton limbs and their necks so weak that they could not support the bony, lolling heads.

When they were seated in the cars, they fell against one another like rag dolls, and the orderlies in the front seats had to lean backward and support them.

The walking cases came next, men and women draped in clothes that hung like scarecrow garments. When they walked it was with the shambling, disjointed movements of the very old. Some of them slipped and fell on the icy ground, and when the watchers started forward to help them, they saw the scarred faces and the knotted hands and the shaven scalps and the dead, lustreless eyes.

Last of all came the children, pitiful little bundles with old monkey faces and gapped teeth and twisted, rickety limbs.

When they saw them, the people wept. The women covered

their faces with their hands and the men stood, dumb and horror-struck, with the tears rolling down their cheeks. When Hanlon and Miller drove off in the jeep and the troops followed, silent and stony-faced, they fell apart, heads bowed, to hide the shame that was in them. After a while they turned their faces homewards, walking slowly and silently, like folk who have seen a vision of damnation.

In the manager's office at the Bella Vista, Hanlon and Miller were talking over the coffee cups. The tall American was more relaxed now. He sat sprawled in his chair, chewing on an old pipe, drawling his approval of the preparations that had been made for his patients.

"You've done a good job, Major. I'm grateful. I'll say so in my first report."

Hanlon shrugged.

"It's unnecessary."

"I'll do it just the same." His lined face puckered into a smile. "Quite a shock, wasn't it?"

"That's an understatement."

"It's all an understatement," said Miller laconically. "This is nothing to what we saw in the camps. These are the lucky ones."

"You said half of them would die. Did you mean that?"

Miller nodded and took the pipe out of his mouth.

"It's a conservative estimate. They've got TB and damaged hearts and ruptured kidneys and a list of ailments as long as your arm. They've been starved and beaten for so long they've got nothing left to fight with. Even the ones who survive will be damaged for life. Still . . . we've got to do the best we can."

He put the pipe back in his mouth and sucked on it thoughtfully. Hanlon drank the last of his coffee and lit a cigarette. Then he said, simply:

"If there's anything you want, anything I can do, let me know."

"First thing we've got to do, Major, is talk to the staff."

Hanlon looked at him, surprised.

"I don't understand."

"They won't either," said Miller in his drawling fashion. "We've got to teach 'em some of the facts of life."

"What, for instance?"

135

Miller laid his pipe down on the lip of the ashtray and leaned forward, gesturing with his long, knotted hands.

"In twenty-four hours, Major, this place will look more like a madhouse than a hospital. Remember that most of these people have spent years in concentration camps. They lived like animals, fighting for food, sleeping with the dead, envying the dying. Normal life is a strangeness to them. They don't understand it any more. Some of them still eat with their hands, cramming food into their mouths in case it's snatched away from them. They urinate in the corridors, they sleep in their own filth, they scream and struggle when their clothes are taken away to be washed, they fight the orderlies who come to give them injections because that's the way they saw people killed. We're dealing with broken minds as well as broken bodies. We need patience and lots of understanding. Even for my staff it's difficult. But for the locals . . ." he broke off and leaned back in his chair, watching Hanlon with quizzical, ironic eyes.

"Who'll talk to them, Doctor—you or me?"

"I'd prefer you to," said Miller flatly. "You hired 'em. You know 'em better than I do."

"There's a man who could do it better than either of us."

"Who's that?"

"Father Albertus."

"Let's get him," said Miller laconically.

Hanlon reached for the telephone.

Twenty minutes later they were sitting at the back of the big lounge of the Bella Vista, behind the rows of peasant women and elderly men who listened silently to the old priest as he explained their duties as servants of the sick and the problems they would have to face in their daily execution.

He talked simply, persuasively, and Hanlon was struck once again by his compassion and his understanding of the people who were his flock. He told them of his own life as a prisoner: how he had been beaten and starved and his hands broken, so that by repeated torment he had been reduced to the same sub-human state as the others; how after a session of torture he had fouled himself and lain for hours, helpless and filthy, until a scarecrow hand had reached out to help him; how a man's dignity could be so damaged that only patient charity might restore it; how the sick became like children, petulant, ungrateful, obstinate; how the Christus himself had been debased so that he had to depend on his creatures to wipe the blood and spittle from his face and make him clean even for burial. He told them how they must act when they were cursed and struck, how the maimed and the debased were the proper images of Christ, so that a service to them was a service to the Creator. . . .

The old man's eloquence held them all, even Miller, who sat moodily sucking his dead pipe, his eyes fixed on the luminous face under its crown of white hair.

Suddenly Hanlon's attention was wrenched away.

Halfway down the room, wedged between two stout peasant women, sat Anna Kunzli.

From where he sat he could see her golden hair and the profile of her face tilted upward in an attitude of attention. The sight of her shocked him. A child like that in a sad galley like this one! What part had she in all this wretchedness? What had brought her, and who had permitted her to come?

He was filled with sharp resentment towards Father Albertus, and the deep, compassionate voice began to irritate him. No one had the right to lay these burdens on the young. Let the old carry them. They had had their youth and their laughter. This girl had never known either. She was no nun to be bound to such service, she had no sins to demand such penance. Let the others pay their debts first, those who had eaten the fruits of the old triumph—Holzinger's wife, Traudl. . . .

Then he remembered, and was ashamed to see how easily he had been tricked. Holzinger's women were waiting for him back at the Sonnblick. They were beyond criticism. They were in service already—the clean, comfortable, dignified service of Cæsar's friend. He could dispense with them of course. He could tell them with bland regret that they must go, that there were others who needed them more than himself.

Even as he thought it, he knew he would not do it. No man puts off willingly the panoply of power. He who sits under the eagles has need of comfort in his private rooms.

When Father Albertus had finished speaking, Miller went up to thank him and take him on a tour of the hospital. The small crowd dispersed about their duties, and Hanlon followed Anna out into the corridor and down to a small room stacked with buckets and brooms. She turned suddenly at the sound of his voice and saw him standing in the doorway, blocking her exit. Her face lit up with pleasure.

"Mark! I didn't expect to see you here!"

"I didn't expect to see you either, Anna," he told her, unsmiling. "What are you doing? Why did you come?"

The harsh note in his voice puzzled her. She stared at him.

"Why not, Mark? You saw these people. You know how much they need help."

"There are others to give it to them, Anna." Her innocence angered him now. "You're—you're too young for it. You don't understand . . ."

"Didn't you see the children?"

"I did, but . . ."

"They need somebody young. Don't you see that? They've got to learn to smile again. I may not be very good at scrubbing floors, but I do like children. They like me too. Why are you angry, Mark?"

The fact that he could not answer her made him angrier still. He said roughly:

"I don't agree with it, that's all. When your uncle comes back I'm going to tell him to keep you at home."

"Mark!" There was so much hurt in her voice and in her eyes that he softened immediately and reached out his bandaged hands to touch her.

"I'm sorry, Anna. I didn't mean to be rough. But you don't understand what you're taking on. Why do you think we brought Father Albertus here, except to prepare people for something rather terrible? I'd rather you didn't have a part in it."

For a long moment she did not answer him, but stood holding his hands in her own, looking at the raw discoloured flesh just visible at the edge of the bandages. Then she said softly:

"If it were you that needed me, Mark, I would come gladly. But you don't, do you? It was true what I told you the other night. I must have someone to care for. Without that I am empty. If not you—then the children. Don't deny it me. Please tell me you understand."

As suddenly as it had flared, the anger was quenched in him. He stood looking down at her with love and pity, smiling wryly at the simplicity of his own defeat. He told her gently:

"Very well, *Liebchen*. Do what you want. The children will be lucky to have you."

Then he turned away swiftly and walked down the echoing corridor and out into the raw cold of the afternoon.

CHAPTER 13

THE SUN came swinging northward, off the Horns of the Goat and into the Claws of the Crab. The north winds died in a last flurry of snow, a final patter of sleet. The air was warmer and the skies were duller and the days were longer. The first avalanches thundered down from the peaks, dashing themselves into snow-spume on the barriers of pines.

Then the south wind came, shouting up the defiles, and the snow peeled off the lower slopes like a skin, revealing the green flush of the new grass. The bare brambles along the river sprouted into life, the pine sap flowed, and every valley was full of the noise of water flooding down into the flat country.

The cattle came out of their winter stalls and wandered into the upland, their clappers making a music between the rocks where the late snow was piled in shining drifts. The townsfolk put off their winter grey and the women went shopping in bright dirndls and starched aprons, while the men put on *Lederhosen* and white stockings and hats with jaunty cockades of pheasant tails or chamois hair.

The meadows were dappled with cloud shadows. The girls walked proudly, swinging their skirts, and the cripples sunning themselves on the promenades whistled as they passed.

Spring was striding over the mountains and the people were opening their hearts and their windows to welcome it.

From his high balcony at the Sonnblick, Mark Hanlon looked down on his small empire and found it good.

He could see the progress now, as he could see the first green shoots that mocked the long death of winter. There was work for the men and food for the children. The first rough patterns of commerce were beginning to shape themselves.

Timber was being cut in the mountains. He could hear the ring of the distant axe strokes. The logs were trundling down the slides and there were three mills working on the fringes of the town. Raw and unseasoned as it was, the milled pine was being snapped up before it was cut, to rebuild the bombed areas of a dozen towns. By a system of inter-zone barter, which Hanlon had designed, half the proceeds of the sale must be delivered in goods—foodstuffs, clothing material, shoes, medicine. The other half was paid in Occupation credits which were blocked for future reconstruction. The schilling was at a discount in the markets and Hanlon refused to sell good timber for devalued paper.

Out of these credits he had bought two antique stone-crushers which were now clattering away in the quarries, so that the town had gravel to sell for springtime road repairs. The first lapidaries were coming in from Vienna and Rome and Geneva to buy up the bloodstone and the rock crystal which were being chipped out of the old workings.

New bloodstock had been bought on a co-operative scheme to revitalise the local herds. One of Hanlon's troops was a West Country farmer and Hanlon had given him a sergeant's stripes and set him in charge of agricultural enterprises.

The first speculators had appeared with rock-bottom offers for the empty hotels and guesthouses. He had blocked all sales until titles had been cleared and had exacted a deposit with any official quote. The deposits were paid into a trust fund whose interest gave him a little more credit for local industries.

Miller's DP hospital was functioning smoothly at last. As the first bad cases died off, others were sent up to replace them, and those who recovered were now beginning to move about the town, remote, a little ghost-like, but at least alive—which was no small triumph in the years of the hecatombs.

Huber was getting a small ration of the new drugs, and this victory had made a bond of friendship between the two men. A Red Cross official was working in the town, trying to trace the hundreds of missing men from the Quellenberg Regiment.

His own staff had been increased. An intelligence team had moved in to investigate Party affiliations and property titles, and with the increase had come promotion for Hanlon and Johnson.

Batteries of typewriters had been indented for and local girls recruited to deal with the mountains of paperwork.

A newcomer to Bad Quellenberg would not have noticed a tenth of it. He would have seen a shabby resort, peopled by mountain folk and sick men and a small colony of troops, with empty hotels and rationed goods, and at best a marginal living.

But, standing on the balcony, looking out over the circling town and the green patchwork valley, Lieutenant-Colonel Mark Hanlon saw the truth of it. There was progress. There was life. There was hope to match the new coming of spring.

One thing still irked him. He had not yet found the man behind the gun. In spite of Johnson's raised eyebrows he had insisted on continuing the house searches. When the intelligence teams moved in, he had made it part of their assignment. But the man had not been found. There were rumours, vague hints and tags of gossip, all of which pointed to the fact that the murderer was still in the area. But his name and hiding place were still a mystery.

It was the one sour taste after the sweet wine of success. It was a damage to his pride. If he could not bring the Quellenbergers to submit this case to a just trial, then he had failed. The principle of justice was still in breach.

That was what he told himself.

The truth lay deeper than he dared to probe. Huber had touched it sharply in one of their frequent talks. The big Tyrolese had grinned at him and said in his slow, provincial burr: "You do so much, my friend. You have so much intelligence. And yet you are blind in this matter."

"How?"

"You are not content to be the consul, the friendly governor. You want to marry yourself to this people."

"What's wrong with that?"

Huber made a wide emphatic gesture.

"Mixed marriages never work. There is always the reserve, the area of—of incomprehension. Nations are like families. They have their own privacy. They have their own jokes— about the follies of Aunt Matilda and the lecheries of Uncle George. The stranger cannot share them, not ever. They have their scales of judgment which have nothing to do with absolute justice—or perhaps come closer to it than any you can dispense. You will never bring them to this final surrender. They will break your heart first."

It was sound sense, but Hanlon could not accept it. The memory of his youth in Graz was still strong, still rosy with the afterglow of the lost paradise. The years between had been too barren of comfort. He had no yardstick to measure either hope or illusion.

The door opened behind him and Traudl Holzinger stepped out on to the balcony.

She was dressed, spring fashion, in a swinging skirt caught at the waist with a belt of tooled leather and a light blouse moulded over her firm breasts. The skin of her face and neck and arms glowed dully with youth and health. Her perfume reminded him of that first night when he had played the piano in the Bürgermeister's house.

She was his secretary now, and though they had come neither to hand's touch nor to kiss, there was a bond between them, a sense of sharing and companionship. Her frank sensuality provoked him, but he was too wary to commit himself to an affair with her. He knew that she was wooing him, carefully and slowly, and the knowledge was a vague comfort, a daily balm to his hurt pride. While she worked with him he was comfortable and good humoured. When she was away he found himself uneasy and irritable. They were still formal with each other. He called her Fräulein and she addressed him by his title; but he always welcomed her with a smile and she ran his office with efficiency and consideration for his comforts.

Now she had a message for him. Doktor Huber was on the phone. He thanked her and went back into the room and picked up the receiver. Huber's big voice was sharp with interest:

"I think I have something for you, my friend."

"That sounds promising. What is it?"

"Theft," said Huber bluntly. "It's been going on for some time."

Hanlon frowned in puzzlement.

"That's a matter for Fischer. I can't override his authority in local matters."

"I think you should know about it before Fischer."

"Why?"

"Better we don't discuss it on the telephone," Huber told him carefully. "How soon can you get down here?"

"How important is it?"

"It could be very important—to you."

"Twenty minutes," said Hanlon. "*Auf Wiedersehn.*"

"*Auf Wiedersehn.*"

The line went dead in his ear, but Hanlon still stood there

with the receiver in his hand, while Traudl Holzinger watched him thoughtfully. She asked no questions. When he was ready he would tell her, as he told her most things nowadays.

In his small garden at the end of the Mozartstrasse, Rudi Winkler lay sunning himself. He was naked but for a pair of trunks, and his bright, restless eyes were hidden behind a pair of glare glasses. His fat, pink body was stretched on a rug, his head pillowed on a rubber cushion, and he stared drowsily at the clouds drifting slowly over the pinetops. The warmth soothed him, and the tang of sap and fresh grass was pleasant in his nostrils. The birds made him a private concert and like a true hedonist he was content with the slow delight of the moment.

He had other reasons for satisfaction as well. Inside the house his patient was sleeping off the anæsthetic. The final operation had been done, the last scar tissue had been pared away, the last new skin had been planted, and, given continuing luck, he would be a new man inside a month. Not quite a man perhaps, but a reasonable facsimile. Now that the scar had been erased, now that he had been fed and rested and calmed into security, his face had lost the wolf-look, and the blue tinge of the grafts was the only sign of the old ravages.

His eyes had changed too. The terror had gone out of them, the hostile animal glare. They were sombre now, but calm. They showed neither eagerness nor hope—but a man who had dodged the hangman should not expect too much. Even a surgeon like Rudi Winkler could not turn a eunuch into a lover or a father of sons.

He smiled at the thought and rolled over to take the sun on his shoulders and the flabby muscles of his back.

In a month he would be rid of this embarrassment. Johann Wikivill would be gone and Rudi Winkler himself would be a new man. Fischer had kept his promise: fresh papers, a fresh identity. His past was safely buried, his future comfortably assured.

Yet even this prospect had its small sour regret. When his patient had gone, he would be lonely. He had come to have a fondness for him, as an artist has for his own creation because it is the best part of himself. And, in his odd fashion, Rudi Winkler was an artist.

There was sensuality in it too. He was a sensual man

addicted to refined perversities of pleasure, because the normal passion was beyond him. He had found satisfaction in his service of this damaged body. He had treated it with tenderness and care, denying himself the sharp impulses to cruelty that came on him as passion comes to more normal men. And this denial was itself a pleasure because it affirmed his dignity and seemed to absolve him from the excesses of the past.

It did not trouble him that there was no response to his tenderness and no gratitude in the sombre eyes of his patient. His pleasures had always been solitary ones. They demanded company but not sharing.

Suddenly he began to feel restless. The itch of spring was stirring under his pink hide. Discretion and the demands of his patient had kept him at home these last months. His walks had been confined to the back valleys and the less frequented paths. Now he needed something more—the movement of a town, the sight of new faces, the search for a new friend who might be complaisant to him.

He thought about it for a little while, lazily, chewing on a grass stalk. Then he got up, folded the rug and walked back to the house.

He found Johann Wikivill awake, lying on his back, staring up at the brown beams of the ceiling. The upper part of one cheek was covered with a lint dressing strapped with adhesive tape. He turned his head painfully and looked at Winkler, then asked him in a flat toneless voice:

"How did it go this time?"

Winkler bent over him smiling and touched the fresh tight skin at the side of the bandage.

"Fine. No trouble at all. Unless we get secondary infection, that's the end of it."

"You're a good surgeon." It was a statement of fact, not an expression of thanks. Winkler gave a high, shrill chuckle.

"You're a lucky man. I used to charge a lot of money for a job like this."

"I understand you've been well paid for this one too."

"Enough." Winkler was still smiling. It was hard to put him out of countenance. "You'll be able to start making plans for your future."

"What sort of plans?"

"Where you'll go, what sort of work you'll do. Unless of course . . ." He let the sentence hang a moment unfinished.

"Unless you'd like to stay with me. We get on well together. We understand each other. . . ."

Somewhat to his surprise, the man on the bed did not reject the suggestion. He nodded slowly and said in the same dead voice:

"I've thought of that too. I've thought about all the things that might be left to make me feel a man again. Even that. But there's nothing."

Winkler bent to him eagerly.

"There could be. There are so many things. . . ."

"There's nothing," said Johann Wikivill. "Unless a man believes . . ."

"In what?"

"In God perhaps. The soul."

Winkler's red lips curled in contempt. His voice was a silken mockery.

"I have had many men under the knife, my friend. I have explored to the limit their capacity for sensation—and suffering. I have never yet found evidence of a soul. I have heard them scream for God but I have never known Him answer. There is only one reality—this!" He sat down on the edge of the bed and drew the tips of his fingers along the smooth new skin of Wikivill's cheek. "This body with its million nerve ends, each susceptible to its own delight. When it dies, there is nothing. While it lives, there is still a joy to be coaxed out of it. Why reject what is left, even now?"

The man on the bed made no movement. For all the response he gave he might have been made of stone. He said simply: "Because there is nothing left for me. Nothing."

Winkler wrenched away his hands as if he had been burned. He stood up.

"Then I've wasted my time," he said in a high, harsh voice. "I should have let you hang."

He turned abruptly and walked out of the room. The man on the bed lay back and closed his eyes. Five minutes later Rudi Winkler walked out, dressed in his light spring clothes, to take the air in Bad Quellenberg.

On the broad, paved terrace of the Spiderhouse, Sepp Kunzli too was taking the air. He was pacing slowly up and down, hands clasped behind his back, head thrust forward, busy with a long and complicated thought. Below him the garden fell away in banks of lawn and shrubbery to the screen of pines that gave him privacy from the road. Beside him were the big french windows that gave on to his study, where an elderly Britisher with two Austrian assistants was working through a pile of documents.

They had been there for weeks now, from nine in the morning till six at night, sorting, classifying, indexing, patiently building a schedule of Sepp Kunzli's assets and those of the men, living and dead, for whom he had acted. They were lawyers, like himself, dry, meticulous men appointed by the Occupation Authority to trace expropriated estates and restore them to their rightful owners, provided they were alive.

Now and again they spoke to him, gently, respectfully, as to an honoured colleague. When they needed advice he gave it to them. When there were gaps in the records he supplied them out of his own card-index memory. And all the time he knew that the schedule they were building would be the text of his own indictment.

Yet he was calm about it, almost content.

It was as if he had come to a crisis, survived it, and lived thereafter in a state of syncope, a suspension of all effort and all emotion.

The crisis had come on his journey to Zürich. He had left cheerfully enough, convinced that in the week at his disposal he could sort out his affairs, to leave himself comfortably rich and preserve his standing with the Allied authorities. It was a move he had prepared a long time, and, even at the worst, the salvage would be handsome.

In Zürich he had met a woman. She was charming, witty, willing, and recently divorced from a wealthy exporter. Kunzli was a cool philanderer and the affair had been simple to begin. Its ending had shocked him profoundly.

After their first night she had left him, dry-eyed and bitter, and her last words had rung in his ears ever since:

"It was like mating with a corpse. I hate you for it and I hate myself!"

In the past he had found pleasure in the fear he inspired in the wives of Party men and the daughters of generals. It was all part of his revenge. But this one was different. He had no need to revenge himself on her. He had even looked to her as the beginning of new free life, the first fruits of the waiting years.

Then, suddenly, he understood. There would be no fruit, ever again. The tree was barren. The taproot was cut. The sap of passion would never run again. There was only the figment of life, the dead symbol, stark and leafless, better cut down before it became a mockery.

Despair is a strange sin, committed in a strange fashion. Sepp Kunzli surrendered to it in the sad passionless hours of his second morning in Zürich. He saw quite clearly what his end must be, and, like the tidy fellow he was, he set himself to prepare for it.

He met his bankers, arranged for the liquidation of his safest assets and their payment into an account in the name of Anna Kunzli. Then he gathered all his remaining papers together and took them back to Bad Quellenberg. When the inquisitors came, he launched them on their investigations and sat back calmly to await the outcome.

To his niece he presented the same mask of courteous indifference. He neither forbade nor encouraged her work with the displaced persons. He was content to drift through the empty days towards the blank, inevitable future.

The thing that puzzled him now was how he had come to this vacuous state. Other men he knew had lied and cheated and lusted and killed and intrigued and had still retained their taste for living. They still had goals to reach, desires to satisfy. Some of them arrived at love—or a fair copy of it. They still had fears. They still had moments of exaltation.

Yet he, the sanest and soberest of them all, had lost, somewhere along the way, the key to life. Perhaps he had never had it. Perhaps it had dropped out of his hand the day his wife had died. Perhaps this was a reason for her dying—that she knew he was dead already. Now it was all so long ago, so hard and fruitless to remember.

Far back in the house he heard the shrilling of the bell that announced a caller at the iron gate. He stopped his pacing and looked down towards the road. A few moments later Bürgermeister Max Holzinger came hurrying up the steep path.

Kunzli beckoned him on to the terrace and greeted him with a distant smile:

"*Grüss Gott*, Herr Bürgermeister! This is a pleasant surprise. What can I do for you?"

Holzinger cast a quick nervous glance inside the study.

"A word in private, Herr Doktor. A personal matter."

Kunzli took his arm and led him off the balcony to a sunlit lawn where rustic chairs were set about an iron table.

"Sit down, Herr Bürgermeister. Let's be comfortable. Now . . . ?"

Holzinger coughed and fidgeted unhappily. He was never an eloquent man, but now he was tongue-tied with embarrassment. Kunzli encouraged him with gentle irony:

"Come, my friend! Out with it! Times are bad for all of us. Why should we be uneasy with one another?"

"Well then . . ." The Bürgermeister took a deep breath and plunged ahead. "You—you know the investigations that are going on—into property, into Party affiliations?"

"None better," said Kunzli dryly.

"You know that I—well, that my record has been at least fairly clean."

"Cleaner than most." Kunzli nodded agreement. Then he smiled with a hint of the old malice. "With luck you might hold your job."

"I—I am less concerned with that than with my reputation. You will understand that I am in a delicate position. The Occupation authorities trust me. Colonel Hanlon has been a guest in my house."

"And your daughter works for him."

"That's right."

"Fortunate for you—and for her."

"Quite. But . . ." Holzinger tugged at his collar.

"But a trifle indiscreet of Hanlon. Is that what you mean?"

"Not at all, not at all," Holzinger assured him hastily. "There is no question of a liaison. Everything is very correct and official."

Kunzli cocked a sardonic eye at his visitor.

"Any hopes of marriage?"

"The . . . the subject has not been raised. Later, one might hope, perhaps . . ."

"Then why so sad, Herr Bürgermeister?" Kunzli put it to him bluntly. "You have more reason than most of us to be glad."

Holzinger told him, stammering:

"There—there is this question of my house. The title, as you remember, was transferred to my wife on a pre-dated deed. If that were to become known . . ."

Kunzli eyed him coldly.

"How should it become known, my friend, since you and I are the only ones who know it—and the witnesses were unaware of its contents?"

"I—I thought you might give me your assurance . . ."

"Would it make you any more secure? Would it?"

Holzinger was sweating now. The matter was in the open, but he had bungled the diplomacy. Kunzli was baiting him. Later he would set a price. The next question startled him even more.

"Why should I want to betray you, Herr Bürgermeister?"

"Please!" Holzinger held up a shaking hand in deprecation. "I did not mean that."

"You did," Kunzli told him mildly. "And you should not be ashamed to admit it. There was a time when it might have flattered me."

Holzinger said nothing. He was trying to read the thoughts that went on behind the metallic, spider's eyes. Kunzli let him sweat a few moments longer, then an idea seemed to strike him. He said briskly:

"I'll make a deal with you, Holzinger."

Holzinger winced. This was the moment he had dreaded. He asked uncertainly: "What sort of deal?"

"I shall give you my solemn word of secrecy, in return for a small favour—a personal favour."

"I don't understand."

"It's quite simple. I'd like you to ask my niece to dinner, very soon—and have her stay the night with you."

"Is that all? I mean . . . it would be a pleasure in any circumstance, but . . ."

"In the present circumstance, it would be the biggest favour you could do me."

"May I ask why?"

"Better you didn't, Herr Bürgermeister."

And, for the first time in all the years of their acquaintance, Holzinger knew he was getting the truth from Sepp Kunzli. In a secret, shamefaced fashion, he was very glad of it.

To Father Albertus spring brought a new labour—the visitation of his flock. During the winter he was cut off from many of them. He was too old and too frail to make the rounds of the outer farms and the isolated communities in the back valleys.

But when the sun shone and the tracks were dry, and his tired heart beat a little more strongly, he was able to move more freely, sometimes on foot, sometimes riding on a peasant cart.

He had much to do. There were children to be baptised, confessions to be heard, sick folk to be comforted with the Sacraments, bundling couples to be churched. In the outlying villages he would lodge in one of the farmhouses and say Mass in the big living-room where the onions and the smoked hams and black sausages hung from the blackened rafters.

This was his own interpretation of the allegory of spring: the sap of grace beginning to flow again, from the root which was Christ through the trunk which was the Church, out into the spreading branches which were the scattered community of the faithful. Some of the branches seemed dead; and this was a sadness to him. But he never lost hope for them, or ceased to pray. Spring had its miracles every year. Buds broke out on the driest twigs. The oldest trunks pushed out young branches. And on the roughest scree slopes the gentian found room to grow.

On this bright afternoon, while Rudi Winkler was stepping out to see the town and Mark Hanlon was hurrying down for his conference with Meinhardt Huber, the old priest was coming home from a two-day tour of the southern area of his parish.

The woodcutters had given him a lift to the top of the rise. Now he was strolling quietly down a narrow track that gave on to the Mozartstrasse. Sometimes he stopped to feed the birds with a handful of crumbs from his pocket, or coax the little grey squirrels that clung to the treeboles and stared at him with bright, wary eyes. The sound of water was all about him, and the low hushing of the wind through the new foliages. The peace of it seeped into him, the warmth stirred his ageing blood. Life was renewing itself, hope too. Flowers would grow out of the mouths of dead men. Children would play on the charnelheaps and never know that they were there.

When he came out into the Mozartstrasse he stopped and looked up at a small chalet of yellow pine with a trim terrace of lawn in front of it. He fished in his pocket and brought out a small notebook, the register of his parishioners. The entry for this house said simply: 'R. Winkler. Visitor. Religion unknown.' He looked up again and saw that the front door was open and the curtains looped back from the windows. He slipped the notebook into his pocket, opened the gate and walked up the stone steps.

When he came to the door, he knocked lightly. There was no answer. He knocked again and waited a moment, then he walked inside.

The first thing he saw was the housekeeper, scared and gaping, framed in the doorway that led to the kitchen. Then he saw the man lying on the bed. He was sleeping, with his face turned to the wall, so that Father Albertus saw the dressings on his cheek and the new skin growing round them.

He turned to the housekeeper and demanded in a low voice: "How long has he been here?"

She was too frightened to lie and she told him.

"Since St Nicholas's Day. The Herr Doktor has been caring for him. I had nothing to do with it, Father. I am only a servant here and . . ."

He silenced her sternly.

"Hush, woman! You have nothing to fear from me. Leave us."

"But the Herr Doktor . . ."

"Leave us!"

She went out, closing the door behind her, and Father Albertus sat down to wait until the sleeper should wake again. Silently he began to pray: "Open Thou my lips, O Lord, and set wisdom on my tongue. . . ."

Rudi Winkler leaned on the parapet of the bridge and looked down at the waterfall that plunged down from the crags and cut clean through the centre of the town. It was swollen now with the melting snows and the thunder of it filled the street and the spray was flung up in a fine mist between the blank walls of the buildings.

There was something hypnotic in this tumult of water and he stood there a long time, watching the patterns of foam and the tossing of the spume about the rock faces. Then he had the uneasy feeling that someone was watching him.

He looked up and saw another man, half a dozen yards away, standing with his back to the water, studying him intently.

He was thin as a beanpole and his clothes hung on him loosely. He had a long bony face and sunken eyes and a shock of hair that stood straight up on his head like a birch broom.

Winkler tried to outface him, but he went on staring. The little Bavarian shrugged with annoyance, turned away and walked up the street in the opposite direction, conscious of the bleak eyes fixed on his retreating back.

After a while the shock-haired fellow moved off too. And when he came to the Bella Vista he gathered his friends about him and told them:

"The Butcher's in town! I saw him with my own eyes."

CHAPTER 14

IN THE shabby office at the 121st Feldlazarett, Mark Hanlon conferred with Reinhardt Huber.

The Doktor was angry. His broad good-humoured face was clouded, his mouth was grim. As he talked he toyed restlessly with a steel paperknife, now scoring the blotter, now thrusting it, like a scalpel, at Hanlon's intent, sober face.

"I told you once, my friend, I have no local loyalties. I don't belong to this town. My world is inside the walls of this hospital. So I am not concerned to make myself an informer for you or anyone else. If this were any other sort of theft, I should deal with it as a military matter or hand it over to Fischer. But this . . . this is a vile thing. You know how little we have here—how men wake under the knife because I must ration anæsthetic. How I must reserve the sulphas and the penicillin only for extreme cases and let the others fight out their pain for weeks and months. When the little we have is pilfered, then I begin to think of the thief as a murderer. I call on you. Do you understand?"

"Partly." Hanlon was non-commital. "I still point out that in the absence of other circumstances Fischer is the man who has jurisdiction."

"To hell with Fischer!" Huber exploded. "Fischer's in this too, up to the neck."

"If you can prove that," Hanlon said with a grin, "I'll be happy to move in."

"Right!" Huber slammed down the paperknife and heaved himself out of his chair so that he stood towering over Hanlon, a big angry man, hurt and ashamed. "Here are the proofs. First, the thefts have been taking place over a long time."

"Since when?"

"The first losses were noticed just after St Nicholas."

"Why didn't you do something about it then?"

Huber shrugged unhappily.

"It was the first time. We could not be sure it was theft. The quantities were small—a quarter of a litre of ether, antiseptic solution, a small quantity of sulpha powder. They could have been explained by a careless stocktaking. After that, as you know, things began to be much harder to get. You helped us over the worst. But the small unexplainable losses were there—all in the same categories. Anæsthetic, antiseptic, dressings. Now"—his stubby finger thrust emphatically at Hanlon—"second, the inroad begins on the last and most precious commodity of all. Two capsules of penicillin were taken from the refrigerator. There is no doubt about this one, believe me."

"Do you know the man who took them?"

Huber nodded.

"This time, yes. A wardmaid saw him leaving the dispensary at a time when he had no right to be there."

"Have you questioned him?"

"Not yet. I should like you here for that."

Hanlon frowned and shook his head.

"Not without a reason. Why do you want me to handle it?"

Huber gave it to him, succinctly.

"Our thief has a mistress in the town. Her husband is a patient of ours—incurable, poor devil. She comes to visit him and goes home with a bedfellow . . ."

"What's her name?"

"Gretl Metzger. She holds one of the tobacco licences here."

"We've got nothing on her in our books."

"I don't think anybody has," said Huber with a weary grin. "But the liaison is significant. It becomes more significant when you know that Gretl Metzger is an old flame of Karl Adalbert Fischer."

"Can you prove that?" Hanlon shot it at him sharply.

"It shouldn't be hard. It's a small town. Everybody knows

the smutty bits about everybody else. So now we have it. Our thief, his girl friend, Karl Fischer and a handful of drugs in three categories—where do they all point?"

"To my first guess," said Hanlon tersely. "Fischer's shielding a murderer and someone's trying to do a plastic on his face. There are no medical supplies on the open market—this is the only way he can get them. Fischer's been using the Metzger woman to seduce your staff."

"Right again, my friend!" Huber eased himself back into the chair. "Now do you handle the case?"

"I handle it."

"Good," said Huber. "And you also pay me for information received?"

Hanlon looked at him in surprise. The request was so blunt and yet so alien to the man's character. Huber's mouth relaxed into a wry, unhappy smile.

"You are going to replace my drugs, Hanlon, and you are going to increase my supplies. I'm not very proud of myself, you see. I'm selling out my countrymen to the Occupying Power. I want to see a profit in it—for my boys at least."

"You'll get your supplies," Hanlon told him quietly. "And I don't think you should blame yourself. Why should a killer be saved when twenty men die of shock or septicæmia because their supplies have been stolen?"

"No reason at all," said Huber bleakly. "But I'm a doctor, not a judge."

"Like it or not," said Hanlon grimly, "we're all judges. You're better off than I am. I'm the hangman too . . ."

"The price of victory," said Huber with thin humour.

"It buys nothing but a headache," Hanlon told him sourly.

"And the Mayor's daughter."

He said it with a smile, but it took Hanlon like a smack in the mouth. His face flushed and he thrust himself out of his chair and stood staring down at Huber. Anger boiled over in a stream of passionate abuse:

"You bastard, Huber! You cruel, dirty bastard! I trusted you. I tried to help you—and that's the muck you fling in my face. Be damned to you! Get your man up here and let me question him. After that you can run your hospital without help from me."

The big Tyrolese did not move. He sat slumped in his chair, staring at his hands. It was a long time before he raised his head. When he did so, Hanlon saw that his eyes were misty and his face was suddenly aged. The words came out, stumbling and strangely penitent:

"I—I have said an unforgivable thing . . . a malicious joke. I am humiliated by what has happened here, with my own people. I am ashamed of my own part in it, so I try to shame you too. I destroy at one stroke a friendship that is precious to me. I am sorry—God only knows how sorry!"

With a sudden weary gesture he put his head down on his arms and slumped forward over the desk. Hanlon stood looking down at him with cold, bitter eyes. His words cracked like a lash over the lolling head:

"I came in friendship, Huber. I came to build, not destroy, to co-operate, and not to rule. What did I get? Murder, cheating, lying, insult. I'm tired of it. I've had enough!"

Slowly Huber raised his head and looked at him, haggardly. His voice was flat and weary.

"That's the trouble, Hanlon. We're all tired. We don't think straight any more. I'm tired of living with all this misery, sick to death of my own helplessness against it. I'm tired of patching bodies that are wrecked beyond repair, tired of preaching a hope I know is a lie, tired of begging for drugs and instruments, sick of the butchery I have to do without them. I can't unsay what I've said, but please believe I'm sorry for it."

He stood up and faced Hanlon across the desk. Then he held out his hand. After a moment's hesitation Hanlon took it and they looked at each other, shamefaced as schoolboys, until a slow smile broke over Huber's drawn face.

"Nobody believes she's your mistress. And they resent the fact that she isn't. They're afraid of saints, and celibates are dangerous men. We're a primitive folk. We like our rulers comfortably drunk and happily bedded. They're easier to manage."

"I'm a romantic," said Hanlon with a crooked urchin grin. "I'm still crying for the moon. I want a lover more than a mistress."

Huber's big hands waved away this Celtic folly.

"The moon is cold, my friend. But if a woman is warm in bed you are already halfway to love."

On that tart little tagline they were friends again, and they bent themselves to the business in hand: the tracing of stolen drugs and the search for the man behind the gun.

Karl Adalbert Fischer sat under the wine-stained map, with its drooping, melancholy flags, and contemplated his own dubious future. Spring was breaking out all over the mountains, but he was still sunk in a sullen winter of anxiety and disillusion.

His eyes were bloodshot, his mouth was stale with liquor and his body spent from the passion of the night before. He was getting too old for lechery, but the drive of habit was still strong, and hope died more slowly than the loveless ecstasy.

He had spent last night with Gretl Metzger. She had telephoned him late in the afternoon, with the news that there would be no further supplies from the hospital, and that her boy friend was in daily fear of discovery.

Fischer had gone to see her. She had wept and railed and threatened so that, in sheer weariness, he had had to take her. She had sobbed on his breast and sworn that she would never betray him; but when she had fallen asleep he had lain awake for hours, staring into the darkness, knowing that when the inquisitors came she would tell everything.

That they would come, he had no doubt at all. What he must do was equally clear to him. He must smile and submit and answer no questions until they brought him to trial, when, with luck and a good lawyer, he might assume the character of a martyr, a man driven to petty crime by loyalty to his family and his country. It would make a good case. The Press might even build it into a famous one.

The Occupying Powers were in a neat dilemma. They preached democracy and the right of fair trial. In practice they were committed to local autocracy and a doubtful legality in the processes of justice.

He was more troubled about his nephew than about himself. The boy was very near the end of his treatment. Freedom was just around the corner. It would be sweet sarcasm to send him away now. Time was against it, and circumstances too. But somehow a way must be found.

He tilted himself back in the chair, put his feet on the table and lit another cigarette.

Before it was halfway smoked there was a knock on the door and Father Albertus came in.

Fischer swung his legs off the table and stood up to greet him. The old man waved aside the formalities of greeting and came straight to the point.

"I saw your nephew this afternoon, Karl."

"The devil you did!" Fischer stared at him, irritated and bewildered. "But I told the young fool to stay inside the house."

"He did, Karl. I met him by chance. I was making the visitation of the parish, and it brought me to Winkler's house."

"Oh . . ." It was a long-drawn sigh of relief. "For a moment you had me frightened, Father."

Fischer was smiling now, but the face of the old priest was grim. He said crisply:

"There is nothing more Winkler can do for him. I am taking him away from there."

"What?"

Father Albertus faced him with stubborn dignity.

"The boy is almost healed in body; but in mind he is sick, near to despair. Winkler cannot help him, being so near to damnation himself. I propose to take Johann into my own house and care for him."

Fischer looked at him stupidly, fumbling for words.

"You mean you would dare . . ."

"For a wandering soul," said Father Albertus simply, "a priest should dare anything. Besides, the sanctuary of the Church is a better protection than you or Winkler can give him."

Fischer shook his head and smiled regretfully.

"There is no sanctuary now, Father. This is the twentieth century, the Secular state. The church has no immunity any more."

"Perhaps God may supply what the State refuses," said the old man mildly. "In any case, I am taking him. Tonight, after dark, I shall bring him down to my place. He can stay there until he is cured, in body and in spirit."

"And then . . . ?"

"Then he will make up his mind what to do."

Fischer eased himself slowly back into his chair; then suddenly he began to laugh. The old priest watched him, frowning.

"Perhaps you should tell me the joke too, Karl."

Karl Adalbert Fischer stopped laughing and waved him irritably to a chair. Then, quite dispassionately, he told him.

The old priest listened intently till the story was finished, then he leaned back in his chair, joined his hands fingertip to fingertip and stared musingly at the policeman. His first words were characteristic.

"There is hope for you yet, my friend."

Fischer shrugged and shook his head.

"There's no hope, believe me. I shall be arrested this evening."

"I was not thinking of that," said Father Albertus mildly. "I was remembering that, for the first time for many years, you have done an unselfish act, at considerable cost to yourself. That is the real hope."

Fischer cocked a sardonic eyebrow at the old cleric.

"You think you'll get me to confession, Father?"

"I'd like to get you to heaven," said Father Albertus with a sudden smile. "That might be less difficult."

"Get the boy out safely," Fischer told him sourly. "That's the big thing."

"No, Karl. The big thing is to give him hope and a goal. The rest is unimportant."

A wintry admiration showed in Fischer's canny eyes.

"You priests will never learn, will you?"

"It depends on the lesson, Karl."

"And what would you have me learn, Father? I'm an old dog. I don't take kindly to new tricks."

"It's the oldest lesson in the book." The priest stood up, ready to go. He paused a moment, then quoted softly:

"*'Vanitas vanitatum . . .'* Vanity of vanities, Karl. Everything is vanity but the love of God and the love of His creatures."

It was a timely thought, but a bitter one. Karl Adalbert Fischer was still chewing on it when Captain Johnson came with two soldiers to place him under arrest.

Rudi Winkler was returning from his walk. He had made the circuit of the town and the lower promenades and now he was retracing his steps, thinking cheerfully of the prospect of a beer in the Goldener Hirsch and a warm bath when he reached his house.

He was tired but relaxed, and he walked slowly, whistling a drinking song and inhaling the last pine-scented warmth of the day. The shadows were lengthening and the shopkeepers were putting up their shutters, but the long winding street was strangely active.

Little groups of promenaders strolled along the narrow footpaths and spilled over on to the roadway. Others stood in the doorways of the shops, talking in low voices.

At first he was hardly aware of them, lapped as he was in a pleasant weariness and in his habitual self-contemplation. Then the strangeness struck him. The time was late for strollers. These were not townsfolk. They looked different; their faces were odd and angular, their eyes hostile, their skin sallow and unhealthy. Their voices were odd too, soft and secretive, tinged with unfamiliar accents. They did not walk freely as the mountain folk did, but shambled, almost furtively, with bent shoulders and heads thrust forward.

Winkler began to be uneasy. He quickened his step, striding out more strongly, looking neither to right nor to left.

The strollers reacted immediately to his change of pace. Those in the doorways stepped out on to the footpath and began to walk steadily in the same direction, keeping pace with Winkler so that they formed a human screen between him and the safety of the doorways.

Those behind strung out in line abreast across the roadway, cutting off his retreat. He dared not look back, but he heard the measured tramp of their feet. Then they began to chant and the beat was in time with the thudding rhythm of their boots—"Butcher! Butcher! Butcher!"

Panic seized him and he began to run, panting and stumbling, up the cobbled road. The others began to run too, not bothering to catch him, but dogging his tracks, outflanking him. They were still chanting, breathlessly but insistently, so that the sound drummed into his ears in a crescendo of terror.

Faster he ran and faster, up the slope that led to the open square where there was usually a policeman on duty. Then he realised that before he reached the square he must cross the bridge over the tumbling waterfall. When he turned the corner he saw it.

Each parapet was lined with lean scarecrow figures, and the exit was blocked by another double rank. Hope died in him and he stopped running. His pursuers stopped too. He stood, motionless in a wide square of people—skeleton faces, scarecrow limbs, dead, hating eyes.

They watched him, silently, as he turned this way and that, looking for a way of escape. They saw his mouth open and heard his scream. Then, without haste, they began to move in on him.

Five minutes later a torn and bloody bundle was hoisted above the heads of the crowd and flung over the parapet. They watched it tossing and leaping in the torrent, then they turned away and shambled back towards the Bella Vista.

The police had refused duty after the arrest of Karl Fischer and Mark Hanlon's troops had not yet arrived to picket the town.

It was seven in the evening before the news of Winkler's murder reached Occupation Headquarters. More than a dozen people had seen it happen, from shop fronts and upper windows. Some had telephoned the police, but authority had collapsed, and none was prepared to apply to the Occupying Power.

Miller, the American, was the first to come at the truth. When his inmates returned, half-scared, half-gloating, the news spread quickly through the wards, and a white-faced nurse came hurrying to the Director's office to tell him the news.

He had acted quickly. All patients were confined to the hospital and a detachment of troops had been called to picket the entrances. Then Miller had driven up to the Sonnblick to make his report.

Hanlon heard him out in silence, approved his prompt action and then settled down to question him closely.

"The name first—you're sure it was Winkler?"

"No doubt of it." Miller assured him in his flat drawl. "I got it from half a dozen witnesses. 'Butcher' Winkler they called him. He'd served in two camps, Dachau and Mauthausen. Anyway, you'll be able to identify him when you recover the body."

"I doubt it," said Hanlon with dry distaste. "From what you've told me, they must have torn him to ribbons. How many of your people were involved?"

"Upwards of fifty."

"Can you identify a leader?"

Miller shook his head doubtfully.

"No. I'm not sure we'd be wise to try."

"Why do you say that?"

"It was a collective act. A scapegoat gives it a different character. It's easier to handle this way, easier to hush up."

Hanlon gave him a swift, shrewd look.

"What makes you think I want to hush it up?"

"You've got no choice," Miller told him. "It's justice of a sort—rough justice if you want—but neither your Headquarters nor mine will want to make a song and dance about it."

"They can't have it both ways," said Hanlon abruptly. "You can't have the courts for some and lynch law for the others. It's a negation of everything we're trying to do here."

"I agree," said Miller with a sour grin, "but I'm talking from experience: this isn't the first case I've seen. There were others, much worse. All of them were hushed up quietly. They'll do it with this one too."

"This is an area of British jurisdiction," said Hanlon tartly. "I think my people will take a different view."

"I wouldn't bank on it. There's a Four-Power policy involved. Besides, there's a practical point. What are you going to do with fifty DPs? Give them a collective trial and a collective sentence? Hand a readymade propaganda piece to the Russians and the Old Guard? Better bury Winkler and the case too."

"I'll have to make a report on it," said Hanlon stiffly, "and ask Klagenfurt for a directive. I'll send someone down to take depositions and a list of participants. I'd like you to make facilities available."

"Happy to help," Miller told him casually. Then his scrawny neck jutted forward and his lined face became unusually grave. "Don't misunderstand me, Hanlon. I know your views and the situation here. I'm just trying to save you some embarrassment."

Hanlon grinned lopsidedly and made a small shrugging gesture of helplessness.

"I'm embarrassed already. I've just arrested Fischer and the police are on strike."

"The hell you have!" Miller threw back his head and laughed. "What's the charge?"

"Receiving stolen goods. Concealment of a criminal. Accessory after the fact in a murder case."

"Think you'll make them stick?"

"Not all of them. My intelligence team is sweating him out now. This Winkler business will help them and me."

"What's the connection?"

"That's what I'm waiting to find out. I've sent Johnson to search Winkler's house and pull in his housekeeper. If she talks, as I hope she will, I'll confront Fischer with her and see what we get."

Miller stood up and held out his hand.

"I wish you luck, Hanlon. And a smooth passage with Klagenfurt!"

"To hell with Klagenfurt!"

"To hell with the whole lousy mess. I'd like to go home."

"Wouldn't we all?"

It was one of the clichés of the Service and Hanlon tossed it off lightly enough. But the truth was quite different. He had no home to go to, and he was too near to triumph to want it, anyway.

Karl Adalbert Fischer was sweating under the lamps.

They had him propped in a chair in a cellar room of the Sonnblick, with lights glaring in his face and the steam heater turned up to full pressure a foot from his back, while three stony-faced interrogators hammered him with questions, hour after hour.

It was a technique familiar to him and he counted on his years of experience to turn it into a harmless if wearisome ritual. For the first two hours he had done very well. He had stepped round the pitfalls and shrugged off the traps with the bland derision of a man who knows them all by heart.

Then, slowly, the strain began to tell. His clothes became sodden with sweat, his mouth dried out, his fingers twitched, his eyes burned and his head buzzed painfully under the dull repetitive impact of the voices. He had to clamp his mouth shut to stop screaming aloud. He tried vainly to close his ears and withdraw into a state of selfhypnosis, but the lights blazed and the voices drummed on and on so that he wished, in spite of himself, to tell them everything and be done with it.

Then, surprisingly, the inquisition stopped. The lights were switched off. They gave him coffee and a plate of sandwiches and talked genially and casually while he ate them. Then they gave him a cigarette and let him smoke it through to the end, while they reasoned with him like an equal.

The telephone rang and one of the men answered it. Fischer pricked up his ears, but all he heard was the indistinct crackle of the receiver and a non-committal series of answers. The interrogator put down the receiver and turned to him with a smile.

"You're a lucky man, Fischer. That was Colonel Hanlon. We're going to release you."

Fischer looked at him, stunned.

"What did you say?"

"We're going to release you. There's no case."

A warm wave of comfort swept over Fischer's body. He had won. He had told them nothing. He would emerge from this brief ordeal with added prestige and added power. He asked for another cigarette and they gave it to him without question. When he came to light it his hands were trembling violently, but one of the inquisitors leaned forward courteously and snapped a lighter. They poured him another cup of coffee and began gathering up their papers in the shamefaced fashion of men who have finished a distasteful task.

Then the door opened and Mark Hanlon came in—with Rudi Winkler's housekeeper.

In a long bare room at the top of the Pfarrhaus, Father Albertus was dining with Johann Wikivill.

It was a meal the like of which had not graced the presbytery table for many long years: *Rindsuppe*, a trout fresh-caught and stuffed with mushrooms, a roast of chicken, *Apfelstrudel* and fresh whipped cream. There was a Nussberger for the meats and a Muscatel with the sweet, and a long Dutch cigar to match the coffee. The old man had coaxed the ingredients out of the local shopkeepers and handed them all to his grumbling housekeeper, hoping that her skill might not be atrophied after years of ascetic cooking. He had made no secret of the identity of his guest, but had cautioned her to silence and sent her back to the kitchen.

When Wikivill had arrived, furtive and panicky, he had made him bathe and change his clothes and settle himself in a small bedroom with a view over the town and the valley. By the time dinner was served the visitor was calm again and they dined in leisurely fashion, by candlelight, like men remote from disaster.

Father Albertus steered the talk into harmless channels, and his guest responded gratefully, as to a forgotten pleasure. He talked well but with detachment, as if he, like the priest, were no longer part of the world which they discussed. His hands were steady and his eyes were clear but sombre like those of a man accustomed to the contemplation of immense distances, treeless and barren.

It was not until the last of the wine was gone, and the last drops of coffee had been poured, that he asked the critical question:

"You have brought me here, Father. I'm grateful. But what do you hope to do with me?"

The mild, deep-set eyes looked out on him from the luminous face. The grave voice answered him:

"You have come—as every man comes sooner or later—to the end of a road. Behind you is a wreckage. In front, blankness. It is the beginning of despair."

"It is despair."

"No." The priest's voice was gentle but very firm. "Despair is the loss of hope."

"I have no hope."

"I want to try to give you one."

"Can you?"

It was a clear challenge, but, strangely enough, the old man did not rise to it. He said simply:

"If I promised it to you, my son, I should be lying. Hope springs from faith. At present you have no faith. You do not believe in God—you cannot believe in yourself. I cannot give you faith—it is a gift of the Almighty. The most I can do is bring you to desire it, help you to prepare yourself for it."

"I desire it," said Johann Wikivill heavily. "I need it, as I need love and passion and a whole body—all the things I can never have."

"You need it more than these, my son. Because the soul endures even after the body is destroyed."

"If there is a soul."

"If there were, and if you could believe it, would you bear more easily the maiming and the loss?"

"I—I think so."

"We begin from there." The fire seemed to leap up behind the transparent face. "We reason together. We meditate together. We pray together."

"I cannot pray. How can I, not believing?"

"You pray as a great Englishman once prayed—he who came from faith to unfaith, and back again, and came to wear finally the dignity of a prince of the Church: 'O God—if there be a God—give me light!' "

The sombre eyes of Johann Wikivill were downcast to the table. The candle flames threw strange shadows on his lean, bandaged face. After a while he said softly:

"It is a long journey, Father. I doubt I have courage to make it."

"There is light at the end of it. And you will not be walking alone. I shall go with you, all the way."

"You may not be able to. The Englishman wants my head."

"He shall not have it, unless you choose to give it to him."

There was so much strength and conviction in the old man's voice that his guest looked up in sharp surprise.

"You can't promise that, Father!"

"I can. I do."

"You can't. Behind the Englishman is a whole nation—four nations! You cannot fight them all."

"Not I, my son." Father Albertus held up his gnarled and broken hands. "But God Almighty who lifts up the humble and topples the mighty from their seats . . ."

Suddenly the telephone rang, its sound shrill and shocking in the bare room. Father Albertus got up to answer it and his guest sat, tense and upright, listening. He heard nothing but the disjointing answers of the priest.

". . . No, I had not heard of it . . . a shocking affair. . . . Yes. . . . I understand that. . . . No. . . . I should prefer to leave it till the morning. . . . I shall be there without fail. . . . Yes, I guarantee that. . . . *Auf Wiedersehn.*"

He replaced the receiver carefully on the cradle and turned to face his guest. He said quietly:

"That was Colonel Hanlon, Occupation Commander. Winkler was murdered this afternoon. Your uncle has been arrested. Hanlon knows you are with me."

"No . . .!" The sound came out on a long-drawn breath of horror. He pushed back his chair and struggled out of it, shattering a wineglass as he did so. "I've got to leave. Get out of here!"

"No!" The deep voice snapped like a thunderclap. Fire leaped up in the old man like lightning. His frail body seemed to grow in stature, dominating the room and the tense crouching figure of his guest. "I made you a promise. I shall keep it.

They shall not have you, my son. Trust me—in the name of God!"

"I don't believe in God."

"Then believe in me."

Slowly, inexorably, the seconds ticked by; the candle flames flickered and the silence crackled with the tension between them. Then, quite suddenly, Wikivill's taut body relaxed and he sat down, resting his trembling hands on the edge of the table. His mouth twisted into a strange smile, half resigned, half despairing. His voice was almost a whisper.

"I believe in you, Father. I don't know why, but I do. I'll stay."

CHAPTER 15

"FOR GOD's sake, Mark! Have you gone crazy?"

Hanlon had hardly finished his conversation with Father Albertus when Johnson exploded into shocked anger.

"You've been griping for months about this fellow. You've turned the town upside down to get him. Now, when he's in your hands, you leave him free—to spend the night with a bloody priest! What do you expect him to do—make his confession or something? Walk in here tomorrow morning and hold out his hands for the bracelets? God Almighty! By tomorrow morning he'll be over the hills and far away. And how are you going to explain *that* to Klagenfurt?"

"Finished, Johnny?" Hanlon turned a bleak, unfriendly eye on his subordinate.

"I'm finished, yes. And so will you be if you carry on with this crazy comedy. I know you're a Catholic. I know there's some connection between you and the priest. Fine! It's none of my business. But this is. I don't like it. Burn your own fingers if you like, but not mine."

"Finished now?"

"Yes, and be damned to you!"

"Then sit down and listen."

Johnson hesitated a moment, then lowered himself into a chair and sat glaring across the desk at Hanlon. Hanlon reached for a cigarette, lit it and tossed the case over to Johnson. Johnson caught it and put it back on the desk unopened. Hanlon smoked for a few moody moments, then he began to talk, crisply and irritably:

"Item one, Johnny. I'm in command here. If there are orders, you obey 'em. If there are kicks, I take 'em. Right?"

"Right," said Johnson sullenly.

"Item two. There was a second murder this afternoon. It was committed by people under our protection—the DPs. I don't know how to deal with them until I get a clear directive from Klagenfurt. It's high policy, political dynamite. Which brings us to item three. If I arrest Johann Wikivill tonight, I've got to put him through the hoops, immediately! I have to charge one man and let fifty others go free. How's that going to look? What are the people going to say to our protestations of democracy and justice?"

"I—I hadn't thought of that."

"Item four. The fact that Father Albertus has taken our man under protection means there's more to the case than you or I know about. I don't want to make any move until I get the score."

"By then it may be too late."

"I'm taking Father Albertus's word that it won't be."

"Why do you put so much stock in him?"

"I've known him a long time, Johnny. He's a bigger man than you and I will ever be, and a wiser one. I trust him."

Johnson sat quietly for a few moments considering the proposition. Then he said apologetically:

"The only item that carries any weight with me is number two. I see we're in a jam. It could be your way is right, though I'm still not convinced. Anyway, I'm sorry."

"That's OK, Johnny. Forget it."

"What are you going to do about Fischer?"

"Hold him till I can see where we're heading on the whole business."

"What if he screams for a lawyer?"

"He hasn't yet. I don't think he will."

Johnson reached for the cigarette case and lit up. Through the spiralling smoke rifts he studied the lean, intelligent face of his commander, noting the deepening carelines and the new grey hairs and the ugly scar along his temple. He said seriously: "You puzzle me, Mark."

"Why so?"

"You're too subtle for me. You think off-centre. I don't say it's a bad thing. In a situation like this it's probably the approach we need. I find you hard to follow, that's all."

Hanlon nodded thoughtfully and began to worry the thought aloud.

"It's fair comment, Johnny. I think it's a difference of approach, of attitude. You see this job one way, I see it another. We think about it in different terms. To you it's a military operation to be handled according to a certain set of rules. Fair enough. To me it's . . . it's a human enterprise, a problem of people—more than people, persons. You're detached from it, I'm involved. I'm not sure that's a good thing either, but it's a fact and I've got to start from that fact. Can you see that?"

"I can see it, yes. But you're not involved right down the line."

"How come?"

Johnson smiled a little shamefacedly.

"Take the rest of the officers. Take Wilson, James, Hanneker. We're involved in a different way. They've got their girls and a place to take 'em and a nice cosy domestic setup. I'm playing the field in a half-hearted sort of way. You're still playing the celibate. You're involved with Fischer and the priest and Holzinger, and even Traudl doesn't get a tumble in the hay, much as she wants it. I'd be happy to give it to her myself, if I thought I had half a chance."

Hanlon shrugged indifferently.

"Don't let me stand in your light, Johnny."

Johnson's face creased into a puzzled frown.

"That's what puzzles me, Mark. You're more detached than I am, yet you're risking more than I'd ever risk."

"Maybe that's it, Johnny," said Hanlon with a crooked grin. "Maybe that's why I don't want to be involved with a woman. I'd risk more than you and profit far less. Now get to hell out of here. I want to go to bed!"

Johnson made no move to go, but sat back, grinning at him with the old jaunty impudence.

"You need a change, sonny boy. You need to get out on the town once in a while. I've got a date with a girl at the Zigeuner Café. Why not ring Traudl and have her along? It'd do you good. You'll be dead a long time."

"Too damn long!" said Mark Hanlon; and, after a moment's hesitation, he reached for the telephone.

The Zigeuner Café was neither a café nor a resort of gipsies. It was a two-storeyed log house, about a mile from the town, perched on the lower pine slopes and looking out across the valley. It took the afternoon sun and was sheltered from the winds at night. There was a terrace in front, planted with blossom trees, and the lower floor was occupied by a kitchen and a long dining-room with a log fire at one end and a big porcelain stove at the other, and half a dozen small guest-rooms.

Its proprietor was a long-headed Carinthian with a stout peasant wife and a quartette of bouncing daughters. They lived on the upper floor, and gave the lower one over to the entertainment of the Occupation troops and their local escorts.

When the proposition had been presented to him, Hanlon had been dubious, but Johnson had sponsored it with enthusiasm. It was quiet, remote from the town. If the boys got drunk there'd be no local disturbance and they would have time to sober up before they came back into the built-up area. It was a useful place for local leave. There were the guest-rooms, the fishing, the mountain walks. . . .

Finally Hanlon had approved. The permit was signed and the Carinthian went away, waving his ration cards, while the more conservative townsfolk muttered unhappily about influence and interlopers.

When the officer staff had been expanded, Johnson had proposed a shrewd amendment. Three nights weekly the place should be private to officers. The rest of the time it should be open to other ranks. This too Hanlon had approved, and the Carinthian was quick to adapt his service and his prices to the different needs of the military castes.

From the official point of view it was a good arrangement. There was privacy for presumptive gentlemen and freedom for those of lower degree. The ladies who accompanied the former could enjoy their seduction in comfort. The soldiers' girls could relax in a more rowdy prelude. The tipple for the troops was tapped from a big cask in the kitchen. The officers' wine came in bottles at double the price. And the bouncing daughters were instructed to keep their mouths shut and their virginity intact, while their father raked in the currency tokens and cashed them at a premium rate.

When Hanlon and Johnson arrived with the girls it was already late. There were half a dozen couples on the floor, dancing to the music of the zither player, a tall blond fellow in *Lederhosen* and a bright peasant shirt. They nodded a perfunctory greeting and settled themselves in a corner near the fire, while the daughters of the house bustled up to light the candles and pour out the wine and lay the table for a meal.

They drank and talked and ate and smoked and laughed and fell silent, watching the dancing couples, while the music played on and on and lost itself in the shadowy, carved beams of the ceiling.

They were restless at first, selfconscious and uneasy with one another. Their talk concealed their thoughts and their laughter had a metallic ring to it. They were lonely, yet not prepared for intimacy. They courted one another yet dared not think of the consummation. But, as the drink relaxed them and the music beguiled them and they watched the hypnotic leaping of the fire, they drew closer to each other and talked more quietly and smiled in the candlelight, but did not laugh any more.

These were the gentle moments: the prelude to passion that had no passion in it; the beginning of love in which there was no thought of love at all.

Then Hanlon took Traudl's hand and led her on to the dance floor. The zither player changed his rhythm to a slow plaintive waltz that swept them into each other's arms in a symbolic surrender.

They danced cheek to cheek, breast to breast, lapped in a mutual harmony of sound and movement. Their lips brushed sometimes, then parted again to whisper small words of satisfaction and endearment.

The other couples fell away from them, then sat down to watch, while they danced on, unconscious of their solitude, of everything but the music and the slow, mounting beat of desire.

Then, abruptly, it was finished. The music stopped. A small clapping broke out. They looked around them in surprise, then walked selfconsciously back to the table, where Johnson and his girl were waiting for them.

The room was uncomfortably warm now, heavy with the smell of pine smoke and cigarettes and food and spilt wine.

Johnson suggested a walk in the garden before they went home. They paid the bill and strolled out into the sharp, scented air under the blossom trees. Then they parted and walked, two and two, into the shadows under the lacing branches.

The moon was riding high over the sleeping valley. The peaks were silver with it, ghostly battlements looking down on the black march of the pines. The river wound brightly through the grey, sleeping meadows, its sound a muted counterpoint to the nostalgic tinkling of the zither.

Hanlon and Traudl Holzinger stood together by the low stone wall looking down over the bright emptiness and upward to the soft scattering of stars, round the fringes of the moonfield. The air was cold, but full of the scent of blossoms that brushed their faces as they turned to kiss and cling to each other.

When the first long kiss was over they drew apart and looked at one another. Their voices were a soft whisper.

"*Du bist so schön, meine Liebe . . .*"

"*Und du, Schatz . . . so schön . . .*"

They were both passionate, both ripe for this moment of starlight and perfume; but neither was ready to make the first demand nor the first surrender. Their passion was strong enough and frank enough, but each, for a different reason, held it in curb. For Hanlon the curb was his marriage and his proconsular status. For the girl it was the age-old admonition of the Sisterhood: 'Give them everything, yet give them nothing until you have the ring and the promise. We are still unconquered, remember. We must make them pay for our surrender.'

So regretfully they retreated from one another, and after a moment Hanlon said gently:

"Where do we go from here, dark one?"

He looked away from her across the valley and she saw the line of his jaw, tight and stubborn, and his eyes, distant and brooding in the grey moonlight. Her answer came back lightly enough:

"Where do you want to go, Mark?"

"I'd like to go back ten years and start again."

"With your wife?"

"No. With just myself—with all the world a garden and the girls in it bright as flowers."

"Why not start now?"

"I might—one day."

"I'll wait for it, Mark."

"Kiss me again."

"*Ach, mein Liebster.*"

After a while the music stopped and they heard the clatter of engines and the laughter of homing couples. Then they too walked slowly out of the perfumed orchard and drove back to Bad Quellenberg under the cold stars.

The following morning, on the stroke of ten, Father Albertus presented himself at Occupation Headquarters. Hanlon received him alone and plunged straight into business.

"You've committed an indiscretion, Father. You've created a delicate political situation. You owe me an explanation."

"I came to give it to you, Colonel." The answer was given with careful formality.

"Let me show you where you stand, first. Yesterday three people were arrested—Gretl Metzger, an orderly from the Feldlazarett and Karl Fischer. The charges against the first two are theft and receiving stolen goods. The charges against Fischer are receiving, concealment of a criminal, and being an accessory after the fact of murder. At least one of these charges could be laid against you also."

Father Albertus nodded thoughtfully, then a faint smile twitched the corners of his mouth. He answered mildly:

"I see your point, Colonel. On the other hand there are circumstances of which you are ignorant. I felt you should know them before—before any decisive action is taken."

"I am not as ignorant as you suppose, Father," said Mark Hanlon coldly. "Karl Fischer made a statement to me, remember. I was prepared to investigate the extenuating circumstances in his nephew's case. Your action in taking him into your house has made that much more difficult."

"Fischer told you everything? What had happened to the boy? What had been done to him?"

"Yes."

"And you saw these things only as extenuating circumstances?"

"I saw that they would make a strong defence at his trial."

"He must not go to trial, Mark!"

Fire snapped in the mild eyes. The old voice rang with

passion and authority. Hanlon stared at him, astonished.

"Do you understand what you're saying, Father? This is a legal matter now. The wheels have begun to turn. I couldn't stop them even if I wanted to."

"Will you hear me out, Mark? Will you answer me some questions and listen to me before you make a final decision? Will you forget for a while that you are Cæsar's friend and remember that—that you were once my son? Please."

Hanlon got up from his desk to walk to the window and stood staring out at the green shoulder of the mountain and the last snow banks near the summit. Without turning round, he said flatly: "I promise nothing. But I'll listen."

"Thank you, my son." The priest paused a moment, as if searching for an opening gambit. Then, almost apologetically, he put the first question: "Are you still a Catholic, Mark?"

Hanlon swung round to face him.

"What's that got to do with it?"

"Everything, Mark. Before we can talk we must establish a common ground of argument. Otherwise we are both wasting our time."

"I'm still a Catholic."

"You don't go to the Sacraments."

"Let's get it straight, Father." Hanlon's voice was harsh and irritable. "I made an unhappy marriage. It gave me none of the things implied in the contract. I've been looking for them ever since—outside the contract. If you want it in moral terms, I'm living in a state of sin. But I'm still a believer. I can recite the Nicene creed and subscribe to every term of it. Is that enough?"

"For the present, yes. I am sorry for you, Mark. I wish you were happy and at peace with your conscience. But that is for another time. You still have the faith. You believe in God. You believe in the soul, in salvation and damnation."

"Yes."

"You will admit that the salvation of a human soul is a greater matter than the fate of empires?"

"As a principle, yes. In practice, the one often depends on the other. It's a paradox and a mystery, Father. You should know that."

"I do, believe me. But now I am concerned with the principle."

"I'll admit the principle. Where does it lead us?"

For a while the old man was silent. He seemed to be gathering his strength, praying perhaps for the wisdom to present his argument. Then he bent forward in his chair and with deep, passionate conviction began to speak:

"Johann Wikivill committed this murder in a state of temporary insanity induced by shock and a long accumulation of terror. Whatever a court might decide, I believe that he is morally guiltless. I believe too that he is now completely sane. What concerns me at this moment is that he is a man on the edge of despair. Hope was destroyed in him with the destruction of his manhood. He sees himself as an object of pity and derision, incapable of giving or receiving love because he is incapable of its physical expression. You know, none better, what the denial of love means to a man. You at least have faith in a spiritual destiny, even if you fail to attain it. He has no faith. Life is a blankness to him. The hereafter is a myth and mockery. If he could come to belief, hope might be restored to him. He might even attain, with the grace of God, a great holiness, accepting his loss with patience, bending himself to the service of his fellows. I—I should like to try to lead him on this road. I know that I cannot do it if he still remains in a state of flight and fear. I want to keep him with me, pray with him, talk to him, spend love and courage on him. If you take him away I cannot do it. He will be lost in a black night of disillusion. You see what is at stake, Mark? Not the small symbolic justice of a military court, but a man's soul—his saving or his damnation? Give him to me, my son! Give him to me in the name of God!"

Mark Hanlon was moved. The eloquence and sincerity of his former mentor touched him deeply. His own moral dilemma disposed him to pity. Every impulse urged him to clemency. But he knew that these were traps for the unwary. He was a man under stringent commission, bound by oath to administer a policy. If he made a mistake, he would compromise himself and the man he was trying to save. He began to cast about for a compromise.

"Tell me, Father. If—and it's nothing more than if—I leave Wikivill with you, will you guarantee to surrender him on demand? We might get round the situation by releasing him into your custody, for health reasons."

The old priest shook his head.

"No, Mark. It is not enough. Don't you see, I cannot begin

to help him with a lie? Sooner or later he would discover it, and the whole work would be destroyed. I would hope that one day he might come to you himself and offer to purge himself by trial, being happy in the outcome because of faith and new hope. But I cannot guarantee it. I must leave him free to choose between flight and surrender, between faith and despair. Can't you see that?"

"I see it," said Hanlon thoughtfully, "but I don't see what I can do about it. I'm a man under authority. Any decision I make can be reversed overnight. If there were some formula acceptable to Klagenfurt, I'd be happy to give it a try; but I can promise nothing, nothing at all. I'll have to think about it."

"And in the meantime . . . ?"

"Keep Wikivill with you."

"On what conditions?"

A slow, weary grin broke over Hanlon's lined face. He shrugged and spread his hands in resignation.

"I leave those to your conscience, Father. I'm sure it's more delicate than mine."

There was no answering smile from Father Albertus. He stood up, twitched his cloak round his thin shoulders and said with grave gratitude: "Thank you, my son. We understand each other. You are doing more than I expected, if less than I hoped. You are a good man. I pray that one day soon you may come to peace."

In a cellar room at the Sonnblick, Karl Adalbert Fischer lay on a camp stretcher and stared up at the ceiling. The room was no more than a concrete box in the foundations of the building, with bare grey walls and a blank door and a weak unshaded bulb in the centre of the roof. There was a wash basin and a toilet can and a bare table and a kitchen chair. There was no window and the only sound that penetrated was the measured pacing of the guard in the corridor outside. His isolation was as complete as if he had been whisked off to another planet.

He was not too disturbed by his situation. He was warm, he was well fed. The charges against him were formal ones, hard to sustain effectively in the sympathetic atmosphere of a civil court. He had lost his job—but there was comfort even in that for a middle-aged intriguer tiring of the backstairs reek of soiled linen.

What troubled him most was his nephew. The lad was in a

mess, mentally and physically. Any new pressures might tip him over the edge into insanity. He would be under arrest by now, possibly in the hands of the interrogators, as he himself had been. He was beyond help, because Karl Adalbert Fischer had no bargaining power left.

Or had he?

A new thought struck him, a new hope, small and weak like the first buds of spring. He nursed it a long while, carefully, then he got up, hammered on the door and demanded to be taken immediately to Hanlon.

He was greeted with ironic courtesy, given a chair and a cup of coffee, and left, at his own request, alone with the Occupation Commander.

Hanlon quizzed him comfortably:

"Well, Fischer, what did you want to see me about?"

"I'd like to make a bargain with you, my friend."

"You can't." Hanlon's refusal was blunt. "Your credit's run out."

"Nearly, but not quite." Fischer leaned back in his chair, his small bird-like head tilted jauntily on its long neck. "You're in a difficult situation, Colonel. More difficult than ever now that Winkler has been killed. I, on the contrary, have nothing more to lose. The scores are even, you see."

"What have you got in mind?"

Fischer laid the tips of his fingers together in a fastidious churchman's gesture and made his point:

"You told me a long time ago, Colonel, what you wanted to make of this town—'an example of co-operation', wasn't it? 'A showpiece for the rest of Austria.' You've never been able to do it, because you were never able to touch the wires that make it work. You are further from them than ever now. All you have are scapegoats for your own failure—me and my nephew. When you get us into court, the failure will be shown up very clearly."

He paused, waiting for the warning to sink in; but Hanlon said nothing. After a moment he took up the thread of his argument.

"For myself, I am not concerned. I shall go through the performance like a well-trained monkey. I might even make some profit out of it in the end. But my nephew is a different matter. He's had enough, poor devil. I don't want to see him crucified again. I know you've got to bring him to trial. I know too that a recommendation to clemency would make things much easier for him. That's what I'm asking. I think I can offer you a good price for it."

"What's your offer?"

"The keys to this town. The private history of every one of its inhabitants. The knowledge that has kept an incompetent like me safely in office for fifteen years. I know you, Colonel. I know what you need—power. I'm prepared to hand it to you, all in one book. It's worth the price, believe me. I took fifteen years to write it."

"Where is this book?"

"Hidden. But give your promise on behalf of my nephew and I'll tell you where to find it." His ridiculous head wagged and his bright eyes shone with malicious humour. "Tempting, isn't it?"

Hanlon's face was blank, his eyes were hooded, but inside he was bubbling with excitement. Once again Fischer was over-reaching himself; and this might be the beginning of the biggest victory of all. He said coolly:

"You might give me the book and I might sell you both down the river."

Fischer smiled and shook his head.

"I know you better than that. It is an English failing to justify the big betrayal by the small loyalty. If you give me your word, I shall believe you."

"You've got yourself a deal," said Hanlon calmly.

When he raised his head, Fischer saw that he was smiling, and the smile chilled him with sudden fear. He had made his last stroke. He had thrown away his shield. Now he was naked to the sword of the invader.

It took Hanlon five hours to draft his report to Klagenfurt, but by seven in the evening it was ready. It was a small master-piece of concise reporting and meticulous balancing of political possibilities. It ended with a recommendation which he hoped would appeal to the British preference for a workable com-promise against a dramatic decision between alternatives.

'. . . We are thus in a neat dilemma. If we proceed against Johann Wikivill, we must perforce proceed against the mur-derers of Winkler. If we cite one and not the others our credit as impartial administrators is destroyed. If we arraign both parties we find ourselves prosecutors of actions against the sympathies of large numbers of powerful people. The court would undoubtedly return a merciful verdict and award minimum sentences. Shrewd propagandists would make profit out of both cases in the Eastern and the Western press. We ourselves would lose much and gain nothing.

'My recommendation is that both affairs be dealt with quietly at the discretion of the local command. DP inmates are now under disciplinary restraint and Johann Wikivill is under the care of the parish priest, a discreet man with a good Resistance record. He is being advised by local medical authorities on the therapeutic treatment of a difficult mental case. I am convinced that no further incidents need be feared.

'We are still considerably in profit. No press disclosures have been made and with the removal of Karl Fischer—a troublemaker—I have been enabled to remodel the police force and appoint a more co-operative official, without running foul of the interim Austrian Government. I hope you will agree with these recommendations and confirm my discretionary powers in both cases.'

He signed his name with a flourish over the typed subscription, folded the letter, sealed it in a triple envelope and tossed it into the tray for posting.

He had had a big day. He was looking forward to a bath and a cigarette and dinner with Traudl at the Zigeuner Café.

Then the telephone rang. He lifted the receiver.

"Hanlon here."

A precise, wintry voice answered him.

"Colonel Hanlon? This is Sepp Kunzli."

"Yes. What can I do for you?"

"If you would be good enough to listen for a few moments, without interruption, I should be very grateful."

"Go ahead."

"My niece will be dining with the Holzingers this evening. She will sleep the night in their house. My housekeeper has been given leave to visit her mother. I am therefore alone . . ."

Mark Hanlon frowned at the black mouthpiece but said nothing. The cool, prim voice talked on steadily.

". . . You have, I believe, an affection for my niece. At least you owe her a small gratitude . . ."

"Yes, but I don't understand what . . ."

"Please, Colonel, no interruptions.

"I hope therefore that you will be kind to her during the

next few days. Your investigators have done a good job, Colonel. In a week at most they will have traced nearly all the expropriated property that has passed through my hands. You will then be forced to take action against me. I propose to save you the trouble. In a few moments I shall kill myself."

"For God's sake, man!"

"Don't try to do anything, Hanlon. By the time your people got here I should be dead anyway. I am trying to leave you a clean desk. I have made provision for Anna and I know you will believe that the property I have left her is all of clean title. I'd like you to see that she gets it without trouble."

"I'll do that. But listen, Kunzli, this is crazy. You can't just . . ."

"On the contrary, Colonel, it is the sanest thing I've ever done. I'm saving everybody a lot of trouble, myself included. You'll thank me for it later. You can repay me by being kind to Anna." There was a moment's pause and the voice came back again, cold and measured as ever.

"I have just taken a cyanide capsule. I expect to be dead in three minutes."

"Kunzli, listen to me!"

"Goodbye, Hanlon."

The receiver went dead in his ear. For a long moment he sat there staring stupidly into the black mouthpiece, then, slowly, he put it back on the cradle and walked out into the corridor to find Johnson.

CHAPTER 16

SEPP KUNZLI was buried the following day in the Lutheran cemetery. The coffin was carried to the graveside by four peasants and the only other mourners were Holzinger, Hanlon, Kunzli's housekeeper and Anna herself. It was a drab, hopeless little ceremony and they were all glad when it was over.

Anna wept a little when the coffin was lowered, and Hanlon put his arm around her shoulders to comfort her. Then he walked her out of the churchyard and along the sunlit promenade, where the birds sang in the overhanging branches and the children played on the dappled carpet of pine needles.

She was strangely calm. It was as if she had anticipated the tragedy and had prepared for it a long time.

"He was a cold, unhappy man, Mark. His life was very empty. I think he is better quit of it."

He was wrenched with pity for her, touched with admiration for her small, bright courage, but he had no words to use. He questioned her gently:

"What will you do now? Where will you go?"

"Where should I go, Mark? This is my home. I have work here."

"Won't you be lonely?"

"I'm used to that. I'd be lonelier somewhere else. I have friends here."

"I'd like to help you, if I could, Anna."

"You've helped me already, Mark. Things would have been much worse if you hadn't taken over. There was nothing for me to do, nothing to fear."

"There was nothing in that. Official routine."

"You're a good official, aren't you?"

"It's a matter of debate." He grinned in spite of himself. "Myself, I'm inclined to doubt it."

"Herr Holzinger says you are. And Traudl too. She works with you all the time. She should know."

Her face was turned away from him, so that he could not see whether it was innocence or jealousy that prompted the words. He shrugged them off and said simply:

"If you're in need of help—any kind, any time—I'd like you to come to me first."

"Please, Mark. . . . Let's not talk about it any more. Here, I want to show you something."

She laid a hand on his sleeve and drew him off the path into a small bay where there was a stone seat and a bird cote where the birds came to feed in the hungry winter. She made him sit down on the seat, then she scooped up the grain and the nuts which were scattered on the floor of the cote and moved to stand a few yards away, hand outstretched, beckoning the birds.

"Be very still," she told him. "Otherwise they won't come."

She pursed her lips and threw back her golden head and began to whistle a low trilling call. A moment later the birds came fluttering about her, just out of reach. They retreated immediately, then came again, closer this time, while she stood motionless and beautiful in the broad shaft of sunlight, offering the grain in the cup of her hand. Finally they lost their fear and came to settle on her shoulders and on her wrists and to feed from her palm, while Mark Hanlon watched with wonder and delight.

She woke a deeper passion in him than Traudl did; but her innocence was a barrier to courtship. He could not practise on her the soft deceits of love that other women welcomed. Yet he was in love, as he had never been in love before—and this might well be his only memory of her: a dreaming girl, face tilted into the sun, with the birds fluttering down to her hands and their wings an aureole about her golden head.

Traudl's thoughts on the same subject were rather more prosaic. She gave them to him at length when he returned to the office after driving Anna back to the Bella Vista for her day's duty with the DPs.

"Little Fräulein Kunzli's nicely set up now. She's her own mistress. She's got a house and a sizeable dowry. She'll be a good catch for someone."

"She won't marry for a long while yet," said Hanlon irritably. He was tired and cross grained, and vaguely uncomfortable under Traudl's cleary-eyed scrutiny.

"Why not? She's old enough to carry the milk pails. And she's a big girl too. Or hadn't you noticed?"

"I hadn't."

"You're slipping, Mark," Traudl said softly, as she picked a non-existent thread from his lapel. "She's in love with you . . . or hadn't you seen that either?"

"I've been too damned busy to notice anything," he snapped at her. "A riot, a murder, a suicide and three arrests— All in two days! I should interest myself in a girl's green-sickness."

"You were interested in mine, Mark."

"You're different."

"How different, *Schatz*?"

Her hands were soft on his cheeks. Her perfume was all about him. He took her in his arms and kissed her, just as Johnson opened the door and stepped into the room.

He goggled a moment, then burst into a whoop of joy.

181

"Lovely stuff! Happiest day in months. The lad's human after all. When are you putting up the banns, Mark?"

Hanlon flushed angrily, then recovered himself. The thing was out now. Best to be good humoured about it. Traudl stood beside him, head high and proud, her hand lying on his arm in a gesture of possession. Hanlon disengaged himself lightly and said with a grin:

"Shut the door, Johnny. Get the drinks. We could all use one."

The glasses were filled and they drank, smiling a little shamefacedly at one another.

"To romance," said Johnson.

"*Prost!*" said Mark Hanlon.

Traudl had a toast of her own, but like a wise woman she kept it to herself. It was Johnson who saved the day with his breezy summing up:

"I'm glad the penny's dropped—for both of you. You've been getting damned hard to live with, Mark. All work and no play makes the Colonel very dull company."

"Better keep it to yourself, Johnny," cautioned Hanlon.

Johnson shrugged it off cheerfully.

"Who am I to gossip when there are a hundred others to do it for me? Why should you care, either of you?"

"There's Traudl to be considered . . ."

"Not me," said Traudl firmly. "I want to shout it from the mountains. I will too."

"No," Hanlon told her bluntly. "I'm still married, remember, and we're in the middle of a ticklish political situation. The less said the better until it blows over. Same for you, Johnny. You know the score."

"Yes, Colonel."

He said it so demurely that they all laughed and the awkward moment was over.

Hanlon had no intention of being jockeyed into a full-scale love affair and it was fortunate for him that Traudl was not prepared to go beyond the comfortable routines of courtship without a firm promise of marriage. She was as passionate as Hanlon and she had had her own brief encounters with the young bloods of the Reichswehr; but now she was playing for bigger stakes—a marriage that would take her out of this defeated land and into the wider pastures of the West. There were barriers to the leap—Hanlon's marriage, his unwillingness to commit himself to a new gamble, his position as the Occupying Power. None of them was insuperable, but she must lead him gently to the jumps lest he balk and refuse them altogether.

So they settled down to comfortable companionship in work and in playtime, broken by daily passionate interludes that brought them each a little closer to the final surrender. They submitted, willingly enough, to Johnson's amiable conspiracies to bring them into company and force them out again into the spectacular privacy of acknowledged lovers.

They worked late on the accumulated documentation of the Kunzli affair. They dined and danced at the Zigeuner Café. They drove out in the moonlight as far as the roads would take them and bundled for an hour or two in the jeep. They parted at the Holzingers' gate and Hanlon went back to his big bed in the Sonnblick to continue his nightly study of Fischer's black volume of the sins of Bad Quellenberg.

The book fascinated him. The secret life of the town was spread before him like the underside of a carpet—a shabby pattern of lies and cheating and adultery and incest and political bargaining. All the men were there, all the women, even the misdemeanours of their children. Their public successes were set down, side by side with their personal failures. At first he was ashamed of his interest. Then he began to succumb to the fascination of it.

Here, as Fischer had promised him, was the essence of power; to know the sins of all, and the price at which they could be bought. The book was a talisman, like the lamp of Aladdin. Turn one page and a councillor would pour money in your lap. Turn another and his daughter would come to your bed. Point to this line and that and a dozen fearful human beings would run to your most degrading service.

Holzinger was there, the weak, good man making his shoddy compromises between comfort and conscience, never quite sure whether he was wearing the cuckold's horns or the blinkers of a fool.

But Fischer was sure. Fischer had picked up the rumour and traced it back to Hamburg, and proved it for a fact that Liesl Holzinger had lived with a British soldier and possibly become pregnant by him on the eve of her husband's return.

Traudl was there too. Her young wartime loves were listed one by one: the Panzer lieutenant, the official from Vienna, the

Luftwaffe pilot who had promised to marry her but had never come back. The geography of her passion was meticulous: the ski huts were named, the hotel rooms, the glades and glens where she had given herself, and the times were set beside the names of the men who had possessed her.

As he leafed through the sorry little chronicle, Hanlon was touched with horror at his own prurience. He was not in love with this girl, but he had a comradely fondness for her, and a hearty sensual urge for her willing body. Yet here he was peeping like a *voyeur* at the intimate commerce of her bed-room.

It took him a little time to understand why he could read and read and read and not be jealous. There was nothing to be jealous about. Her past belonged to him, even more than her present. Like all the other citizens of Bad Quellenberg, she was in his power.

Fischer had paid dearly for what he might have had free. He had handed over the keys of the city. He had made Mark Hanlon master of Bad Quellenberg and all the folk who lived there. And yet, not all. There were the few innocent, the many ignorant but unimpeachable. There were the simple ones who were born and loved and married and begot and died unmind-ful of the greatness they had achieved. They were beyond the reach of malice—like Father Albertus, whom he respected, like Anna, whom he loved but could not have.

They made him ashamed of himself and of his new creeping itch for power. Because of them he closed the book and locked it away in the lowest compartment of the safe, to which he alone had the key.

One night, shortly after the death of Sepp Kunzli, he walked down into the town to call on Reinhardt Huber. A small parcel of replacement drugs had arrived from Klagenfurt and he wanted to give himself the pleasure of delivering them personally.

Huber's broad face lit up with pleasure at the gift and he insisted that Hanlon share a cup of coffee and the last of a bottle of schnapps. They talked and smoked and drank for the best part of an hour, and when Hanlon stepped out into the street again the clock in the church steeple was sounding nine.

The street was deserted. The burghers were all at home supping behind closed blinds. The DPs had been under curfew since the murder of Winkler. The troops were drinking in the *Stüberls* or necking with the girls on the promenades or dancing in the Zigeuner Café. Hanlon's footsteps rang hollowly on the cobbles and the moonlight was ghostly on the blank walls and on the pinewoods above the town.

Suddenly, far ahead of him, he heard a woman's scream, high, panic stricken, quickly stifled. He began to run, swiftly and silently on the balls of his toes. The road narrowed and twisted sharply into the old town, where the shopfronts were set back under the low shadowy arches.

Then he saw them: the woman backed helpless against a stone pillar, the man holding her with one arm locked against her throat while the other tore at her clothing. The man heard him coming, wrenched away and bolted up the narrow street. The woman crumpled at the foot of the pillar.

When Hanlon bent over her he saw that it was Anna Kunzli.

He lifted her gently and carried her the rest of the way to the Spiderhouse. She woke in his arms, trembling and incoherent with shock, but she gave him the name of her attacker and a rough description of him. When they arrived at the Spiderhouse he handed her over to the housekeeper to be bathed and put to bed, while he himself sat at Sepp Kunzli's desk and telephoned to Johnson.

"I want you to find me a man, Johnny. His name's Anton Kovacs, a DP from the Bella Vista. Phone through to Miller for a full description of him. Comb the town, call in every man jack of the troops and the police if you have to, but get him tonight."

"What then?"

"Arrest him—and don't be gentle about it. Close confinement."

"What do I charge him with?"

"Attempted rape."

"My God! Who's the girl?"

"Anna Kunzli."

Johnson's whistle of surprise shrilled in his ear.

"Who's the witness?"

"I am."

"We'll get him, Mark. When will you be back?"

"I don't know. Expect me when you see me. If you want me I'm at the Kunzli house."

"Roger. Oh, by the way, Traudl rang and wanted you to . . ."

"To hell with Traudl. Jump to it, Johnny."

"I'm on my way."

"*Wiedersehn.*"

He put down the receiver and sat with his head on his hands staring down at the burled polished wood of the desk top. He was angry and weary and dispirited. One by one the illusions were being stripped from him. The cynics were proving right. His own blind idealism was a deceit and a sham. Fischer had warned him that the DPs would bring murder and rape and violence. All three had happened. Huber had warned him that a man could not be a lover of the people and a good administrator at the same time. The proof of it was on every page of Fischer's black folio. How could one love the rutting, snarling, treacherous animals pictured there? They could be controlled only by strength and cunning. Survival—that was the driving motive. Trample the weak, seduce the strong, take what you want and if you can avoid paying for it, so much the better.

Johnson was right when he derided the compromise of his position. He was involved, but not far enough. He wanted power but was not prepared for the final ruthlessness. He wanted love, but solaced himself with a juvenile courtship. He was neither a contented celibate nor a cheerful lecher. He wanted the best of both worlds and was stuck with the worst of each.

He was still mumbling over his tasteless cud when the housekeeper came and told him that Anna was ready to see him.

He found her propped against the pillows in the same bed where he himself had lain during the days of his illness. She was pale and heavy eyed and the bruises were beginning to show on the white skin of her throat. He sat down on the edge of the bed and bent to kiss her lightly. Her arms went round his neck and she clung to him in a sudden paroxysm of sobbing.

"Oh, Mark! Mark! It had to be you. There was no one else . . . no one!"

He held her close, soothing her with lover's words until the weeping was over and she was calm again. Then he dried the tears from her face and settled her pillows and sat looking down at her with love and pity.

He told her softly: "It was a bad dream, *Liebchen*. It's over now. It will never come back."

She shook her head.

"It was horrible, Mark. He was like an animal. I feel as though I shall never be clean again."

"You are as you always were, Anna. Clean and beautiful."

"Am I beautiful, Mark?"

"Very beautiful, *Liebchen*."

"Will you kiss me please?"

He bent and kissed her lightly on the lips.

"Not like that, Mark. I'm not a child. I'm a woman. I want to feel like a woman. I—I love you so much."

"I love you too, Anna."

"Kiss me, then."

Her arms were round him again and their lips met and she made him lead her through all the soft, wild rituals of love, as if only his hands could cleanse her, and only his body could waken her from the nightmare.

When they woke in the morning, the room was full of sunlight. The housekeeper smiled when she brought them their breakfast on the terrace and, when they looked about them, the world was bright and new as if spring were breaking out a second time on the green flanks of the mountains.

When Traudl Holzinger heard the news, she laughed in his face.

"For God's sake, Mark! I thought you'd know better. These mewing virgins are all the same. They're white as milk and soft as butter and so damned innocent you have to teach them the words. They wilt in your arms and beg you to be tender with them—and six weeks later they're yelling that they're pregnant. Men are such fools!"

"It isn't like that, Traudl."

"It never is, *Schatz*, until they start waving marriage lines under your nose! You wait and see! I'll give you two months, then you'll be back with a bad hangover and indigestion from too much sugar cake."

"I'm sorry, Traudl. I'm going to marry her."

"You won't, you know," she mocked him cheerfully.

Hanlon was touched by her bright, cool courage. He said gravely:

"Johnny's more than half in love with you."

She made a small shrugging gesture of resignation.

"He's still a boy, Mark. But I'll probably make a man of him. Don't worry about me."

She bent forward suddenly and kissed him full on the lips, biting them till the blood flowed and he forced her away from him.

"That's for remembrance. I think you're making a big mistake, Mark, but I wish you luck. Meantime . . ." She was suddenly serious. "You won't want me round here any more, I suppose."

"If you're prepared to stay, I'm glad to have you," said Hanlon stiffly. "No point in making a song and dance about it. I still need a secretary."

"You need more than a secretary, Mark," she told him with sudden malice. "You need someone to teach you the facts of life. I'm probably the only one who can do it. I'll stay."

And stay she did—an efficient assistant, a sardonic observer of all the follies of this new mating of May and September.

The first reply from Klagenfurt on the murder cases, reached him the next day:

'Your report received and noted. If possible maintain present position until after High Command Conference Vienna, when further directive will be sent. . . .'

Hanlon smiled sourly at the bland official equivocation. He was still in command of the situation, but if he made a mistake they would have his head on a chafing dish.

He sent a copy of the telegram to Miller and to Father Albertus, then, weary of so many crises, he settled back to the comfortable routine of administration.

He kept his evenings and his weekends free and he spent all of them with Anna Kunzli. They tramped the back valleys, they fished the trout streams, they sunned themselves in the grass of the uplands, where the gentians bloomed and the small rock orchids and the early columbines. Often he slept in her house and walked back to headquarters in the first warmth of the morning, wrapped in the soft sad contentment that follows after love.

He had been married to one woman. He had slept with many others, in vain pursuit of what the first had refused him. He understood that enjoyment is easily attained, while contentment is as elusive as a marsh light.

With Anna he had both, and a renewal of his youth as well.

They were in tune with one another—as leaf with wind, as water with the pebbles over which it runs.

Passion rose in them at the same moment, they were calm together and they laughed and kissed and were silent to a common impulse.

Hanlon's young days had been spent in a monastery garden. He looked back on them with a sense of loss. A man has a lifetime to collect wisdom. He has only a few years to store up memories of spring.

Anna Kunzli made good his loss; and because he was wiser now, he was able to be grateful, so that she too was content— at least for a while.

But as the weeks passed, an element of uneasiness began to show itself in the smooth score of their pastorale. In the beginning they had talked, lightly enough, of divorce and re-marriage, yet the more they returned to the subject, the more the difficulties showed themselves. Anna had a Catholic conscience on divorce and a fear of the moral sanctions involved. Hanlon had it too, but he was older, more cynical, more ready to grasp what the years must soon snatch away from him. Anna thought in a woman's terms—the fate of the children, the security of the bond, the breach with the Church.

At first her doubts were easily stifled. Passion ran strongly between them and the warm propinquity of the lovers' bed was all the security they needed. But custom stales even a springtime affair and often she would wake in the night and cling to him, begging for reassurance which he could not give without a lie, so that he could only make love to her and lull her into a temporary forgetfulness. They had small quarrels, quickly healed with a kiss; but the scars remained, a small accumulation of doubts and indecisions and unspoken regrets. They loved each other but the security of possession was denied them. The bloom was dusting off the flower. The gilt was wearing off the gingerbread house. Traudl Holzinger saw it all and said nothing.

Finally, one night, Anna faced him with it, squarely.

They had dined and drunk a little and made love; but for the first time they were out of harmony and the loving was brief and unsatisfactory. They were lying apart from each other in the big bed in Sepp Kunzli's room, which had become their marriage chamber. The light was burning and they saw each

other's faces, strained and dubious. Anna said quietly:
"Mark?"

"Yes?"

"I want to be alone for a few days."

"Just as you like."

"Don't be angry with me, Mark. I love you. You know that. I want nothing better than for us to be happy always and always. But I've got to be sure."

"You can't, you know," said Hanlon gravely. "Life isn't like that. Nothing's sure. People drop dead in the streets. Gasworks blow up. Children are crippled with disease. There's war and flood and famine and cankers in the guts. Tomorrow is the most doubtful word of all. The best one can do is live for the day. Take the cash in hand and be glad you've got it."

"Can you do that, Mark?"

"Nobody can completely."

"No. . . . That's why I want time to think, to decide. . . ."

"Decide what?" The fear pricked like a sharp knife around his heart.

"Whether to go on with this. Whether to take the cash . . . or play for the future."

"It's your right, my dear. I don't quarrel with it. How long do you want?"

"I don't know. How can I? Will you leave it to me to get in touch with you?"

"If you want it like that."

"I do, Mark."

Without another word he threw back the covers and got out of bed and began dressing himself. The girl lay back on the pillows watching him.

When he was dressed he bent over her and kissed her gently, then walked out of the room without another word. When the door closed behind him, she buried her face in the pillow and sobbed.

Shoulders bent, head thrust forward, Mark Hanlon walked slowly back to the Sonnblick under the cold moon. *Post coitum omne animal triste.* Man is the saddest animal in the world. The act which gives him the keenest delight is the one which brings him closest to death.

CHAPTER 17

FATHER ALBERTUS sat in his high-backed chair, under a wooden statue of St Julian, and looked down at the swollen, tear-stained face of Anna Kunzli. She sat opposite him, pale and straight backed, her fingers picking nervously at the edges of a small lace handkerchief. The old man's voice was warm with understanding, and even in his chiding there was a gentleness.

"What do you want me to tell you, Anna? That black is white, that adultery is a good thing, that happiness can be built on a lie and an injustice?"

"I want you to help me, Father." All the youth had gone from her voice. It was weary under the weight of experience. "You talk about adultery and lies and injustice. These are words to me. All I know is love. I love Mark. He loves me, It's not a dirty word like the others. It's beautiful. How can I make you understand that?"

"I do understand it, child, believe me."

"How can you, never having felt it?"

"You think not?" A ghost of a smile woke in the mild eyes. "I'm an old man now, but I was young once like you and Mark. The vows of the priesthood don't destroy one's manhood. Only age does that. Do you think I have never felt desire? Do you think I have never held a child in my arms at the baptismal font, and wished that it were my own? What do you think I hear at the confessional? Fairytales?"

"Then why are you so pitiless?" She flung it at him desperately.

"I am not pitiless, but I cannot change the truth. Look, Anna . . ." He bent to her, gesturing with his broken hands. "For the first time in your life you are face to face with the real meaning of religion—the thing that binds, the thing that restricts. People talk of it as if it were a gentle thing, a source of consolation. So it is, but only in part. For the rest, it is a burden, a cross on our backs."

"Who lays it there?"

"Not I, child, but God Almighty."

"Then he too must be without pity."

The wise, luminous face clouded. The white head bent in deprecation.

"He has pity, Anna. He has love too. He framed your lips for kissing and your body for love and child bearing."

"And then denies them to me in the end."

"Because they belong to another woman, Mark's wife."

"She doesn't want them. She never has."

"Did Mark tell you that?"

"Yes."

"How do you know he wasn't lying to you?"

"You've got no right to say that, Father. I know Mark. He hasn't lied to me."

Father Albertus nodded gravely.

"No, I don't believe he has. I'm sorry. Mark is a good man but an unhappy one. It is hard enough for anyone to be continent when he lives for years away from his wife. It is harder still when there is no love left to preserve loyalty."

"That's it, don't you see, Father." She seized eagerly on the tag of argument. "There is no love left, there is no injustice. Life will be awfully long for him and for me too. Why shouldn't we enjoy it while we can?"

"You're young, Anna, you can enjoy it with another man— and with a safe conscience."

She raised her head and faced him squarely. Her young eyes were suddenly cold, her mouth was firm. She said very deliberately: "Understand something, Father. Whatever I decide in this matter, there is only one man I can ever or will ever love. That man is Mark Hanlon."

Looking at her then, Father Albertus knew with moral certainty that he was hearing the truth. Anna Kunzli was, in the absolute sense, a simple person, one of those who see quite clearly and choose quite coldly and who hold for ever to their choice, even if it leads to ruin and damnation. This was no country bundling with tears and repentance and marriage lines at the end of it. The girl had come to him in good faith for help in an irrevocable decision. If he failed her now, the damage would be irreparable. He closed his eyes and prayed as he had prayed with Johann Wikivill, for light in his eyes and wisdom on his tongue. Then, very gently he told her:

"I have no consolation to offer you, child. I can only tell

you the truth and pray that you may find strength to follow it. If you and Mark stay together you may come to happiness. I say you may, because I know Mark better than you, and I tell you that no woman will ever satisfy him completely. He is one of those touched with a hunger for the lost paradise. He will search for it until he dies, and then, if God is kind to him, he may attain it. I say again, you *may* be happy. If you are, it will be at the expense of your faith, which is the only thing when passion dies and the body begins to wear out."

"And if I give him up?"

"You will be lonely for the rest of your life."

"What about his child?"

"His child?"

"I'm pregnant, Father," said Anna Kunzli calmly.

The old man said nothing. He got up, walked to the window and stood a long time staring out over the roof tops of the town. When at last he turned to her again, she saw that his eyes were misty. His voice was tired and hesitant.

"With all my heart, Anna, I wish I could say to you now, 'Go and be happy with your man. Bear his children. Keep his house. Build yourself a new life in the valley.' I love you both, you see. I—I think of you as the son and the daughter I have never had. In your children I might see the continuity which my vows deny me. But I cannot do it. In the camp they beat me and starved me and broke my hands to bring me to betrayal." His voice faltered. "I tell you truly it was easy, compared with this."

Anna Kunzli was touched with sympathy for the old man, but she looked at him with her bright, clear eyes and challenged him:

"You say you love us both, Father. Yet you condemn us to death, a long, slow death, lonely and without love."

"Not to death, child, to life."

"Show me anyone who could survive it."

"I'll do that," said Father Albertus quietly. "Perhaps he can help you better than I."

Without another word he walked from the room, and, a few moments later, he was back with Johann Wikivill.

Two days later Mark Hanlon had a visit from Father Albertus, who handed him a letter from Anna Kunzli. It was short, simple and final.

My dearest Mark,

I have decided. I can't go through with it. I know you will understand why. I love you still. I will love you till I die. But please, please don't come to me.

Anna.

Hanlon read it through in silence; then, quite deliberately, tore it into small pieces and dropped it in the wastepaper basket. Then he looked up at Father Albertus and said with grim courtesy: "Thank you, Father. Was there anything else?"

"Except to say that I feel very deeply for both of you."

"If Anna can survive it," said Hanlon ironically, "I've no doubt I can. I've had a good deal more experience."

The old man brushed aside the irony and answered him warmly: "You try to hurt me, Mark, but in reality you are tormenting yourself. I did not take Anna from you. I showed her both roads. She made the choice herself. You know that's true, don't you?"

The sardonic mask dropped from Hanlon's face, to reveal the hurt and heartbreak beneath it. He flung out his hands in a passionate appeal.

"Why did she go to you, then? Why didn't she tell me herself? I wouldn't have tried to hold her. Do you think I'd want her unhappy? I know too well what it means. I can't forgive you for that, Father."

"She was afraid to come, Mark. If she had to hurt you she didn't want to do it with a kiss. Besides, she loved you too much to trust herself in your arms again."

"Which makes me a pretty sort of lecher, doesn't it?"

"You're not a lecher, Mark," Father Albertus reproved him mildly.

"What then?"

"A man looking for love," said the old priest calmly, "wanting it so much that he may well lose it eternally."

"Or have it snatched from him." Hanlon's voice was bitter. "You took her from me, Father."

"I did not take her." The old voice was touched with anger. "She surrendered you freely. And I tell you now, you will never be happy until you make the same free surrender of her."

Hanlon's first slammed down on the desk. His eyes blazed and he shouted at the old priest:

"You want too much for too little. You take everything and give nothing. I gave you Johann Wikivill. You've got Anna. You want me too."

"I'm a hunter of souls, Mark." The mild eyes lit with sudden fire. "I cast the nets as wide as I can."

"And what do you give to those who surrender, Father?"

"Peace, my son."

"Peace!" The word was flung back in harsh mockery.

Hanlon heaved himself out of his chair and began to pace angrily up and down the long room, pouring out the resentment and disappointment of years.

"Peace, you tell me! You promised it to me in the monastery close. I never found it. I found pride, ambition, jealousy, and lack of love. You sent me out to look for it in the world. I didn't find it there either. I came, as I came to this place, with love and kindness, and had them tossed back in my face. I loved a woman and was left unloved. I loved my children but their love for me was poisoned. I fought a war to found a peace. I came to this town to establish it. There was no peace. There was murder, rape, suicide, and the death of love. You promise me peace, Father. Where is it? Where?"

The priest was silent a long time. His pitying eyes were fixed on the ravaged face of his old pupil. Then he quoted softly: "Thou has made us for Thyself, O God, and our hearts will never rest until they rest in Thee."

"It's too late, Father," said Hanlon in a dead, flat voice. "It's too late and I'm too tired."

"It is never too late, my son."

"Let's forget it." Hanlon's voice was crisp again. His face smoothed itself into the old, official mask. "There's a business matter . . ."

"Yes?"

"I told you, you asked too much and gave too little. It's a bad bargain. You've got Anna. I want you to give me back Johann Wikivill."

For one disbelieving moment Father Albertus stared at him, then he stood up and said formally: "I'll send him to you, Colonel. *Auf Wiedersehn*."

"*Auf Wiedersehn*, Father."

A little while later Traudl Holzinger came in with the afternoon's mail from Klagenfurt. She greeted him impersonally and began slitting the envelopes and laying the correspondence in front of him. He worked through them abstractedly, signing them, initialling them and tossing them into their various trays. All the time he never said a word. At last there were only two letters left.

When he opened the first of them, his face changed. He read it through a second time, then abruptly he threw back his head and burst into a great bellow of laughter. He laughed and laughed till the tears ran down his cheeks while Traudl watched him in puzzlement. Then he tossed the paper on the desk in front of her.

"That's it! That's the last bloody straw. Read it! Go on, read it!"

There was little enough to read. There was a file number and a reference and a curt memorandum from the GOC Occupation Headquarters, Klagenfurt:

'Your recommendations on recent incidents in the Quellenberg area are acceptable to this Headquarters, and in line with recent agreements on Four-Power policies in occupied Austria an amnesty for certain classes of military and political prisoners will be proclaimed immediately after the forthcoming elections. We suggest that you take advantage of this to deal with both the displaced persons and with Johann Wikivill.'

"What's so funny about that?" Traudl handed him back the letter. "You got what you wanted, didn't you?"

"That's the cream of the joke, sweetheart. I got it—and now I don't want it."

"Like Anna Kunzli?"

He looked up swiftly and caught the bright mockery of her smile.

"I want her, but I've lost her."

"And now what?"

He picked up the last letter on the tray and tapped it absently on the desk, while he looked at her with bleak irony.

"It's my own damnation, dark one. I'll work it out for myself. Why don't you get Johnny to take you home?"

For a long moment she stared at him, half pitying, half resentful, then she turned on her heel and walked from the room. Hanlon picked up a paper knife, opened the last envelope and began to read:

My dear Mark,

It has taken me a long time—too long, perhaps—to come to the writing of this letter. I can only pray that you will understand my reasons and be kind.

The children want to see you. They have heard that arrangements are being made for families of Occupation troops to visit Europe and later to live there with their menfolk. They love you, they miss you. And they are beginning to resent their separation from you.

I, too, want to see you. Please, please, believe this! I want it more than anything else in the world. Our marriage foundered a long time ago, but, until recently, I didn't understand that it was I who destroyed it.

You knew and you hated me for it. Your hate was a weapon in my hands, just as the children were. Now I don't want weapons. I have no defence. I've been selfish and cold and cruel. I want to say I'm sorry. Then, if you'll have me, I want to try to begin again. I want to give you some of the love I denied you, and, if possible, to build something out of the wreckage of our lives.

If you can't forgive me, I shan't blame you. You were always a gentle man and I know will still be gentle for the sake of the children. If you want to know what's brought me to this, it's quite simple.

I'm older and wiser—and afraid of the loveless winter. That, too, is a sort of selfishness, but this time at least I'm honest about it. I'm honest too when I say that if we could come together, on any basis, it wouldn't be one-sided, ever again.

Will you please write and let me know whether we may come and what arrangements we should make at this end?

Some day—soon, please God—I'd like to be able to sign myself

Your loving wife,
Lynn.

He laid the letter down on the desk and covered it with his hands. Then he leaned back in the chair and closed his eyes.

This was the final irony. This was the love he had pleaded for, wept for, tried to fire with anger and nurse with patience through all the bleak years. This was the love whose denial had driven him out, a wanderer, into the arms of other women, to the barren pursuit of power. Now it was being offered, freely and with humility—and he did not want it.

It was meaningless to him: a script in a forgotten tongue, a score jumbled into a hopeless dissonance. Once upon a time the mystery had piqued him—to passion, to tenderness, to the thousand labours of a lover, to a sense of guilt for his own inadequacy. Now he understood that there was no mystery. There was just a woman's body, priced too high; a heart too shallow; a mind bent back too long upon itself and suddenly terrified by the first lonely glimpse of reality.

The children? Yes. They were his other selves, his promise of continuity. They gave love and took it, thoughtlessly. They were the supplement, the annotation, without which the record of life was incomplete. But they were not the full text. They were the third aspect of the human trinity—man, woman, child. They proceeded from both, were independent of either. They could neither supplant nor supply the intimate relationship of body and spirit which is the beginning, the middle and the end of love.

There was still a bond between himself and Lynn; but the bond was a legality. It had nothing to do now with the body or the spirit. Long ago they had ceased to be one flesh. His body now belonged by affinity, if not by law, to Anna Kunzli. His spirit would always be restless without hers to voyage with him.

What could one rebuild out of a situation like that? A home for the children? But where there is no harmony, there is no home. Affection, respect, mutual trust? Impossible, unless both hearts surrender and each accepts the repentance of the other.

He picked up the letter and read it through again, slowly. He was moved by the pity of it. But he resented bitterly the new burden of decision it imposed upon him.

In this small divided kingdom, as in Bad Quellenberg itself, he was being called upon to give judgment, on a cause involving his own happiness, his own peace. The scales were weighted against him but conscience still demanded a meticulous equity.

Other men, he knew, shrugged off such responsibilities. Equity, they said, was a small thing compared with the fundamental need to survive and to find some safe harbour to do it in. If you could not live inside the law, then the law must be wrenched, little or much, to make room. Marriage was a contract, but if the contract proved inequitable, then to hell with it.

The rub was that such practical fellows were more often

right in the outcome than men like himself, who clung to the creaky machinery of justice, long after it had seized and lurched to a standstill.

Once again he was face to face with the fundamental problem of his character and education. He needed love, he needed peace. He was not ruthless enough to destroy them in others to guarantee his own attainment.

A word, a visit, a letter, might bring Anna back to him in defiance of Father Albertus, but he would not have her on these terms. A reunion with Lynn would give her security and make a home for the children. It would leave him for ever empty and solitary. Still he could not bring himself to deny her.

For a long time he sat, head on his hands, pondering his situation. Then he drew pen and paper towards him and began to write. It was a long letter, sober, gentle, kind, and it said quite simply: 'Come first and we will talk. The children can follow, later.'

When he scrawled his name at the foot of the page, it was as if he were signing his own death warrant. He folded the letter, sealed it and tossed it into the posting tray. Then he put on his cap and greatcoat and went out to walk in the grey, cool dusk that gathered under the pine trees.

CHAPTER 18

IN THE bare, shadowy room that looked out to the twilight sky and the black humps of the mountains, Father Albertus was taking supper with Johann Wikivill. Their food was almost untouched. They sipped sparingly at their wine and for a long time they did not speak at all. The peace of the moment was precious to them. The wine was like a viaticum—a sacramental preparation for the journey of the pupil and the lonely vigil of the master.

Wikivill's face was in shadow, but the face of the priest still retained its rare luminous quality and his eyes were full of compassion. For him there was a strangeness in the moment. This was his son whom he was sending out to meet that other son who had left him many years since to walk the crooked paths of passion and ambition.

What would happen at their meeting he could not guess. Each in his own fashion had fallen under the harsh disciplines of the Almighty. Each had reacted differently, the one by rebellion, the other by slow submission of the will. One had come to peace, the other was still in torment. He loved them both. He was bound to each by the same paternity of the spirit, yet they might destroy each other under his eyes. He could do nothing but commit them to a common Mercy and wait with resignation on the outcome.

At last he spoke, his voice deep toned in the vesper silence.

"You should go very soon, my son."

Wikivill raised his head, so that the old man saw the calm, distant eyes and the firm set of his mouth.

"I'm ready to go."

"You don't regret it?"

"No. I've always known it must end like this."

"You must not hate this man."

"The only man I have ever hated was myself."

"You must not do that either."

"I know. That is a thing you've taught me—to live at peace with myself."

"Are you afraid?"

"Yes."

The old man got up, walked to the window and stood a long time looking over the misty valley towards the shoulder of the mountain and the first faint stars pricking out in the soft sky. Then slowly he turned, a black silhouette against the window, and began to speak:

"Let me explain Mark Hanlon to you. If you understand him, you will not be afraid. If you come to him without fear, you may be able to help him."

"Help him?" Wikivill's voice was sharp with surprise. "He wants my head. I'll give it to him. After that I've got nothing left."

The deep voice admonished him firmly: "You are a man who has walked, like Lazarus, in the valley of the shadow of death. You have endured the wreck of manhood and the destruction of hope. You have survived to a new hope. In that you are rich. You have strength to spend on this man who walks, as you walked, in the place of the dead, in the abyss of desolation. At core, he is a good man, because there is much love in him and no one is lost until he shuts love out of his life and hardens his will against it. Those he has loved have been taken away from him, so he turns to revenge himself on you. He thinks he hates you, but he has no satisfaction in it. He despises the impulse even as he yields to it. He is empty, lost, solitary, yet his pride will not let him confess his need. Even such a pride is not wholly bad, because it will not allow him to take advantage of a man helpless in his hands. Don't fight him. Don't despise him. Don't set your own pride against his. He is poorer than he knows, and you, for all your loss, are singularly blessed. Remember that, my son."

"But what do I say to him?"

"What your heart tells you."

"I am still afraid."

"If you were not, there would be no merit in what you do. There would be no sacrifice if there were no risk."

"But I risk the only thing left—my liberty." Wikivill's voice rose in urgent pleading. "Don't you see that? It's the walls that frighten me, the stones that hem me in. I killed to escape them. Now I must go back to them, freely, on my own two feet. I'm afraid I may lose courage halfway there."

"There are no walls any more, my son." Father Albertus moved towards him across the dim room. "When you accepted the prison of a maimed body, you came at one stride to freedom. No walls can contain you now. No bars can keep you back from the pastures of contentment. Believe that, in the name of God."

"I believe," said Johann Wikivill softly. "God help my unbelief."

With an odd, pathetic gesture, he leaned forward and buried his face in his hands while the old priest stood towering over him, praying desperately for the infusion of strength in this critical moment. Finally Wikivill raised his head. His eyes were calm again, his face was peaceful. He pushed back his chair and slipped down on his knees at the feet of the old priest.

"Bless me, Father."

Father Albertus raised his broken hands in the ritual gesture of benediction: "*Vade, mi fili*. . . . Go, my son! In the name of the Father and of the Son and of the Holy Ghost, go in peace."

Mark Hanlon sat, chilled to the bone, on the small stone

bench where once he had watched Anna feeding the birds, and thought about his situation.

It was plain to him now. He had reached the limit of living. All he had loved was lost to him. All he had built was founded on sand. His hopes were folly fires, his achievements a blown dust on the desert of the past. The future was a wailing emptiness. He could not go back and there was nothing to beckon him forward. The progression of life had been halted and he was caught in the syncope—a timeless, motionless state of naked disillusion.

He was incapable of consecutive thought. All that was left was a series of pictures, a wild kaleidoscope of people and places, unreal, fantastic, strangely terrifying: Willis lying on the roadway; the wolf mask of the man behind the gun; Anna's face, ecstatic in the moment of love; the claw hands of Father Albertus; the cold, obsidian eyes of Sepp Kunzli; the obscene secrets in Fischer's black book; Traudl in his arms and the movement of her body against his own; Holzinger's weak, handsome face, and behind it the faded, featureless face of his own wife.

The pictures spun dizzily faster and faster until he cried out with the terror of it and buried his face in his hands to shut them out. His body ached as if he had been beaten with rods; his face twitched and his teeth began to chatter uncontrollably. He was deathly cold.

He stood up and began to walk slowly along the promenade in the direction of the town. The trees hung black and motionless in the still air. The sound of running water troubled him like nightmare voices, and when he looked up at the sky he saw only the bleak mockery of the starlight.

When he reached the town it seemed to him that its aspect had changed. The walls were high cliffs; its yellow windows were caves peopled by monsters who mocked him silently. The shop fronts mirrored his stooped, shambling figure so that he looked like a shadowy dwarf.

There were ghosts under the black archways. Goat masks stared at him from behind the chimney pots and Anna's despairing scream rang in his ears over the pounding feet of her attacker. He walked faster and faster until his body was streaming with sweat and an iron band clamped itself round his rib case.

At the entrance to the Sonnblick the guard stared at his wild, yellow face and put out a hand to support him, but he brushed past and hurried into the lift, slamming the steel gates and jabbing the button in a frantic effort to reach the safety of his room.

Gasping and retching, he hung over the basin until the nausea had left him; then he stripped off his tunic, douched his face and hands and walked unsteadily back into the office to pour himself a drink. The raw spirit took hold of him quickly; and he drank another glass and another, then sat down at his desk and lit a cigarette. He choked on the first mouthful of smoke and stubbed the cigarette out in the ashtray.

Then, shrill and shattering, the telephone rang.

Instinctively he reached out and lifted the receiver. Habit and not will dictated the familiar words:

"Hanlon here."

Sergeant Jenning's voice answered him.

"There's a man to see you sir. Name Johann Wikivill. He says you sent for him."

"Send him up—alone."

"Yessir."

He replaced the receiver and sat down at the desk. The comedy wasn't quite finished. There was still the antistrophe, the sour epilogue.

A few moments later the door opened and Johann Wikivill stepped into the room.

To Hanlon's heated imagination he looked like a man ten feet tall. He was dressed in the same uniform which he had worn on the day of their first meeting—square, peaked cap, tight jacket, baggy trousers, and the long, theatrical cloak that reached almost to his ankles. The peak of the cap threw a shadow over his forehead, and out of the shadow his distant eyes shone strangely.

It was the cloak that gave him height, but it was the face that lent him the look of an unearthly visitor. One side of it was rough and stubbled, and darkened by shadow. The other was smooth, new and shining. 'Like Lazarus,' thought Hanlon inconsequently, 'caught halfway between death and the renewal of the resurrection.'

The thought amused him. He embellished it, smiling to himself, while Johann Wikivill stood tall and immobile, watching him. 'At the resurrection there shall be neither marriage nor giving in marriage, but we shall all be like angels of God....

The eunuchs will come into their own, the celibates, the barren ones. They'll all have mild, mystical eyes and baby skin like this fellow. They'd be dull company for us poor devils who are content with three meals a day and a little honest loving at night—if we can get it.'

Johann Wikivill announced himself formally.

"I am Johann Wikivill, Colonel. You wanted me."

"I've been wanting you a long time," said Hanlon. "Tell me . . . Why did you kill Willis?"

"Because I hated myself."

"That's it!" Hanlon's voice rose. "Good! It's always that way, isn't it? I know how you felt, man! I'm feeling it myself now! Tell me, what do you see from your end? What do I look like?"

"Like myself." There was warmth in the voice now, a haunting pity. "You look weary, hunted, sick . . ."

Hanlon looked up sharply. "Of course! You're a doctor. I remember now. What's your prescription?"

"There's only one."

"Name it."

"Hope," said Johann Wikivill softly.

Hanlon's mouth drew back into a tight, cheerless grin.

"Father Albertus taught you that, didn't he? I know . . . he taught me, too. But there's a catch in it—a big catch. You know what it is? To hope, you must have something to hope for, a goal, an end! What do you hope for, Wikivill?"

"To be free one day. To practise medicine again. To spend some skill and kindness on poor devils like myself."

"They won't thank you for it," said Hanlon with cold irony. "They never do."

"I'll be paying a debt. There's no question of thanks."

"You owe me a debt." Hanlon's smile was bitter. "A life for a life."

"I'm here to pay it," Wikivill told him calmly.

"You can't!" Hanlon picked up the letter from Klagenfurt and held it out to him. "Here, read it."

Wikivill stepped forward and took the letter. The approach diminished him to human size. The shadows fell away from his face so that it became symmetrical again. He read the letter carefully, then handed it back to Hanlon. His eyes were mild; his lips were parted in a smile of great gentleness.

"It seems I owe you a double debt, Colonel."

Hanlon waved a contemptuous dismissal. "You owe me nothing. Get out!"

Wikivill did not move. For a long moment he stared at Hanlon, groping for words to convey his gratitude. Then, very quietly:

"I'll look after Anna for you, Colonel. When her time comes, I'll deliver her myself, and care for the child, too. They'll be safe in my hands, I promise!"

Hanlon's head jerked back as if he had been struck in the mouth. His voice was a hoarse whisper. "What are you saying?"

"I'm sorry," said Johann Wikivill gravely. "I thought you knew. Anna Kunzli is going to have your child."

For one disbelieving moment Hanlon stared at him; then all the pain of the years was wrenched out of him in one despairing cry:

"Dear God in Heaven! No!"

Then he buried his face in his hands and wept like a child.

Johann Wikivill took off his cap and his cloak and stood beside him, patting his shoulder and murmuring small words of comfort, as if they were two brothers, united by a common grief.

"You should go to her," Wikivill told him firmly. "No matter what she has said, go to her. Tell her how it is with you and your wife. Tell her you love her and what you want to do for her and the child. That way there will be no bitterness, no regret. . . ."

They were sitting together in the big room where once Hanlon had planned the capture of the man behind the gun. There were drinks between them and the slow, friendly curl of cigarette smoke. Hanlon was still numb with shock, but slowly life seemed to be flowing back to him from the tall, lean man with the calm eyes and gentle voice.

This was not the surrender he had planned, but if there was no triumph in it, there was also no regret. Now they were men together, conscious of mutual deeds, of common debts. There was no shame between them. The shame of victory was wiped out by the dignity of defeat. The shadow of the lictor's axe was replaced by the shadow of a common cross.

Hanlon leaned forward, questioning awkwardly. "I'm

worried about the child. What happens to him? He has no name, no father. How can Anna still live here and . . ."

Wikivill cut him short with a gesture. "You forget how it is with our people. They have respect for life—however it comes. The child will be welcomed, and loved, too. Besides, there will be many like it in this land of ours, where the men are dead and the women are lonely. We shall be grateful, all of us, for this new promise of the future. You will see. The women will make clothes, and the woodcutters will bring toys, and there will be flowers and candles for the baptism, so that it will be like the coming of the *Christkind*. I will see that she has a good delivery. If they are sick I will care for them."

Hanlon was almost stifled by the simple wonder of it.

"I wanted you dead. And now . . ."

"Now you should eat something, then you should sleep, and in the morning go and see Anna."

"I'd like to see her tonight."

"It's late," Wikivill told him soberly. "You've had a bad day. And night is a treacherous time for lovers."

Hanlon nodded wearily. "I know. You're right, of course. I'll wait. But don't go yet," he added hastily. "Stay and eat with me. I'm scared."

"Reaction," said Wikivill professionally. "The mind and the body can take just so much, any more and they reject it, violently."

"That's what scares me. This is only the beginning. There's my work here. There are a dozen personal problems to be worked out. I—I'm so damn tired I'm not sure I can face them."

Wikivill leaned forward and poured more liquor into the glasses on the table. Without looking up he said gravely: "You're stronger than you know. We all are. But we need a shoulder to lean on sometimes. If you would let me help, it would make me very happy."

Hanlon gave him a tired grin. "To pay a debt?"

Wikivill shot him a quick, sidelong glance. "Not to you."

"To whom, then?"

"To Father Albertus." He raised his glass. "*Prost!*"

The old nerve jumped in protest against this shrewd probing. "Drink that one yourself," said Hanlon baldly.

Wikivill drank, deeply.

CHAPTER 19

HE FOUND her waiting in the garden of the Spiderhouse, colourful as a flower in dirndl and peasant blouse. The bloom of new pregnancy was on her cheeks, and when she came hurrying to greet him her eyes were bright with happy tears.

They kissed and clung together, and then sat down on a rustic seat under the spread leaves of a copper beech. They held hands and looked at each other, wordless but content with this first moment of communion after the long days of separation.

Once again, Hanlon was struck by the extraordinary air of innocence which surrounded her. Some women were coarsened by passion. Pregnancy made others uncertain and shrewish. But Anna Kunzli was calm, contained, fearless. The new life that fed on her seemed to add to her strength instead of diminishing it.

When he began to speak, she listened gravely, prompting him where he stumbled, soothing him when he broke out into anger and bitter resentment. Her gentleness was a balm to him. Her courage shamed him; and, when his story was done, she put her arms about him and drew his head down to her breast, so that he felt the beat of her heart and smelt the warm perfume of her body.

Her voice seemed to reach him from a long way off.

"Rest now, my dear. You've talked enough. There are no lies between us any more—no blame, no regrets. When your son comes—and I know it will be a son—I will teach him to be proud of his father. When he is old enough, I will send him to you and you will be proud of him, too."

Hot tears pricked at Hanlon's eyelids and he dared not look up at the unbearable tenderness of her face. Anna talked on:

"Sometimes, when you are back in England, you will write to me and I will write and tell you about your son. Perhaps, even, you may come to visit us—but not too often, nor for very long. I don't think I could bear to have you near me and not love you."

Hanlon straightened up and looked at her. His face was

207

drawn and haggard. He challenged her: "How can you take it so calmly? Doesn't it frighten you?"

Her eyes clouded a moment, but she answered him sanely: "Yes, Mark, it frightens me. I know that I'll wake in the night and cry for you. I'll look at other women with their menfolk and mourn for you. But I can bear it, Mark, because I love you, and I know that this way will be best for both of us in the end."

"I wish I thought so, Anna."

She reached out, imprisoning his hands in her own. "You do, Mark. Otherwise you couldn't have made this decision to go back to your wife."

"I broke my heart when I made it."

"It will mend, my dear," she chided him quietly, "and one day we will both wake up, and find suddenly that we are at peace again." Her voice faltered a little, but she controlled herself quickly. "Let's walk round the garden, Mark, just as we used to do."

They stood up, Hanlon took her arm and they began to stroll up and down the long terrace of lawn between the Spiderhouse and the lower swathe of pines. The sun was warm on their faces; the air was full of pine scent and the songs of birds. The slow harmony of summer took possession of them, and their talk fell into the sober rhythm of their footsteps.

"I'm afraid, too," said Mark Hanlon.

"Of what?"

"Meeting my wife. It's been so long, you see. I can't remember when we talked without contention. We're strangers now. I don't even know how to begin."

"With tenderness, Mark," said Anna softly. "She will be feeling the same way, remember. She won't know how you'll receive her. She wants love, but she too has forgotten how to ask for it. Be gentle with her, my dear."

"What do I tell her—about us?"

"The truth, Mark. But not brutally nor all at once. She'll need time to prepare herself for it. Time to make herself generous. Give her this time, and she will accept it—if only to show you that she loves you."

"Do you think she does?"

"I don't know, Mark." For the first time a hint of dissatisfaction came into her voice. "And—and you mustn't ask me any more, nor tell me when you know."

"I'm sorry, Anna."

"Don't be sorry, Mark." She gave him a small, uncertain smile. "Just remember that I'm still a woman—and jealous of the man I love."

"I love you, Anna!"

"Of course you do. And our boy will be a love child, and all the happier for it. But . . ." She hesitated a moment. "If you and your wife live in peace together, you will in the end find a certain love for each other. Not like ours perhaps, but still—love! I—I'd rather not think of that."

"What if Lynn asks to see you?"

"Send her to me. But don't come with her."

"Just as you like."

"Mark?"

"Yes, Anna."

"Now I'm going to ask you to do something for me."

"Anything—you know that."

Gently she disengaged herself and stood facing him, her hair shining golden in the sun, her face up-tilted to his. She waited a moment as if uncertain how to frame her request; then she put it to him simply.

"Mark, I'd like you to make friends with Father Albertus."

He stared at her, half angry, half puzzled; then he asked her: "Why?"

"He's an old man, Mark. He's suffered a great deal, and he loves us both."

"He's got no monopoly of either suffering or love." Hanlon's answer was harsh. "And I've given him concessions all along the line."

"Have you regretted any of them, Mark? Have you regretted Johann Wikivill?"

"I've regretted you," said Hanlon stonily. "You were his greatest victory."

Anna shook her head slowly. "He didn't take me from you, Mark. He simply pointed out to me what we both believe in—and it broke his heart to do it. Can't you see, Mark? We're suffering—yes. But so is he. He looks on us as his children, you most of all, I think. Can't you bend to him a little, for my sake, for the child's? We must live here, remember. We shall depend on him for so much and you could make him very happy."

There was so much eagerness in her, so much warm wisdom,

that Mark Hanlon was touched in spite of himself. His eyes softened, the taut line of his jaw relaxed. He reached out and drew her to him, holding her against his breast so that his lips brushed the gold of her hair while they stood under the shining bronze leaves of the beeches.

"All right, *Liebchen*," he told her. "So be it. I'll make friends with him."

Then, for the first time, her control broke and she held to him, sobbing as if her heart would break, while Mark Hanlon soothed and coaxed her with words he did not believe and hopes that were already a dusty illusion.

A long time afterwards, when she was calm, and they were both weary, they walked down to the gate and kissed goodbye. Mark Hanlon saluted gravely and turned his face towards the town.

Mark Hanlon lived through the next ten days like a sleep-walker. There were weights on his shoulders and chains round his heart. He had no desires—only needs: the need to eat and work like a galley rower and sleep a little after the white nights, when he tossed and turned and stretched out groping hands for comfort just beyond his reach.

His body functioned like a protesting machine. One part of his mind worked with precision and clarity, accurate in assessment, prompt in decision, but the rest of him, the feeling part, the part that desired and willed, was caught in a cataleptic state between the horror of living and the mercy of dying.

He dealt with his officers politely but curtly, so that they were glad to be out of his room. With Traudl he was brusque and cold, and for all her affection she could not come within reach of him. When Holzinger or Miller or the local officials came to see him, he dispatched their business so quickly that they went away wondering how they had offended him.

None of his friends could break down his icy reserve. Captain Johnson's awkward advances were snubbed. Huber's invitations were ignored and Father Albertus did not come at all. He lived in a sterile vacuum, solitary, self sufficient, and desperately afraid.

In spite of his promise to Anna Kunzli he made no move towards a reconciliation with Father Albertus. Resentment had died in him as hope had died; but he lacked the strength even for a simple act of submission. The little energy he had must be husbanded for the moment of his meeting with his wife.

She had not yet replied to his letter, and as the days spun themselves out in painful succession, he felt his resolve weakening and his fears growing daily greater. Questions began to torment him like squawking birds: How should he greet her? Should he kiss her on the lips, could he command a smile to welcome her, or would she sense the revulsion in his touch? How should he tell her about Anna? If she were jealous, how could he master his anger? Was there love enough left in him to share with his legal children and with his coming son? How could he silence the whispers of the townsfolk when they saw him walking arm in arm with Lynn and remembered the pregnant girl in the Spiderhouse?

There was no answer to any of them, but they fretted him night and day, pecking away at the props of his resolution.

Ten days of this ruthless self-inquisition left him frayed and utterly exhausted. He was smoking too much and drinking more than usual, and his appearance shocked all those who had contact with him.

Then, on the eleventh day, a letter was laid on his desk, franked with a London postmark. His fingers trembled as he slit the envelope and unfolded the thick, scented paper which Lynn used.

My dear Mark,
    I cannot put into words how deeply your letter touched me, nor how grateful I am. I may not be able to do it, even when I see you. I know I shall be awkward at first, but I beg you to be patient with me. The children are, of course, over-joyed, if rather impatient that they cannot come with me.
    The authorities have arranged for me to fly to Munich on Monday. The arrival time is 3.30 in the afternoon. Can you arrange to meet me? I can't write any more now. I am too excited and afraid to hope too much. The rest must wait till I see you.

                    Your loving wife,
                    Lynn.

He laid the letter down on the table and sat a long time staring at it, while Traudl watched him curiously from her desk at the other side of the room.

She was tempted to go to him, put her arms about him in the old, frank fashion, and charm the trouble out of him. But the naked grief in his face frightened her. She saw him reach for a cigarette, light it with shaky hands, and draw on it greedily. She saw him walk to the french windows and out on to the small balcony, where he stood, leaning on the balustrade and looking down over the fall of the hills into the green valley, where the houses huddled in mocking peace round the spire of the church.

When he came back into the room, his eyes were dead and his voice was weary and remote.

"Send a note to Johann Wikivill. Ask him to come to see me as soon as possible."

Traudl scribbled the note on her pad; then, in spite of herself, she stood up and moved towards him.

"Mark! You're ill. What's the matter? Couldn't you tell me?"

He turned towards her, and the dead eyes and the grim mouth stopped her in her tracks.

"I'm quite well, thank you. There's nothing the matter. My wife's coming to visit me. I should be glad about that, shouldn't I?"

"You poor devil," said Traudl softly. "You poor unhappy devil."

Afterwards he remembered that it was the only time he had ever seen her cry.

Early on the Monday morning, Mark Hanlon and Johann Wikivill left Bad Quellenberg for Munich airport. Their way lay northward: over the mountain passes from Carinthia down into the valleys of Land Salzburg, then up again through the Bavarian hills to Munich.

Hanlon drove fast and dangerously, rolling the car round the sharp curves, sliding it through the patches of gravel on the shoulders while the tyres whined and the small echoes whipped back from fence posts and embankments.

Johann Wikivill sat calm and unruffled beside him, lighting his cigarettes, talking inconsequently of legends and landmarks, apparently unperturbed by the danger or by Hanlon's unresponsive silence. There was an odd, reposeful quality in him: the passionless contentment of a man who has seen too much of death to be afraid of it, and too much of life to be disappointed in it.

Hanlon was reminded of the old biblical phrase, 'Strength

went out from him'. In spite of his silence, he was grateful to Wikivill, and as the road spun out behind them, he surrendered himself more and more to the cathartic pleasure of speed and to the enveloping virtue of the man he had once hunted.

When they stopped at Salzburg to lunch and refuel, the sky was grey and lowering. By the time they reached the Bavarian foothills a slow drizzle was falling; and when they came to Munich the weather had settled down, cheerless and faintly sinister, after the full blaze of Alpine summer.

The air terminal was like a military installation. A scowling GI checked their passes and waved them into the parking area, where trucks and staff cars were stacked three deep, and gum-chewing drivers lounged under a tin shelter. The aircraft huddled round the aprons. All carried American markings and the waiting-room was a babel of accents from Maine to New Orleans.

To Hanlon, fresh from the isolation of Bad Quellenberg, the scene was a sharp reminder of the nearness of the war and the uncertainty of peace in the scarred cities of Europe. He checked the arrival time on the schedule board, found that the plane would be twenty minutes late, then pushed his way up to the bar with Wikivill to buy coffee and brandies.

Now that the waiting was nearly over he was beginning to be calm again. The sight of the uniforms and the clamour of voices soothed him with a sense of community and comradeship. These men, too, were far from home. They had seen death and disaster as he had. Many of them were involved in war-time loves and post-war heartbreaks. They were his brothers, as Wikivill was. He was neither singular nor separate. He was a unit in the human family, needful, like all the others, of pity and love and wisdom and strength.

He looked up suddenly, to find Wikivill's calm eyes fixed on him. He gave a small, bleak grin. "It's all right, my friend. I'm ready for it now."

Wikivill nodded and smiled gravely. "I told you, didn't I? You were stronger than you knew."

Hanlón shrugged ruefully and turned back to his drink. He, too, was conscious of the small, solid core of strength that remained to him, but he knew that he must nurse it carefully against the moment of Lynn's arrival.

The babel of voices began to sort itself out into snatches of dialogue. A corporal from Brooklyn was talking about a girl in Vienna; a dry-voiced major discussed Four-Power politics at command level; an UNRRA official checked off a list of medical supplies with a hatchet-faced woman in Red Cross uniform. A French captain made passes at the fräulein behind the counter.

Hanlon listened, now to this one, now to that, grateful for the distraction, while the minutes ticked away on the electric clock above the schedule board. Suddenly he looked up and saw, with a small shock of surprise, that it was already long past the new arrival time. He pointed it out to Wikivill, who smiled and shook his head.

"In this weather it can be dirty flying from Frankfurt to Munich. Perhaps they will make an announcement soon."

"The sooner the better," said Hanlon irritably. "I wasn't prepared for this."

"Another drink?"

"Why not?" Hanlon swirled the dregs of liquor in his glass and tossed them off at a gulp. "Dutch courage! I never believed in it before."

"So it be courage, who cares?" Wikivill grinned and pushed the glasses across the counter to be refilled. Before Hanlon had time to answer, the speakers crackled into life and a flat, impersonal voice made the announcement:

"Attention, please! Would all personnel waiting on passengers from Flight 123, London, Frankfurt, Munich, please come to the Controller's office immediately."

The crowd in the waiting-room fell silent, and they looked at each other uncertainly as the metallic voice repeated the announcement. Then small knots of people began to disengage themselves and move hesitantly towards the glass-panelled door at the end of the waiting-room.

A few minutes later they heard the news that Flight 123 had crashed fifty miles east of Frankfurt and that there were no survivors.

Johann Wikivill had driven him halfway across Bavaria before Hanlon fully understood what had happened to him.

CHAPTER 20

IT WAS a Saturday afternoon, late and drowsy with the heat of high summer.

Father Albertus sat, cramped and tired, in a room a little larger than a coffin, but not quite as big as a grave. In front of him was a velvet curtain, purple in colour, musty with age and human exhalation. On either side of him were walls of pine slab, darkened by age, each pierced by a small grille, which was covered by a Judas door. Behind him was the grey stone wall of the church.

Every week he came here, stifled by the heat or frozen by the winter cold, waiting for his people to come to the shriving of sins. Every week a succession of shadowy faces pressed themselves to the grilles, and their halting whispers counted out the tally of commissions and omissions for judgment and forgiveness.

Children's voices told him of the first small lapses from innocence. Young men, hoarse and ashamed, stumbled through their tales of passion under the pine trees. The married told of their angers and their hates and their occasional adulteries. Spendthrifts came and misers, proud men and humble girls, the wise, the foolish, the selfish and the sorrowing; and over each he pronounced the words of absolution and the counsel suited to their needs.

There were moments—all too few—when his narrow room seemed to grow and lighten like the courtyards of heaven and he was humbled by the manifest workings of God among his creatures. There were other times when the walls closed in on him, like those of the punishment cell at Mauthausen, and he was broken and beaten down by the weight of misery laid on his old shoulders.

He was a priest, like his Master. Like his Master he must make himself the scapegoat of the people. When they did not repent he must count it a failure in himself. When they refused to do penance, he must chastise their follies in his own flesh. This was the meaning of priesthood—a lifelong crucifixion, to merit for others the gratuitous mercies of which he was the channel and the minister.

Sometimes, as it did today, the sheer repetition and continuity of human folly drove him to the brink of despair. In spite of two thousand years of redemption, of renewed martyrdom and crucifixion, the sum of sin never seemed to diminish. A thousand absolutions issued in ten thousand new transgressions. The very patience of God was made a mockery.

When he waited in the stuffy darkness for a new penitent to present himself at the grille, it seemed to him that the years of celibacy and discipline were a monstrous waste. When he struggled to pray against the temptation his lips framed only the desolate words of the dying Christus: 'Eloi, Eloi, lama sabachthani. . . . My God, My God, why hast thou forsaken me?'

Long years ago the Bishop had anointed his fingers and given him all men for his children. But his children left him to follow strange gods, and even after he had forgiven them they went back, like dogs to the vomit, and he could do nothing but wait and hope, and pray for their return.

Age lay on him like a cross and he asked often for the mercy of release from it. But the mercy was withheld, so that he sat here still in the room that was like a coffin and waited for his next patient.

He heard the creaking of the confessional door and the rustle of clothing inside the booth. He slid aside the Judas door, bent his face to the grille, averted his eyes and waited. Then he heard Mark Hanlon's voice, low but firm in the ritual preamble:

"Bless me, Father, for I have sinned."

The old man's heart leapt, but he kept his face averted and raised his broken hands in blessing.

"*Benedico te, mi fili*. . . . How long since your last confession?"

"A long time, Father. Five years, six maybe."

"You know that this is itself a great sin, that a man should turn away from the grace that is offered to him daily?"

"I know that."

"Tell me your sins, my son."

Then it began—the long count of the locust years, the slow reconstruction of the complex relationship between the old man and the pupil who had left him so many ages ago: the brotherhood of the faith, the fatherhood of the Spirit, the sinner and the judge, priest and penitent, Cæsar's friend and the follower of the Crucified.

To each, the moment brought its own pain and its own consolation. The failures of the pupil were the failures of his master. The penitence of the one was humbling to the other. The hands that would confer forgiveness were shaky with gratitude for the restoration of simple, human affection.

When the long recitation was over, Father Albertus asked him: "Is that all, my son?"

"All I can remember."

"It is enough."

The broken fingers were raised and Mark Hanlon bowed his head to receive the absolution. "*Deinde ego te absolvo....* I absolve you from your sins in the name of the Father and of the Son, and of the Holy Ghost. Amen."

"Thank you, Father."

"For your penance, you will recite the sorrowful Mysteries of the Rosary."

From the other side of the grille came a small, ironic chuckle and Father Albertus looked up sharply, but Hanlon's face was an indistinguishable blur against the wire mesh.

"As easy as that, Father?"

"Forgiveness is always easy, my son," said Father Albertus soberly. "The hardest thing of all is to bend the will to ask for it. It has taken these years and a singular mercy to bring you to this moment."

"There's a harder thing yet," said Mark Hanlon dryly. "To live with the memory of the past."

The old, deep voice admonished him firmly. "That is part of the penance. To perform it you will need new courage and a new mercy. You dare not despise yourself, because that would be to despise the greatness of God and the good that He has made to flower under your hand. You may regret the past, but you must not resent it. You must not brood upon it, else you may poison the happiness of those with whom you live. You will accept it, humbly, as you will accept what the future offers. You will be grateful that the design of God, through a physical accident, has resolved a dilemma that you could never have resolved yourself. Let the dead bury their dead—but pray for them, because the dead still belong to you, and you to them, through the Communion of Saints. Do you understand?"

"I understand."

"Go in peace, my son."

Mark Hanlon stood up and the door creaked again. After he had gone the old priest sat a long time, praying quietly and waiting for the next visitor; then, as no one came, he too got up, stretched his cramped limbs and walked out into the shadowy nave.

The church was empty except for Mark Hanlon, who knelt in the front pew, looking up towards the sanctuary where the dim taper flickered in its bowl of crimson glass. Father Albertus went up and knelt beside him. In a low, clear voice he began to recite the canticle of the Mother of God.

"*Magnificat anima mea Dominum....* My soul doth magnify the Lord."

"*Quia deposuit potentes...*" answered Colonel Mark Hanlon. "Because he hath put down the mighty from the seats, and hath exalted the humble."

Together, master and pupil, victor and vanquished, they finished the recitation of the hymn. Then they walked out together through the forest of headboards, past the wooden Christus, out through the lych gate and up the dappled hillside to the Spiderhouse, where Anna Kunzli was waiting for them.

Winston Graham

'One of the best half-dozen novelists in this country.' *Books and Bookmen*. 'Winston Graham excels in making his characters come vividly alive.' *Daily Mirror*. 'A born novelist.' *Sunday Times*

His immensely popular suspense novels include:

Take My Life
The Sleeping Partner
Fortune is a Woman
Marnie
Greek Fire
The Little Walls
Night Without Stars
The Tumbled House
Night Journey

Winston Graham has also written The Poldark Saga, his famous story of eighteenth-century Cornwall:

Ross Poldark
Demelza
Jeremy Poldark
Warleggan
The Black Moon

And historical novels including:

The Grove of Eagles

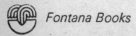 *Fontana Books*

Herman Wouk

One of the most talented novelists writing in America today.
All his novels have been highly praised, and *The 'Caine'
Mutiny* won the Pulitzer Prize.

His books include:

Don't Stop the Carnival

Aurora Dawn

The 'Caine' Mutiny

The Winds of War

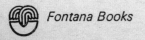 *Fontana Books*

Howard Spring

In 1938 his most famous book, *My Son, My Son*, was published; it was a world-wide success. Since then all his books, without exception, have been best-sellers and have earned Howard Spring a high reputation as an author of universal appeal.

'Howard Spring is a novelist of solid and considerable talent, whose ability to tell a story, sense of character, craftsmanship and industry should put hollower and more pretentious novelists to shame.' *Spectator*

'He is not afraid of stark drama, and he writes with real feeling.' *Sunday Times*

I Met a Lady

A Sunset Touch

Winds of the Day

These Lovers Fled Away

My Son, My Son

There is No Armour

 Fontana Books

H. H. Kirst

Sometimes very funny, often bitingly satirical, Hans Hellmut Kirst's novels describe Germany and the Germans, from the Nazi era to the present day. 'Kirst's oblique, deadpan gaze is deeply revealing, deeply compassionate.' *Sunday Times*

Camp 7 Last Stop

Hero in the Tower

A Time for Truth

A Time for Scandal

The Return of Gunner Asch

What Became of Gunner Asch

Officer Factory

The Night of the Generals

The Wolves

 Fontana Books

Fontana Books

Fontana is a leading paperback publisher of fiction and non-fiction, with authors ranging from Alistair MacLean, Agatha Christie and Desmond Bagley to Solzhenitsyn and Pasternak, from Gerald Durrell and Joy Adamson to the famous Modern Masters series.

In addition to a wide-ranging collection of internationally popular writers of fiction, Fontana also has an outstanding reputation for history, natural history, military history, psychology, psychiatry, politics, economics, religion and the social sciences.

All Fontana books are available at your bookshop or newsagent; or can be ordered direct. Just fill in the form and list the titles you want.
